The Enchanted Kingdom of
Sir Thomas Tattletale
by Johnathan Hallgrey

Johnathan Hallgrey
2017

Special Thanks to Stavros Basis for technical assistance in the making of this book.
Cover Art: Adam Sokolowski
Cover Art Direction: Johnathan Hallgrey
Interior Art Illustration: Johnathan Hallgrey & Gin Yu

First Printing: 2017

ISBN 978-1-387-06230-0

CHAPTER 1
Sir Thomas Tattletale of Surrey

Our story opens in Surbiton, Surrey, England in 1922. Children are laughing and playing kickball in a school yard when a 1918 Renault limousine passes by the school yard. Two voices in the motorcar can be heard talking to each other.

"Oh, my dearest Arborvitae, what medicinal music to the ears a child's laughter makes!" exclaimed an elderly gentleman in a silk top hat.

"Indeed it does, my dearest Pineapple!" an elegant lady in a large hat with pheasant plumes replied. "Shall we introduce ourselves to them, my love?"

"I'm too weak to make the introductions, this time, my dearest Arborvitae. Could you do me the honor?" With grey morning gloves, he held her hand as he looked at her with warmth.

"Oh, my dearest love, it would be indeed a pleasure and honor to do so," cried the lady in a large hat with pheasant plumes with delight. The elderly gentleman in the silk top hat smiled and kissed her hand. "Click Und Snap, stop the motorcar! I'm getting out."

The chauffeur stopped and parked the automobile, then hurried to open the door for the lady. As the grey-gloved woman exited the automobile, she held out her hand. The chauffeur, wearing black driving gauntlets, helped her from the motorcar.

"Danke, Click Und Snap. What a magnificent day it is!" exclaimed the lady in the large pheasant plumes hat. "Click Und Snap, quickly bring out the gramophone player!"

Click Und Snap of Gemütlich Germany, was a paraplegic from a tragic automobile accident in 1918. He was saved by mechanical prosthetics that made up both of his legs and an arm, as well as part of his face.

Click Und Snap went back to the automobile and carefully pulled out a gramophone player from the trunk. Holding it with great care, he walked around the car slowly. Its cylindrical mahogany base was inlaid with ivory and supported a two-headed brass horn. He began to crank it up after resting it on a nearby stump, and the lovely music began to play.

Back on the playground, a child accidentally kicked a ball over a small fence into a dark wooded area.

"Ugh, Henry! You did it again!" a child yelled.

"I'm always the one that has to go and get it!" cried Henry.

"You did it, so you go and get it!" Henry, shrugged his shoulders as he proceeded to look for the ball through the shrubbery and weeds.

"Hello, Henry!" said a little girl. Henry turned around, "What are you doing here, Jenny?"

"I came to help you look for the ball, Henry. I thought you could use some help. What else are little sisters for?" she smiled. "Little sisters can also be a pain! If you find it, just give it to me and go home!" Henry said.

As they both looked for the ball through the shrubbery, they came upon a gravel roadway. They could hear music playing. It was American ragtime in style. It sounded like an orchestral piece of 'Someday a little bug is going to find you', by Silvio Hein, 1915.

"Henry, do you hear that?" Jenny asked.

"Yes I do, Jenny. Just hold my hand and stay close. I've never heard anything like this before!"

Entranced by the music, they walked further down the gravel roadway. As the music grew louder, they noticed a beautiful lady standing next to a large automobile in the middle of the road. They could see that a two-headed horn gramophone player was the source of the music, and the woman was listening to it intently. She was wearing a large grey hat with pheasant plumes. A long strand of pearls came down her grey flannel walking suit. Draped in a grey fox boa, she stood there with the children's ball resting in her hand.

"Hello Madam, could we have our ball back?" cried Henry.

"Oh my! How adorable you are! And how old are you, young man?" asked the elegant lady in the large pheasant plumes hat.

"I am 10 years old," answered Henry. "Just perfect! Do you care for some raspberry twists? I have enough for you and your sister."

"No, thank you. We just want our ball back."

"That is a lovely dress you have on," said Jenny.

"Oh, why thank you! Aren't you just the dearest thing. And what is your name?" the lady in the large hat asked.

"My name is Jenny, and I'm eight years old. My brother's name is Henry!"

"You both can come closer, I do not bite, but I do giggle a bit! I have chocolate cake with vanilla icing, enough for all your friends to have a party!"

"Oh thank you so very much, but mother has told us never to take anything from strangers," stated Jenny.

"And mother also told us never talk to strangers, too!" cried Henry, looking at his sister.

"Oh! But there is one other thing your mother forgot to tell you," the elegant lady in the large hat with pheasant plumes said, still smiling pleasantly.

"And what would that be, Madam?" Henry asked.

"You should never get close to strangers, either!" she said and her smile turned maniacal. "Click Und Snap, grab them and throw them into the steamer trunk!"

The children were scooped up quickly as they kicked and screamed. "Madam, please let us go!"

"Dear children, you're in very good hands now! No need to worry, my little Peaches," the lady said calmly.

"Please, please, let us go, madam!" yelled Henry in desperation.

"I'm frightened, let us go! Please miss!" cried Jenny.

"My dear children, I am not a miss nor madam, but a baroness. Baroness Giggle Von Tickle to you!" She giggled as the steamer trunk was hoisted to the top of her motorcar, and threw the ball out of the window as the motorcar drove off.

In another part of Surrey in Effingham, a class was just beginning at the Newhavencroft boarding school for boys. Their crisp uniforms consisted of a silk top hat, red tie, high rounded collar outside a fitted black jacket, and accompanied by grey flannel slacks with button up shoes.

"A is for aviators, B is for bowler hat, C is for cat," explained the teacher. All the little boys were sitting in attention except for one, who was looking out the window onto the courtyard daydreaming. Then, a butterfly happened to fly in and landed on his nose. As the little boy tried to swat it away, he began to giggle. "Sir Thomas! Sir Thomas Tattletale!" yelled the teacher from across the room. "There is nothing funny about the importance of learning the alphabet, young man! You are to stop this nonsense this very instant!" the teacher bellowed, as she banged the ruler on her desk.

"Oh, you must forgive me, Ms. Appletwist, but I was trying to swish the butterfly away, and it started to move about my face!" he said, still laughing.

Sir Thomas Tattletale of Surrey is a bright, gentle boy of six and a half years. He is heir to Tattletale Publishing, and the son of Lord Titus and Lady Tatiana Tattletale of Surrey, England.

By now, the whole class, forgetting about the lesson, had surrounded Sir Thomas and was admiring the exotic butterfly.

"I say, that's a rather extraordinary butterfly you have there, Sir Thomas!" cried one of the twin brothers looking on.

Sir Thomas Tattletale replied, "It's quite unique. It's not indigenous of England, Prince Cuatro."

"I've seen better butterflies in Brazil, you know!" cried the other twin brother standing next to him.

"You're just jealous, Cinco, because it didn't land on your nose!" Prince Cuatro exclaimed.

Princes Cuatro and Cinco Chuku of Nigeria are inquisitive and adventurous boys of six and a quarter years, and heirs to the Chuku diamond mines of Nigeria. Cuatro and Cinco were born in Madrid, Spain, their births separated by an hour with one at 4:00 in the evening, and the other at 5:00, which is why their mother Princess Chuku of Nigeria chose their names, four and five, but in Spanish.

"Actually, you're quite right," contested another little boy with tinted horn-rimmed glasses and little black gloves on. "It's an Anna's 88, or the proper name, Diaethria Anna. It's commonly found in Central and South Americas." He stuck out his tongue at Prince Cinco.

"Bow bumble, Phillip. I guess it means good luck!" Sir Thomas exclaimed.

Phillip de Curieuse du France is the scientist of the class. He is very knowledgeable on insects and bugs when he's not eating them. He is the son of Augustin, the ambassador to France, and Antoinette de Curieuse du France.

"I say, Ms. Appletwist, Sir Thomas is a rather funny old chap!" shouted one little boy to the teacher, with a lisp, as he licked a large red lollipop.

"I take it you are Sir Thomas' very good friend."

"Indeed, I am, Ms. Appletwist!" he said with a grin.

Ms. Appletwist was smarter than letting him get away with eating during class. "That's so very good to know, Lord Langley. Lord Langley, are you aware of the time and place for lunch during school?"

"Oh indeed I do, Ms. Appletwist. It's in the main hall promptly at 12:15."

"It is so very nice to know that you are quite aware of this, Lord Langley Lyndon," said Ms. Appletwist. "Before you go back to your seat, you are to dispense that lollipop in the class lollipop box." She added, "It is beyond me how a little boy such as yourself, day in and day out, can consume a lollipop bigger than his head!"

In the corner of the classroom was a box of confiscated lollipops and most of them belonged to Lord Langley. Lord Langley Lyndon is a precocious, though mischievous, little boy of six years, with an inherited lisp from his parents due to the testing of lollipops. He is the son of Lord Linford, a distant cousin of the Queen, and Lady Lancaster Lyndon of Lolly, England. His parents are the inventors and manufacturers of all the lollipops in England.

"Sir Thomas Tattletale!" cried Ms. Appletwist. "Out through the window from which it came, young man, this very instant! Now everyone back to your seats. There is nothing more to look at! Pip-pip!" She clapped her hands, and the class settled as heavy feet were dragged across to their chairs.

As Sir Thomas Tattletale let Anna's 88 fly to his fingertips, he gently put it outside the window and watched it fly away.

Later that afternoon after school as Sir Thomas sat waiting on the school steps for his motorcar, Princes Cuatro and Cinco walked by. They were dressed in little black leather dusters and black aviator caps.

"Great class today, Thomas," said Cuatro cheerfully.

"Have a good weekend, Thomas!" exclaimed Prince Cinco. Waving goodbye, as they got into a double sidecar motorcycle, the chauffeur passed them little goggles to wear.

"Goodbye, Cuatro and Cinco!" cried Sir Thomas Tattletale, smiling.

Sir Thomas happened to look up and see a magnificent hot air balloon about to land. "Bow bumble!" The hot air balloon, red in color, was painted with bright purple stars and yellow moons.

He wondered who the balloon was for, then Phillip de Curieuse came running down the steps, crying, "Oh my goodness, I do hope I'm not late!" He noticed Sir Thomas sitting on the steps. "Oh, Bonjour Sir Thomas, can't talk now, but have a great weekend!" The boy's chauffeur helped him into the balloon. Up, up, and away they went.

Sir Thomas was still waiting for his ride, when with a smirk on his face, Lord Langley came walking over. "I say, Sir Thomas. What a row in class today! I have two very good pieces of news for you, old chap!"

"Oh, bow bumble! Lord Langley, what could it possibly be?" asked Sir Thomas, with a most somber face.
"Number one, I have my lollipop back!" He said, showing Sir Thomas the red lollipop with a grin on his face, as he gave it a lick.

"I say, how did you get your lollipop back?" Sir Thomas asked. "Let's just say, old chap, that I'm a rather crafty old boy! But wait till I tell you the second piece of good news. I've located your smashing butterfly!" he said, turning the lollipop around to reveal the exotic butterfly stuck to it.

"Lord Langley Lyndon! How could you? What did you do! I never want to talk to you again!" cried Sir Thomas Tattletale.

Lord Langley said calmly, "I say, old boy! No need to be upset. I did not put it there! It must have flown back into the classroom after we left looking for sugar to eat, I say. When I broke into the classroom, the window was already open, you know. Oops!" Lord Langley said with another grin.

With that said, Lord Langley's motorcar pulled up. It was a 1921 Burgundy and Grey English Finch driven by two chauffeurs. "Oh, Sir Thomas Tattletale, please don't be cross with me," he said as one of the chauffeurs picked him up and placed him into the automobile. "I do hope you could still make it to my birthday party, Sir Thomas. Lady Fiona Gainsborough of Hats will be in attendance and you know how much she adores your stories from abroad, old chap!"

As Lord Langley's motorcar drove off, Sir Thomas Tattletale's limousine arrived, kicking up dust down the gravel way. It was a 1918 hunter green steam powered Dormer Dashington. The chauffeur greeted him with a warm smile, "Oh, Sir Thomas, so glad to see you! Your mum misses you so. As does all of Tattletale manor!"

"It's very nice to see you too, Pistachio!" Sir Thomas said, excitedly giving him a hug.

"Your mother is holding a grand dinner party tonight to celebrate your grand aunt's new husband."

"Whatever for?" asked Sir Thomas.
"She wanted to get to know him better. I hear he is one of wealthiest men in Europe. Your aunt Amanda will be attending, as well!"

"Bow bumble that sounds just fantastic! Perhaps aunt Amanda will take me up in her flying machine!" answered Sir Thomas.

"Perhaps she will!" he responded with a lighthearted laugh. "And how was school today, Sir Thomas?"

"Just smashing!" he was quick to reply.

Meanwhile, Henry and Jenny were fast asleep in a French steamer trunk that approached the autumn manor of the Baron and Baroness von Tickle in Heaver, Kent. All the servants stood at attention outside awaiting their arrival. These were not just any servants, however, but a fleet of small trolls, who were dressed in clothing too small for them. They were quite a desolate sight with their bluish-green complexion, bulging eyes, missing teeth, and thinning hair.

As the motorcar slowly stopped in front of the steps of Tickle manor, all the troll servants rushed over, grunting and slobbering, to help with the luggage by climbing up onto the motorcar. The noise of the trolls carrying the trunk woke up the children, who were frightened by the horrible sounds and started to scream.

The Baroness exited the automobile and walked up the steps while holding onto the Baron's arm. The trolls carried their luggage behind them. Upon hearing the children screaming inside the steamer trunk, the Baroness turned around. She bellowed at the trolls, "My little ghastly trolls of the night, take this steamer trunk to the Hexagon Ballroom. Mind you, there shall be no sour milk nor raw fish to eat for you if any damage comes of the contents of this trunk!"

The Hexagon Ballroom of Tickle manor was a room of exquisite hand-carved magnificence. The original 20-foot tall vaulted ceiling was supported by blue sodalite marble columns procured from Bolivia. The massive windows were shaped as hexagons and matched the designs on the floor. The floor included colorful inlaid strips of marble imported from Italy. The walls were imported from France and were made of stained red mahogany with brass inlay that accompanied the hexagonal theme throughout the room.

Six trolls brought in the French steamer trunk on their backs and placed it on the side of the room. As Click Und Snap unlocked the trunk, the Baroness approached it and in a soft voice addressed the children to come out. "Dearest little Peaches, welcome to Tickle manor."

The children slowly opened the trunk and peered out onto a magnificent ballroom. There was a brass pedestal decorated with Egyptian water lilies in the middle of the room. In between each column was a little wooden chair with the seat cushion upholstered with a burgundy damask. As they got out of the trunk, they pleaded with the Baroness to take them home.

"Oh my darlings, I shall indeed, but before I do, you must dance for the Baron and me. Do you know how to foxtrot?" the Baroness asked.

"A little," the children replied, looking at each other.

"Well then I shall show you!" the Baroness said eagerly. After a short period of instruction, the children got the hang of the foxtrot.

Click Und Snap brought in the two-headed horn gramophone player and placed it on the brass pedestal in the middle of the room and began to crank it up. The Baroness then instructed the children to dance around the gramophone player in circles and asked for the Baron to be called to the Hexagon room. The Baron, too weak to walk, was wheeled in a wheelchair by one of the troll servants.

"Just delightful, my dearest Arborvitae. Just delightful!" cried the Baron, clapping his hands.

As the children started to foxtrot around the gramophone player in circles, the Baroness, very pleased with her efforts, cried out, "A little faster my darlings, a little faster! But do try not to laugh, my dearests."

Around and around the children went, to the rhythm of the rickety sounds of ragtime music. Just then, Henry started to laugh. Seeing him laugh, Jenny couldn't help herself and followed suit. "This is not so bad after all. This is rather fun!" exclaimed Henry.

"Indeed, this is fun," cried Jenny. "I can't stop laughing!"

Faster and faster they went, around and around the gramophone player.

Looking on in utter enjoyment were the Baron and Baroness. "Shall we join them, my dearest love?" asked the Baroness. "Oh yes indeed, the time is just right, my dearest Arborvitae!"

The Baron, trembling, inched himself out of his wheelchair and gently grabbed the Baroness' outstretched hand. They both began to slowly dance the foxtrot counterclockwise around the children. The second time around the children, the Baron and Baroness began to move a bit faster. They circled again and again, and moved even faster with each counterclockwise circle. They started to laugh, which seemed to make them move even more quickly. However, something was odd, and the Baron began to look a bit different. After a few more minutes of dancing, they finally stopped and looked at each other. All the Baroness could say to the Baron was "you are as handsome as you were 60 years ago." The Baron was no longer old and sickly, but young and handsome once again.

All this time the children had been dancing unabashedly and when they were too exhausted to dance anymore, they fell to the floor, out of breath. As they looked up at each other, their eyes widened in horror. They were no longer children, but instead were transformed into ghastly little trolls!

As the Baron and Baroness walked over to them, the Baroness pitifully exclaimed, "Oh my darling little ghastly trolls, I can't take you home to mummy now! Why, what would she say? But I have just the most delightful idea. You can both work and earn your keep in one of our charming steel mills." She looked over to the Baron. "What do you think, my dearest love?"

"Oh, what would I do without you, my dearest Arborvitae? As they say here in England, just smashing. Just smashing, my dearest Arborvitae!" He howled with fiendish laughter.

With their hands to their faces, Henry and Jenny were escorted out by the other troll servants.

"Oh my dearest love, look at the time! We have a grand dinner party to attend."

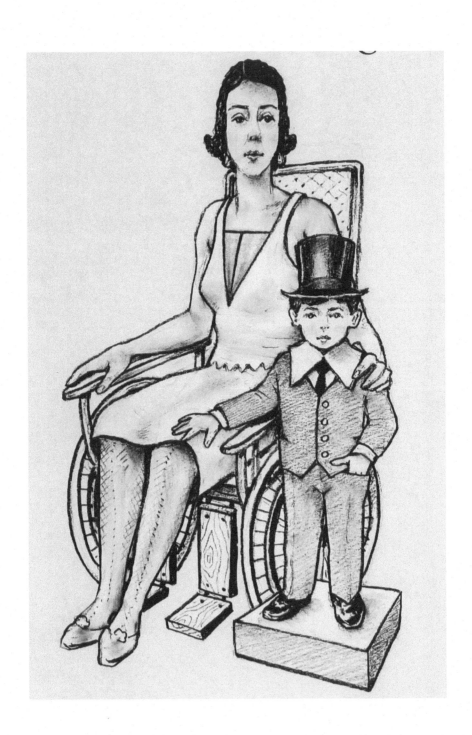

CHAPTER 2
The Grand Dinner Party

The first guest to arrive at Tattletale manor was a most delightful gentleman by the name of Sir Henry Humphrey of The Humphrey Steam Powered Motorcar Company of Londinium. He drove up the gravel roadway in a Canary yellow four-door sedan. Sir Henry Humphrey could be described as a rather colorful man with a nasal laugh and dressed in a red hunting jacket with gold buttons, grey flannel vest, high collar, purple tie, Hound's-tooth cuffed trousers with a black aviator cap.

As he exited his automobile to walk up the steps of Tattletale manor, Sir Henry could not help but notice, looking up into the sky, a rather odd-looking flying machine that was hovering above the house! He could see white smoke coming from its tail. The odd-looking flying machine was making loop-de-loops and sharp turns in mid-air as it tried to spell something in the sky. Looking closely, after a while Sir Henry was able to make out what the aircraft was trying to spell:

HELLO HENRY!

He realized who was doing it! Henry began to laugh. "Muha Muha!!! Haha!" and then he cried, "I say! By Jove! It's Amanda!! Just Smashing!"

Amanda Cruikshank was the second delightful guest to arrive at Tattletale manor. She is the middle sister of Lady Tatiana Tattletale. Amanda is the tinker of the family, who loves to build and repair anything to do with aviation. She was a flight instructor and professional stunt flyer in Austria and today, the proud owner and founder of The Cruikshank's Flight Academy for Adventurous Young Ladies. Sir Henry Humphrey, on the other hand, was famous for his steam-powered motorcars. He was also an advisor and good friend of Lord Titus Tattletale, who himself is an avid collector of automobiles.

Lord Tattletale's collection consists of motorcars from every part of the world. There were some that ran on electric power, while others were powered by steam, and some ran on gasoline. He even had one that ran on peanut butter and raspberry cream!

"Welcome back, Sir Henry! It is so nice to see you again. Lady Tatiana is waiting for you in the solarium."

"Indeed a pleasure Mary, you're looking properly oiled and maintained. Just smashing, you are!" Henry said as he followed her down the hallway to the solarium.

You are probably wondering as to why Sir Henry is talking about Mary as being oiled and maintained. Well, you see, Mary is mechanical: clockwork, you could say. She is an Art Deco masterpiece of ingenuity and one of three clockwork servants at Tattletale Manor. Chris the butler and Mass the caretaker were the other two clockwork servants at the manor. Their outer shell is sculpted in polished brass to simulate skin with interior clockwork mechanisms. On their abdomens, there is a beveled glass door that can be flipped open for repairs if needed.

These mechanical servants can be activated by two mechanisms. One mechanism contains a small crank, which is placed into the side and is used for winding them up. The other mechanism consists of a brass flip switch covered in mother of pearl, which is on the other side. This flip activates an internal self-winding mechanism. Upon activation, it starts bobbing back and forth with a soft "boop-tick" sound. These clockwork people, were a holiday gift by some unknown patron to help Lady Tatiana around the manor.

Sir Henry walked down the marble black and white checkerboard floor and passed Calacatta marble Corinthian columns that lined the Romanesque-style hallway on his way to the solarium. He heard some rather exotic music as he passed by one of the Maplewood doors along his route. He asked leave of Mary, "One moment, Mary. I shall like to investigate this familiar sound. I can find my way to the Solarium thank you."

"Of course, Sir Henry," Mary replied, and proceeded to walk down the hallway.

Sir Henry had heard this music before. But where? He thought to himself. "I say! Its Moroccan, how delightful!" He approached the Maplewood doors and slowly opened them to reveal a magnificent octagonal-shaped portrait room. Grey-veined marble columns lined the room with portraits of Lord Tattletales' family and The Cruikshank family of Scotland (Lady Tatiana's family).

In the middle of this opulent room, he saw a horn gramophone playing the Moroccan music. A little boy in a top hat and burgundy and gold kaftan was dancing around it, laughing. As Sir Henry looked over with sadness, he knew who the little boy was but deliberately did not say a word. Clearing his throat, Sir Henry decided to address the boy, "I say! That is jolly good music you are dancing to, young man!"

The boy turned around in surprise, "Bo bumble! You gave me quite a startle! Welcome to Tattletale manor. You must be Sir Henry. My Name is Sir Thomas Tattletale", he said with a joyous smile as he tipped his top hat, and removed his kaftan. "I am so glad you like my taste in music. Thank you."

"I'm going to meet your mother in the solarium. Would you care to escort me there?" Sir Henry Humphrey asked.

"I shall indeed!" replied Sir Thomas Tattletale.

As they were walking down the hallway, Sir Thomas asked, "Is it true, Sir Henry? You not only make motorcars, but race them, too?"

"Indeed I do young man, in all of England!" replied Sir Henry Humphrey. "I say old boy, have you ever been in a motorcar race be-fore?"

"Why no, I don't believe I have. Sir Henry, is it a fun thing to?" asked Sir Thomas eagerly.

"Indeed it is a fun thing to do!" said Sir Henry, and he began to de-scribe the feeling of racing to Thomas. He got down on one knee, put one arm around Sir Thomas, and held out his other hand in front of them. "My boy, it is truly one of the most exciting things to do in the world of automobiles! Racing down the roadway with the wind in your hair and the roar of the motor, with your opponent far behind you, and then picking up first prize at the finish line." He looked into the distance. "Oh! I say old chap! There is simply nothing like it!" exclaimed Sir Henry Humphrey.

Sir Thomas jumped with excitement. "Bow bumble! Then I would like to go on a motorcar race one day!"

Sir Henry replied, "I'm sure your mother wouldn't mind if you were to attend a motorcar race with me one day," and added, "I say, why there's one coming up next week in Brighton. Perhaps with your mother's permission, you can join me!"

"OH BOW BUMBLE! Sir Henry, I would like that very much." Sir Thomas started jumping up and down, then grasped Sir Henry's hand gently. He looked up at him with a great big smile and proceeded to escort him to the solarium.

Along the way, Sir Henry noticed that Sir Thomas was humming a rather funny little tune as they were walking down the hallway. He inquired, "I say Sir Thomas, what is that rather funny tune you are humming?"

"Oh, it's just little things that happened to me or I see at boarding school. Would you like to hear?" Sir Thomas offered.

"I shall love to hear it. Go on!" replied Sir Henry.

Sir Thomas started to recite. "Today at school, Bartholomew picked his nose and ate a bug for lunch. On the second day at school, I saw a cat dressed in spats eating a rat with a very large hat! On the third day of school, all the children laughed and thought the teacher sat on a baby pig! Instead, it was and baked beans and cabbage, she had!"

"I say! Sir Thomas funny old chap you are! I'm sure your mother would love to hear this!" said Sir Henry, as they both approached the solarium doors to greet Lady Tatiana Tattletale, singing and dancing to Sir Thomas's funny little tune. They opened the French doors onto a magnificent beveled glass and cast iron solarium, which permeated the smell of tea rose and 18th-century English chamber music. There were all sorts of birds - peacocks, doves, parrots of every color - that flew above their heads! They were gifts from Madam Margret Ming of Monte Carlo. There were plants - ferns, fruit trees, and exotic flowers - from every part of the world.

Lady Tatiana Tattletale was confined to a wheelchair due to a motorcar accident, which had taken the life of Sir Thomas's father, Lord Titus Tattletale, in 1918. They approached Lady Tatiana, who was sitting in a mahogany cane wicker back wheelchair, stroking a magnificent Indian peacock in her lap while listening to the radio playing the 18th century chamber music. She was dressed in a tailored Scottish tweed belted jacket. She had vivid blue eyes and lips red as Japanese oil pastels. Her hair was parted to the side, finger-waved and pushed back, and was complemented by teardrop Barouqe earrings.

Hearing the door open and footsteps approach, Lady Tatiana looked up from the radio and instantly her face lit up. "Oh my! Why if it isn't my two favorite gentlemen in the world!" she cried. "Hello Sir Henry. So nice to see you again! And my Little Thom Thom!"

"Such splendid taste in music, dear Lady Tatiana. Georg Philipp Telemann I believe," Sir Henry exclaimed, putting his hand to his ear.

"Oh Sir Henry, correct you are," stated Lady Tattletale, then looked at Thomas and said, "Thom Thom, come and push Mummy to the fountain." Sir Thomas did so.

Sir Henry had words of great urgency to tell Lady Tatiana, and Tatiana, able to sense this, called over to her son. "Thom Thom?"

"Yes mummy," replied Sir Thomas.

"Tonight shall be quite special. You are going to meet my aunt! Your grand aunt and her new husband, your grand uncle! Could you get ready for dinner while I speak to Sir Henry for a moment?"

"Yes, Mummy," replied Sir Thomas, giving her a kiss on the cheek before running through the solarium doors to prepare.

Sir Henry greeted Lady Tatiana with a double kiss on the cheek and said, "It's just so good to see you again, Lady Tatiana!" Sir Henry wasted no time. He sat on the fountain's edge holding Lady Tatiana's hand and began to explain what was amidst.

"It has come to my knowledge that the motorcar in fact on that dreadful day in 1918 was sabotaged by some unknown assailant. After a few years of thorough investigation of your motorcar after the accident, it seems that someone had impaired the brake system on the motorcar."

Lady Tatiana was alarmed, and cried "Why Sir Henry, who could have done such a thing?" Just then, the birds in the solarium went hay-wire! Tatiana and Henry gazed up at the fluttering birds in their frenzy. "That's rather strange. They've never done this before," stated Lady Tat-tletale.

"It is. As if they are trying to escape from something," stated Sir Henry looking curiously up at the birds with a frown.

Just then, Mary the maid abruptly entered the solarium and also gazed up at the frantic birds before announcing that Lady Galina Cruik-shank has arrived.

"Oh how delightful," cried Lady Tattletale as she wheeled herself at a fast pace toward the exit of the solarium. Lady Tatiana realized that Mary had addressed Baroness Galina as Lady and corrected her, "Oh and do remember Mary, she's is a Baroness now." She further inquired, "Oh and Mary, have all the pier mirrors been covered?"

"Yes, Lady Tattletale, they have been covered," Mary replied.

"I say! Covered? What on earth for?" cried Sir Henry as he trailed behind her.

Lady Tattletale explained the odd request to Sir Henry, "Why? It was a request from Aunt Galina. Before they arrive, all the pier mirrors had to be covered with quilts due to her new husband's sensitive eyes toward reflection of light."

"Nonsense, I say!" cried Sir Henry Humphrey. "My god, he must be over a hundred years old to be married to that sour old lemon of an aunt of yours!"

"Oh come now Sir Henry, Aunt Galina is not all that bad. She's just a lady of a great vintage.

"With all due respect, Lady Tatiana, I was never quite fond of your aunt and nor was your husband Lord Titus. He and I only put up with her because he loved you! I thought she was a fowl woman the very first day I set eye's on her in Paris."

"Oh Sir Henry you are just too much. So glad you are here. Come, let's go and welcome them."

The truth was that Sir Henry knew of Galina Cruikshank's squandering of Lady Tatiana's inheritance in Paris on lavish parties and dresses. This had left Tatiana and her sisters penniless in 1914. But Sir Henry never let her know. Instead, Sir Henry introduced her to the dashing Lord Titus of Tattletale to her, one of the wealthiest publishers in England. In 1915, he fell madly in love with Tatiana. It was love at first sight. They married in 1916 and a year later a son was born by the name of Sir Thomas Tattletale.

You see, Lady Galina Cruikshank was the younger sister of Lord Angus Cruikshank, who was the father of the three Cruikshank sisters. Tatiana is the eldest, Amanda in the middle, and Fanny the youngest. When Angus died unexpectedly without a legal will, Galina inherited the vast fortune and estates and was made to adopt the three sisters until they were of age.

All the servants stood at attention to greet at the door as Galina and her new husband Françoise walked up the vestibule steps hand in hand. Chris the butler greeted them at the foot of the steps in the vestibule, and asked, "What name shall I announce, Madam?"

"The Baron and Baroness Galina and Françoise Von Chatouiller," Galina replied. Galina had the skin of a peach, eyes of hazel green, and lips the color of cherries. She was dressed in 1918 splendor and had long, silky black hair turned up in a large grey hat decorated with three doves, wings extended. She wore a pastel grey walking suit with a six strand pearl choker with a vibrant green emerald surrounded by small diamonds. The Baroness gracefully removed a large pearl stick pin from her hat and placed both on a nearby Italian Giltwood console in the hallway as she walked in.

"Oh! How so very nice it is to be back at Tattletale Manor!" said the Baroness, turning gently toward her husband. Françoise had chiseled features with a small mustache and long blond wavy hair that was pushed back. He was elegantly dressed in a long black wool coat with beaver trim on the collar and cuffs, and sported grey spats. He took off his black silk top hat and placed it by Galina's on the gilt wood console table in the hallway.

As they walked in, rolling up to greet them was Lady Tatiana and Sir Henry. Both of them looked in shock at how youthful the Baroness and the Baron both looked! Sir Henry whispered to Tatiana, "What witchcraft is this? Your aunt is at least 30 years older than me! By Jove, that sour lemon has done it!"

"Oh Sir Henry what has she done?" asked Lady Tatiana with a chuckle. "She's finally managed to sell herself to the devil in order to look that way!" exclaimed Sir Henry.

As they approached, Aunt Galina cried "Oh look my love, this is my dearest niece Tatiana, simply a dearest peach. And how is my favorite invalid niece doing?" she said with pity.

Lady Tatiana replied, "So very nice to see you, Aunt Galina!" The Baroness extended her arms as Lady Tattletale approached, bending down to give her niece a double kiss on the cheek. Lady Tatiana looked at the Baroness with surprise. "I'm very well, Aunt Galina! I must say you look absolutely stunning. You looked as you did when I was 19 years old."

The Baroness waved her hand to dismiss the compliment and said, "Oh come now, nonsense I say!" She turned toward her husband, the Baron. "Tatiana, this is my new husband Françoise."

"Indeed a pleasure to meet you, Lady Tatiana," the Baron said, kissing her hand. With a warm smile, Lady Tatiana said, "Thank you, dear Baron, It is also a pleasure. I've heard so much about you. Welcome to Tattletale manor." Lady Tatiana introduced the two gentlemen, "This is Sir Henry Humphrey."

The Baron smiled. "A pleasure, Sir Henry." As Sir Henry shook his hand with a bow, the Baron asked, "Are you the Sir Henry of The Humphrey Steam-powered Motorcars of Londinium?"

"Indeed I am, dear Baron." Sir Henry replied, his eyebrows raised.

The Baron said, "I simply adore your motorcars. Just so innovative."

Sir Henry still gazed at both of them. "You must forgive us for staring. We had no idea you were so young!" exclaimed Sir Henry.

As they all started to walk down the hallway to the drawing room, Françoise said, looking up at the Romanesque architecture, "Might I say you have a magnificent home."

Lady Tatiana replied courteously, "Thank you, Françoise. I'm sure your castles would put my home to shame. I hear you are also quite a brilliant inventor."

"Why yes, in my earlier days that is," he replied.

Lady Tatiana was surprised, "Earlier days?" she asked.

Galina, immediately alarmed, interrupted them by clearing her throat. She grabbed Françoise by the arm and looked over at Sir Henry to get off the subject of 'earlier days' and tried to quickly mend the slip. With spite in her eyes, she pulled back to her husband's earlier comments on Sir Henry. "Why Sir Henry, I thought your motorcar company went bankrupt years ago." Then she whispered in her husband's ear, "Poor Sir Henry must be here looking for funding."

She then continued to talk to Sir Henry, "Oh Sir Henry, I just thought you'd like to know my husband buys little companies such as yours."

Sir Henry replied with distaste, "Why dear Galina, in the event that I was to go bankrupt or run out of steam to power my motorcars, I would indeed know where to go for an old bag of hot air!"

As they continued to walk down the hallway, Aunt Galina had words with Tatiana. "Oh such a pity to be confined to that dreadful wheelchair, my love, and so pretty," she said to Lady Tatiana as she caressed her hair.

Lady Tatiana softly replied, "Why Aunt Galina it's not a pity nor is it dreadful for me to be in a wheelchair. In fact, it's made me even more independent! My work at Tattletale Publishing in Londinium keeps me active and even the sales are up 45% since I've joined them."

"Oh, that's just so nice to hear, dearest peach. Well in these modern times, my love, I'm sure anything is possible," she replied nonchalantly. She seemed relaxed with the change in topic. "And how are your sisters doing?"

"Amanda's doing very well. She's a flight instructor in Austria," Lady Tatiana replied.

Aunt Galina hid her contempt nicely, "Well, that's just so pleasant to hear. Amanda was always getting her hands dirty. And little Fanny?"

Happily, Lady Tatiana said, "Oh she's a night club entertainer in Paris!"

Aunt Galina recoiled, and then placed her hand to chest said, "My goodness, Fanny can sing? I thought perhaps she would be a clown in a circus."

Lady Tatiana tried to dismiss the ridicule and said, "Oh Aunt Galina, you are so funny. I hear Fanny's quite popular in France and the Americas."

Galina paused for a moment as she peered down the hallway, looking intently at something. "I say! Is that a little top hat coming from behind that marble column I see before me?" she cried.

Lady Tatiana also looked in that direction to see that indeed a little top hat was protruding from a column in the hallway. She smiled and said, "A little top hat you say, Aunt Galina? Oh, my Aunt Galina why that's my little Thomas!!" Then she called out and beckoned Sir Thomas, "Thomas do come out and say hello to your grand aunt!"

"Yes Mummy!" came the reply from Thomas, who then presented himself from behind the marble column. "Hello, Aunt Galina," he said as he tipped his hat with a bow.

"Well now is that all I get from my scrumptious little apple!" She stated with her hands on her hips.

"Yes," Thomas replied with a straight face.

"Now is that any way to treat your favorite aunty," said Aunt Galina as she got down on both knees and extended her arms out to him. She motioned, "A kiss and a hug will do perfectly fine, my little scrumptious."

Sir Thomas appeared unsure. "I don't know," replied Sir Thomas, looking at his mother.

"You don't know what, Thomas?" Aunt Galina asked softly.

"I do not know if you're my favorite aunty!" he replied, running over to his mother and sitting in her lap and hiding his face in her bosom.

Lady Tatiana, in an effort to make up for Sir Thomas's shyness said, "Oh Galina, my little Thom Thom is just being shy."

Then they proceeded down the hallway as Sir Thomas sat in his mother's lap. He looked up to his mother and in a soft voice told his mother, "I'm not shy mummy. I just don't like her."

As they approached the resting rooms for the Baroness and the Baron, Lady Tatiana informed Aunt Galina, "Amanda will be dining with us tonight after she lands and Fanny will be here next month for a visit."

Walking down the hallway coming from the opposite direction was Amanda, still dressed in her aviation gear. Amanda was a big-boned gal with cap and goggles in hand, wearing riding jodhpurs, high boots, and sporting a small strand of pearls.

She burst out, "Well! Whoop de do me, Aunt Galina, what in tarnation are you drinking, or smoking for that matter, to look like that!" She robustly smacked her knee.

Lady Tatiana immediately interrupted, "Oh Amanda dearest! Your nephew is standing right here beside me! Do remember to watch what you say, dear sister."

Aunt Galina looked up into the air and rolling her eyes said, "I see your sister hasn't changed a bit!"

Amanda, unbothered, turned her attention to Thomas, "Oh my, whoop de do! If it isn't my little angel of the skies! Pardon my French! And come give Aunty Amanda a big hug love!"

"Bo Bumble and a boo boo whoop de do, to you Aunty!" Sir Thomas said, running over to give her a big hug as Amanda picked him up and twirled him around.

Then she turned to Sir Henry as she put Thomas down and said, "Hello, Sir Henry." She shook his hand firmly and asked, "How are things at Humphrey motorcars?"

Sir Henry cheerfully replied, "Just utterly smashing like you, Amanda!"

As the resting rooms approached, Lady Tatiana summoned Chris. Then, turning to Aunt Galina, she said, "Galina and Françoise, Chris will show you to your room. We will be dining in the Burgundy room at nine."

The Burgundy room at Tattletale manor was called this because of the deep burgundy damask cloth that covered the walls. It was highlighted with gold leaf baroque framed works of art of the countryside and Sir Thomas' drawings from school that his mother had framed. A Neoclassical grey-veined marble fireplace adorned with two Edwardian nymphs dominated the center of the room and was topped with four blue and white Chinese porcelain jars, with a Regency mantle clock in the middle that chimed every hour. From the painted burgundy and gold leaf vaulted ceiling was one of Amanda's flying machines, hung stylishly by wire cables in the middle of the dining room. This was a new addition to the room. Actually, it was Amanda's first biplane. She had crashed it through the dining room window into the fireplace in 1916. Lady Tattletale had thought it to be quite a smashing work of modern art and so she ordered it to be hung above the dining table.

Soon it was evening and the guests arrived for dinner, all of whom were surprised at the breathtaking appearance of the Baron and Baroness Von Chatouiller as they were announced. All eyes were on the pair as the guests entered the Burgundy room.

The first course served was of onion tomato soup topped with moon-shaped croutons. As the guests drank the vintage wine, it was a rather frightening sight to see Baroness Galina at the dinner table that night by candlelight with not one grey hair, nor a single blemish upon her skin. One could never think of her as the aunt of Lady Tattletale and grand aunt of Sir Thomas Tattletale.

The second course was roasted chicken breast stuffed with a seafood medley of lobster and shrimp, and topped with a garlic vinaigrette sauce. As everybody began to dine, conversation started to flow.

"I say dear Baron, but where did you get such an unusual title as 'Von'? Isn't that German?" asked Sir Henry across the table.

The Baron replied calmly, "Why yes, it is quite unusual my Dear Sir Henry. The title was bestowed upon me in the little town of Gemütlich Germany, when I had purchased one of their main products of export. The people of Gemütlich were so pleased by my charity in saving their town from bankruptcy I was later given the title of Von."

"Gemütlich, you say?" asked Sir Henry. "Why Lord Titus and I knew of a German Prince in that region by the name of Prince Henrik Von Schnapps. He owned an automobile company. Sad to say that the dear man perished in an automobile accident along with Lord Titus, as Lady Tatiana survived."

"Most unfortunate!" answered Françoise.

Just then, Amanda interrupted the conversation, as she looked at her sister and Sir Thomas, then at the Baron across the table, with a grin. "I say Françoise, your last name Chatouiller in English means Tickle! Does it not?"

"Why yes it does!" he replied, "Your knowledge of French is out-standing, dear Amanda!"

"I'm fluent in French, you know!" Amanda replied with a smile.

"Oh, how completely charming," stated Baroness Galina with a smirk.

"I just thought that was the funniest thing when Tatiana told me your last name!" cried Amanda. Holding Sir Thomas in her arms, she began to tell him a story about Aunt Galina. "When Tatiana and I were young, our nickname for Galina was Aunt Giggles because when father would hurt himself, she would giggle and laugh. So Sir Thomas you may now address them as the Baron and Baroness Giggle Von Tickle!" and Amanda began to tickle Sir Thomas Tattletale. Sir Thomas started to chuckle, then he started to laugh and laugh louder and louder!

Amidst this laugh riot, everyone at the table noticed that something was wrong with the Baron. He had started to gag and choke holding on to the edge of the dinner table and was shaking everything on it! He then went into convulsions and fell on the floor.

The Baroness immediately rushed to his aid asking him, "My dearest pineapple what's going on?" As she asked, she put her hand on his chest, trying to loosen his tie.

The Baron gasped, "Take me up to our room quickly my dearest Arborvitae!!"

As the other guests tried to assist them, the Baroness realized that something was seriously amiss. She blamed the Baron's sudden shaking and tremors on the weather and said, "Not to worry! I can handle it form here." Galina covered Françoise's mouth with a lace napkin and put her arm around him, and escorted him back up to their room.

As they were leaving the Burgundy room, Sir Henry cried out, "I say the roasted chicken wasn't all that bad!" and then suddenly, as he remembered something, he mumbled to himself, "I say I do remember someone with an automobile entry by the name of F. Du Tickle? But he was an old man!"

En route to their room, Françoise was still coughing and shaking as he yelled out, "I do believe that dammed boy's laughter shall be a problem for us, my dear Arborvitae!"

As they entered their bedroom and Françoise sat down on the bed, he was still holding the lace napkin over his mouth. Françoise had stopped coughing now and removed the napkin from his mouth. He felt much better. The Baron even started to laugh, "I feel wonderful now!" He then started to jump up and down on the bed laughing! He felt full of vitality.

The Baroness screamed in horror, "Ah! Oh my! My dearest love, look at your face! Go to the mirror!" The Baron could sense her fear and slowly walked over to a long mirror with his hand to his face. Upon reaching the mirror, he simply stared with shock. His clothing hung off him! The Baron was no longer 35 years old, but 15 years old!

"Oh, mon dieu!! How are we going to explain this?" cried the Baron. Suddenly, he started having convulsions once again and fell to the floor.

"Oh my love, is there anything I can do!" cried the Baroness, as she was not affected by this bizarre event.

The Baron covered his face in shame and said, "My dearest Arborvitae, I do think I may need your assistance in getting back up!"

Galina rushed over to help Françoise off the floor, "Oh my dearest, you are old once again!" She screamed in horror. He looked skeletal with pieces of his wavy blond hair in his hands. "How is this possible, my dearest pineapple!" she exclaimed.

Françoise sat covering his face in tears crying on the bed. "It was at the dinner tonight. Your grand nephew's laughter did it without dancing nor music playing! Damned that Thomas Tattletale has extracted my wonderful youth. What am I to do now?"

"Well then my love, we must have Sir Thomas Tattletale over for tea at Heaver Castle and perhaps a dance lesson!" she said slyly.

"Oh my dearest Arborvitae you think of everything!" replied Françoise, as they both laughed.

CHAPTER 3
Amanda's Guest Room

As the sun rose on the misty grounds of Tattletale manor, Sir Thomas was awoken by a flock of birds that were flying past his window. Rubbing his eyes, Thomas slowly walked over to the window to witness the exotic birds fly back to the solarium. It was then Thomas noticed a colorful toucan, resting on the ledge of the window.

"Good morning Mr. Toucan, and welcome back," he said with a smile. Just as he said that, a thunderous crash rang out and the toucan flew off in fright. "Bo bumble, it sounded like one of Amanda's flying machines!" thought Sir Thomas.

He rushed out of his bedroom, through the hallway, and down the steps. He bumped into Sir Henry along the way, who sported a purple nightcap, and was still in his striped blue and white pajamas and a long burgundy paisley robe.

"Why good morning, young Thomas!" replied Sir Henry.

Sir Thomas was brimming with excitement, and hurriedly cried, "And a good morning to you, Sir Henry. Come quickly, I do believe Amanda's flying machine has crashed!"

"I say! What a row this morning, old chap! I do hope the noise did not disturb the Baron and Baroness's beauty rest!" Sir Henry stated in a sarcastic tone, looking over at Thomas with a grin. "Come now, young Thomas, let's investigate!"

As Lady Tattletale approached them, she overheard said, "Oh Sir Henry, I'm afraid they both left in the middle of the night."

"Indeed!" cried Sir Henry, "Well if that isn't the rudest thing!"

"They did leave a note," Lady Tattletale replied. It explained that they had to leave on urgent business and that Thomas should come to visit Heaver Manor one day."

"By Jove! They didn't even have the common decency to thank you for your most gracious hospitality!" said Sir Henry, surprised at their sudden departure.

"Oh Sir Henry, look on the bright side, our wonderful birds are back. I saw them this morning - but oh! What was that horrific sound?" exclaimed Lady Tatiana as they entered the main hallway, where everyone stood.

Chris the butler announced in a calm voice, "Something has landed in one of our Elm trees."

"Hurry! Hurry Mummy! It could be Aunt Amanda!" Sir Henry cried.

"Oh my! I do hope it's not Amanda," cried Lady Tattletale, and called out for a motorcar urgently. "Pistachio! Pistachio, the motorcar if you please!"

The whole house was in a commotion and as Lady Tattletale took the motorcar, Sir Henry and Sir Thomas went on foot. The rest of the servants also bolted out the manor doors and onto the grounds.

As they got closer to the grand elm, they all realized to their surprise that it was not Amanda's biplane after all, but instead another flying machine which they had never seen before. It was painted bright yellow with bold vertical blue and white stripes on its shattered wings. While they all were looking at the crashed aircraft, they heard a voice from behind.

With her hands on both hips looking up at the wreckage at the back of Sir Henry and Lady Tattletale, Amanda cried out, "Well whoop de doo me!"

"Why Amanda you are here! You gave us all quite a startle you know!" exclaimed Lady Tattletale.

"We all thought it was one of your flying machines, Aunty!" stated Sir Thomas, then added, "Indeed you did Amanda, but if that's not your flying machine, whose is it?"

Amanda inspected the wreckage and cried, "I say, why it's Ms. Daisy's biplane, one of my finest instructors at the academy. I wonder what happened? She and four others were supposed to meet me here this morning for air drills for a big race."

As they all approached the grand elm tree to give assistance to Ms. Daisy, she was nowhere to be found. All they could see in the wreckage was the smoldering engine.

"I say, perhaps Ms. Daisy was knocked clear of the wreckage upon impact!" stated Sir Henry.

Everyone split up to search the grounds for Ms. Daisy, and Sir Thomas also decided to help look. Across the way from the grand elm was a blossoming pear tree. As Sir Thomas peered around it, he noticed a long piece of white fabric cascading from one of the branches of the pear tree. Sir Thomas thought to himself, "I say, a clue!" as he walked slowly toward the pear tree to get a closer look. He saw that the hanging white fabric was a long white scarf. He looked up into the tree to see where the scarf led.

Thomas cried out, "Bow Bumble! I found her, I found her! I believe it's Ms. Daisy. Come quickly Mummy! Sir Henry, I think she's dead!" There was a lady hanging upside down from a branch wearing the long white scarf. It was made of silk and covered part of her face.

Suddenly a nonchalant voice rang out from the branch, "I say, dead body? Where, what, and whom does it belong to! Oh, I do hope there were no casualties," she cried.

"Bow bumble, why, you are alive!!" cried Sir Thomas Tattletale.

"What kind of a silly question is that? Of course I'm alive! Why wouldn't I be, silly boy?" Ms. Daisy said as she removed the silk scarf from her face, revealing her bobbed strawberry blond hair, which matched her lips. She wore a tailored burgundy leather aviator's outfit.

A bit startled, Sir Thomas immediately took off his top hat and apologized, "Oh you must forgive me, Ms. Daisy, I did not mean to be rude."

"Darling you are so formal, just call me Oopsi, lovely boy! And what is your name young man?" she asked.

"Oh, my name is Thomas, Sir Thomas Tattletale. Pleased to meet you Oopsi. Welcome to Tattletale manor!" he replied.

"Well, well, it seems I've reached my destination, my lovely. Say, I seem to be stuck. Could I have some assistance, lovely Thomas of Tattletale?"

Everybody started gathering around the tree. Mass the caretaker brought over a ladder and propped it up against the pear tree and began to help Ms. Daisy down.

"Mary mother of applesauce who in the world would have tropical birds in the middle of England, I say!" exclaimed Ms. Daisy, as Mass carried her over his shoulder and down the ladder.

"It's my mummy's birds," replied Sir Thomas, smiling and twisting back and forth.

"Oh I see no worries my lovely, I'm here now," replied Ms. Daisy, as she looked up into the air.

Amanda rushed towards them, shouting, "I say old girl, are you all in one piece?"

"Why, is that you, Amanda? So glad to hear your voice. Just lower it a bit, lovely, I have a splitting headache. I didn't go deaf in the crash, lovely Amanda!"

"Oh, Oopsi! You are such a hoot, but what in the world happened? You're one of my best instructors."

"I thought I had taken a wrong turn until those birds flew up into the biplane. I swerved and missed them!"

"Outstanding maneuver, old girl. Just outstanding, I knew it." she stated, smacking her knee!

Ms. Daisy smiled, "It's going to take more than a flock of birds to discombobulate this old girl!"

Amanda replied, "Ah, that's my girl talking! Nails and bricks you are!" She headed back to Tattletale manor.

As they were all moving toward the mansion, they heard a loud humming sound above their heads which was getting louder. They all looked up in amazement at four magnificent flying machines approaching Tattletale Manor from the sky.

Amanda excitedly cried, "Whoop whoop de do! The other ladies are arriving!" She jumped up and down with excitement.

Hovering above their heads were the instructors of her flight academy. Each was unique in style and color. The first one to land was a single engine biplane with a broad wingspan and short body made of wood and waxed white canvas with only one large propeller in back. It was decorated with large red hearts on each of its wings and side doors. It belonged to Ms. Oki Nocadoki of Japan, who is a nurse and inventor of the translucent Boo Boo lipstick from the kingdom of Ooh nee-booboo Japan. As she exited her biplane in a white cap and black goggles, she applied red lipstick to her lips in long vertical striped black and white gauntlet gloves. There was a large red heart sewn on the right side of her white belted leather aviator coat, contrasted by white pants and black riding boots. Clasping her hands to her chest, she greeted everybody with a soft smile and giggle and said, "Kon'nichiwa, everyone!"

"Hello! Pleased to meet you!" Sir Thomas said with a smile. "I don't mean to be rude, but your last name is rather hard for me to pronounce."

She smiled back warmly and said, "Oh that's ok! Just call me Okidoki!" with a giggle.

Sir Thomas, curious as he was, had yet another question, "Why is there a red heart sewn onto your coat?"

She explained calmly, "You see, when I was little girl, I could not laugh nor giggle so my mother crafted many red suede hearts to be sewn on all my clothes. Whenever I was sad, my mother would poke me with her finger on the red heart that was sewn on my dress and I would giggle."

Hearing the conversation between them, Amanda joined in saying, "Thomas she invented the Translucent Booboo Lipstick."

Thomas turned and looked blankly at her. "I've never heard of Boo Boo Lipstick before, aunty. What it is?"

"What! You never heard of Translucent Booboo lipstick?" exclaimed Okidoki with surprise, "Whenever a child falls down and gets a boo boo on their knee or elbow or on a finger, their mother applies it to her lips in secret. Then, kissing a child's boo-boo immediately afterward removes the pain and suffering."

Sir Thomas was in amazement and took a liking to her instantly.

The second flying machine was a double triplane, made of aluminum painted black with a skull and crossbones motif on the door with exquisite bat-like wings. It had three in the front and three in the back. It was propelled by eight propellers located on top of the wings, four in the front and four in the back. As it landed, the propellers rotated upward and set down like a gyrocopter. This belonged to Countess Fantaisie de Vol of France, an archaeologist and adventure. Her black leather aviator outfit was trimmed in monkey fur on the collar and cuffs. With an eye patch like a pirate holding an unlit cigarette in black suede gloves, she gracefully walked down the steps of her flying apparatus. "Bonjour Amanda! Mon Cher is Oopsi Dead?" she asked in a nonchalant voice while Okidoki lit her cigarette.

"Oh never mind, Amanda. Merci, I see and hear her now! Bonjour Oopsi so glad you are alive and kicking Mon Cheri!"

"Yeah right!" replied Oopsi.

Taking a second puff of her cigarette, the Countess then looked over at Thomas, "Now, now and who is this little flight devil I see before me?" she asked.

"My name is Thomas." Sir Thomas replied cordially.

"I'm Fanta, pleased to meet you. I've heard so much about you from your aunty," she added.

Sir Thomas was still staring at her eye patch, "Are you a pirate?" asked Sir Thomas?"

Fanta was enjoying her talk with Sir Thomas. "Now what would ever give you that idea, young man?"

Pointing at the patch, Sir Thomas replied, "Well I noticed your eye patch, and you have a skull and crossbones on your flying machine."

"Oh Mon Cheri, I was putting on mascara when I hit an air pocket in flight. I lost one eye in the process," she replied.

"Bow bumble! Quite extraordinary," exclaimed Thomas, still unable take his eyes off her eye patch.

Fanta added, "The crossbones motif was my great great great grandfather's. Now, he was a real pirate!"

"I say! It could also mean you're poisonous, dear lady!" cried Sir Henry, with a laugh.

Looking over her shoulder, the Countess replied to Sir Henry's comment, "Mon Cheri, only when I'm double crossed! And to whom do I have the pleasure of addressing in the purple nightcap?"

Sir Henry answered, "Sir Henry Humphrey, my dear Gothic Princess of the air."

"Oh! Of the steam-powered motorcars?" The Countess asked.

"The very person, my enchanted Gothic Princess of the sky," he replied courteously.

Holding out her black gloved hand to be kissed, she announced her name, "I am not a princess, Mon Cheri, but the Countess de Vol. A pleasure indeed!" she said, and smiled.

"Indeed a pleasure, dear Countess de Vol," Sir Henry said, kissing her hand. "I've heard of your many adventures abroad from Amanda. You must tell me more." Extending his arm, Sir Henry asked the Countess, "May I have the pleasure of escorting you back to the Tattletale manor?"

"Why not, Mon Cheri," she replied as she placed her hand in his, and they walked off to Tattletale manor.

The third to land was an elongated baby blue Zeppelin with a white and red bull's eye design on it. On its red base were small wings that held two large propellers. This belonged to Dr. Cumulus Primrose of San Francisco, a meteorologist and a part-time botanist. As she stepped off her airship, everyone noticed her blue hair and darkly tinted goggles. In a most unfortunate accident, while conducting atmospheric research, Dr. Primrose was struck by lightning, which had left her with permanent light blue hair and sensitively to bright light. Hence, she wore the dark flight goggles.

As Sir Thomas looked on, he said to his mother, "Her hair matches her outfit mummy!"

"Why yes indeed it does, my love," replied Thomas's mother.

"Thomas, she's one of the best meteorologist in the world, you know," exclaimed Amanda.

Sir Thomas asked, "What is a meteorologist?"

"It is a person that studies the atmosphere around us, the weather, you can say," she replied, and then added, "Before we take to the skies, we look to Dr. Primrose for our flight conditions."

Dr. Primrose's outfit was as blue as her hair, but the red and white bull's eye motif donned on the back of her aviator's coat and sleeves. As she exited her aircraft and approached Amanda, she cried, "Blueberries and cream corn!" and asked anxiously from Amanda, "I do hope Oopsi is ok. I saw the wreckage from above!"

The fourth aircraft was a quadro plane, built by the owner Ms. Bixby Trumbow of Chicago, an aeronautical engineer and architect. The wings of her flying machine were painted in bold black and white stripes, with the body painted in bright red. They could see that the Bixby's motif on her door was a black square with roman numbers XXI in gold leaf. Powdered smoke came from the tail of her flying machine as she made large loop-de-loops through the air and howling like a wolf before she landed!

Bixby Trumbow was dressed in a green herringbone tweed aviator outfit with brown beaver trim collar that was accessorized by a long strand of pearls that stopped at her knees. As she straightened up her strand of pearls, she walked toward Amanda and her family. Midway, Bixby paused for a moment and took a flask of whiskey out of her boot to take a swig, then cried, "Heidi ho, Amanda!" She reached out to give her a hug, then glanced around. "Oh honey, looking at the wreckage, I think we are going to be a wee bit late for the England to Norway air races. What do you think, Doc?"

"Oh Bixby, it looks like we are all going to have to put on our thinking caps for this one," replied Dr. Primrose.

"Yes absolutely, if we want to be on time for the grand air race," said Amanda.

Oopsi came over and asked Bixby, "Oh lovely Bixby, do have any more of that cough medicine you pulled out of your boot? I could sure use some about now!"

"My god, here take it! You need it more than me, sister. Just use a spoon, honey! I only have two swigs left," cried Bixby.

Twisting back and forth and smiling innocently, Sir Thomas interrupted as he looked on, "Oh don't worry Bixby, mummy has plenty of cough medicine up at the house. She hasn't gotten sick in ages!"

After Sir Thomas's comment, there was a brief silence among the ladies. But as they looked at each other, there was an eruption of uproarious laughter between them.

Brimming with affection, Amanda remarked, "Ladies now, that's my little angel of the skies! Oh, whoop de doo!" Still laughing robustly, she swooped up Thomas in her arms and gave him a great big kiss. "Come, ladies, let's discuss this further up in my guest room." Then as she put Thomas down, Amanda got down on one knee and, smiling, asked, "Thomas would you like to join us? Perhaps you could help us put on our thinking caps."

Thomas was excited. "Bow bumble! I would indeed, aunty" replied Thomas, smiling. Then, he turned toward his mother and asked, "Would it be ok mummy?"

"I don't see why not, my love!" replied Lady Tattletale.

Thomas gave a quick hug to his mother. "Thank you, Mummy."

Amanda caught hold of his hand and said, "Well then, come on my angel of the skies!"

Amanda's guest room was not just a room but a three-story gymnasium dedicated to all of her aviation paraphernalia. Lady Tatiana adored her sister and supported everything she did, and therefore, had given her the northern part of Tattletale manor. The gymnasium was Moorish in style and had a magnificent arched cast iron cylinder glass ceiling. There was a spectator gallery on the second floor, which was used for roller-skating with a running track above it. The third floor, was used for Amanda's motorcycles and bicycle races. As they approached the mahogany-coffered double doors that lead into Amanda's guest room, Sir Thomas admired the crisscross brass aviation propellers that decorated the doorway above. They marveled at the interior as they walked in amidst the Moorish splendor of the gymnasium palm trees planted in blue and white Chinese porcelain fish bowls that complimented the Palladian style windows. They could see all three levels up to the ceiling.

They could hear music coming from the second landing. Just then, Bixby Trumbow cried out, "Say who's playing that music?" which was followed by a loud ring of laughter.

"What's all the commotion about, Bixby?" asked Amanda, hearing the ruckus.

"I brought this record back in Chicago and loaned it out to Fanta two months ago and never got it back! The record sounded like 'This Is the Life, by Irving Berlin,' 1914. Well whoop de doo me, ladies. Thomas, let's all take a gander!"

Upon walking in, they all could see that a gramophone was indeed the source of the music being played, same as the one Bixby talked about. Looking up to the second landing, Bixby was thoroughly irritated. "It's what I suspected all along!" she cried.

It was Sir Henry Humphrey and Countess Fanta de Vol roller skating arm in arm and laughing to the music. "Oh, Mon Cheri Bixby, so sorry, I just love it so. It just makes me laugh!" said Fanta to Bixby as they both glanced at them, seeing them all come in.

With a naughty smile, Bixby said, "Great! So after your finished rolling around up there I should expect it to be given back to me. Oui Oui!!"

"Oh Oui Oui, Mon Cheri," replied Fanta de Vol.

Sir Henry was thoroughly enjoying himself as they skated arm in arm without stopping on the second floor above and exclaimed, "I say! Indeed it does make me quite happy too!"

As they stood in the middle of the gymnasium, the ladies looked up in awe at the arched cast iron glass ceiling. From this vantage point, they had a panoramic view of the landing to the ceiling.

"Just lovely, Amanda. You have quite a spread here!" exclaimed Oopsi Daisy with.

Bixby cried, "I'll say! It must be hell to clean!"

Amanda laughed at Bixby's comment.

"This music makes me giggle too! Are you having fun, Fanta?" cried Okidoki up to the second landing, as she shimmied to the music.

"Oh Mon Cheri Oki there is nothing like it at all!" replied Countess Fanta as she and Henry twirled around and around above their heads.

Still admiring the interiors, Dr. Primrose inquired, "Magnificent indeed but where do you sleep, Amanda?"

Amanda replied, "Ladies my room is on the third floor and your rooms will be on the second."

"You can holler over the banister to my aunt Amanda if you need anything ladies," Sir Thomas added.

Out of the blue, holding up both of her hands in the air, Dr. Primrose cried out, "Blueberry pancakes with bananas and strawberries syrup!"

"I think that's a very funny saying, Dr. Primrose!" Sir Thomas stated with a giggle.

"Funny saying? What funny saying?" asked Dr. Primrose. "Are you mad boy?" she said, looking at Thomas in a most curious manner. "I was talking about breakfast tomorrow morning!"

"Oh, forgive me!" cried Thomas embarrassed by his comment."

Bixby Trumbow swished her hand over to Dr. Primrose. "Apple-sauce, I say" she cried. Then, she put her arm around Thomas to comfort him. "Don't worry about her, Thomas, she's hasn't been the same since she was struck by lightning! Cumulus Primrose used to eat pancakes with just sugar and butter."

"Bow bumble, really! Well, thank God for that lighting!"

"And why do you say that honey?" asked Bixby.

"Well because I really like blueberry pancakes topped with sliced bananas." he said with a large grin.

Bixby replied, "I agree with you on that!"

Bixby and Okidoki covered their mouths as they laughed at Thomas's last comment.

Amanda's room was located at the end of the gymnasium. An ornately polished brass gothic spiral staircase led up to her room on the third floor. In the middle on the left-hand side of the gymnasium was a hand-operated French brass elevator that was decorated with images of Hathor and Jupiter stopped on both floors.

Bixby was still worried over the great air race event and asked Amanda, "What do you think, Amanda? I mean do you think will make it on time?"

Scratching her head, Amanda said with a most optimistic grin, "Well it seems we have been blessed with an aeronautical engineer."

Bixby looked at her and said, "Holy Heidi-ho, Amanda! I did not bring any spare parts, only assembly tools for my aircraft!"

"Oh no need to fret, my dear Bixby! I have plenty of drafting paper and all the aeronautical accouterments you would ever need here," she said, trying to comfort Bixby.

Bixby wanted her to know the limitations. "That's great news, sister, but I still have no major parts to assemble a brand new flying machine!"

The ladies were listening in to the conversation and they formed a group huddle. They decided to put their minds together to sail through the situation and help Oopsi. Indeed, they each came up with a creative idea!

"Oh, Mon Cheri I can spare three of my propellers and various parts, if needed," stated Countess Fanta."

And I can provide a canvas for wings and body if you wish, Bixby," added Oki Nocadoki.

"Well I can still fly without two of my small air-cooled engines," exclaimed Dr. Primrose.

"Whoop de do ladies! That sounds just fantastic. So what do you think Bixby?" Amanda asked exuberantly.

"Amanda, I think this can be done!" cried Bixby as she rubbed her chin and smiled.

Ms. Daisy was extremely excited and said, "Oh lovely Bixby, can you really?" She grasped her hands with joy.

Bixby, now relieved, wanted to begin the repair work as soon as possible. She enthusiastically said, "Indeed I can, Oopsi. Ladies, let's get to work!"

"Just fantastic, Bixby!" said Aunt Amanda as she smacked her knee.

"We can assemble it here in the gymnasium and disassemble it when we're finished. I'm quite sure the ladies will give you assistance in reassembling it outside when we are ready to go, Bixby."

With that said, all the ladies ran out toward their flying apparatus to gather the parts needed for Oopsi's new flying machine.

Then Dr. Cumulus had an idea. "Say ladies, why don't you pack the things we need on my air zeppelin. I could fly up and land on the roof of Tattletale manor with the supplies we need."

Bixby instantly liked the idea. "This would save us a great deal of time! Great idea, Cumulus!"

Oki Doki was thrilled. "Wonderful idea."

"Juste Magnifique, Mon Cheri" stated Countess de Vol as she took a drag of her cigarette.

Oopsi joined in. "Just splendid, Lovely Cumulus, just delightful!"

Lady Tatiana had been listening in to the entire conversation and was pleased with the way ladies had come together to help Oopsi. She looked at Sir Thomas, who was listening intently to the ladies. "What do you think my little Thom Thom?" asked Lady Tattletale.

"Bow bumble, Mummy. It sounds smashingly delightful."

The ladies went to work and gathered everything in Cumulus' air zeppelin as discussed. Then, gracefully landing on the rooftop of Tattle-tale manor, Dr. Cumulus Primrose, and the ladies wasted no time and began to work feverishly. They all worked through the night to build a new flying machine for their teammate Oopsi to the music that sounded like King Oliver's 'Shake It and Break It!' on the gramophone player. When Sir Thomas could no longer keep his eyes open, he fell fast asleep in his aunt's wingback chair.

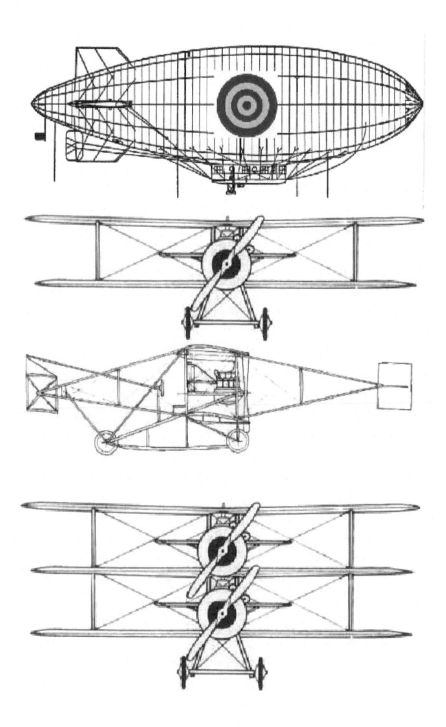

CHAPTER 4
The Next Morning

The next morning as the warm sunlight cascaded through the arched cast iron glass ceiling, a bracket clock with biplane propellers for hands chimed angelically throughout the gymnasium, waking up Sir Thomas. He covered his mouth as he yawned and rubbed his eyes, then slowly removed his hand from his eyes and noticed a magnificent new edition to the gymnasium. "Bow bumble a brand new flying machine," he cried.

It was an exquisite double-winged biplane, with two double wings in front and back made of tin and wood. Atop the first wing span were two polished brass propellers with one other located on the back wings. The tail was round in shape and connected to the last two wings. Four colorful bicycle spoke wheels served as the landing gear. As Sir Henry entered the room, he was quite amazed by their teamwork.

"I say, quite outstanding if I may say so myself. Wouldn't you say, young Thomas?" asked Sir Henry.

"Oh indeed, Sir Henry!" Thomas replied. "I'm sure aunt Amanda wouldn't mind if we were to take a closer look." Sir Henry then began to survey the aircraft. "Looks like it hasn't been fueled up yet, and it also looks like they are not quite finished with some of the interior mechanisms."

"On closer inspection of this flying apparatus, I do believe it would be quite safe for us to take a quick peek inside before the ladies awake, young Thomas," said Sir Henry Humphrey, with a giggle.

Brimming with excitement, Sir Henry helped Thomas up into Ms. Daisy's new flying machine, then climbed in after him. "I say Sir Henry isn't this the most magnificent thing you've ever sat in?" Sir Thomas said with glee.

"Just about, young Thomas. Well, next to my steam powered motorcars that is!" Sir Henry said with a chuckle.

Sir Thomas looked around the cockpit, amazed at how the ladies were able to assemble an entire new flying machine overnight.

Sir Henry then realized it was time for breakfast. "I say, are you hungry, Thomas?"

Thomas replied, "Not at the moment, why do you ask?"

With mischievous eyes Sir Henry replied, "Because we're having blueberry pancakes for breakfast. Can't you smell them? They were imported from San Francisco, you know!"

Sir Thomas took a whiff of air and cried out, "Bow bumble, Sir Henry. Dr. Cumulus Primrose is awake and she's making the pancakes!"

"Come on, Sir Henry. We must leave here at once before she catches us. She's quite sensitive to these sorts of things, you know!"

"I think that would be a wise idea, young Thomas," replied Sir Henry.

As Sir Henry helped Thomas down off the flying machine, his tail coat happened to get stuck on something in the cockpit seat.

"Oh Thomas! I've seemed to be stuck on something!" Sir Henry cried. Still sitting in the cockpit, Sir Henry tried to break free, but was unable. "Oh my, I seem to be in quite a predicament, young Thomas!"

Hearing this, Sir Thomas turned to give assistance. He then began to climb back up into the cockpit to free Sir Henry. "Bow bumble, Sir Henry. It looks like the coat is stuck on some sort of spring."

Just then a voice rang out. Standing in the doorway with a plate of blueberry pancakes in her hand was Dr. Cumulus Primrose. "Gentlemen, if you would kindly remove yourselves from Oopsi's aircraft. It's not yet finished!" She exclaimed.

"We are trying our very best, Dr. Primrose," Sir Thomas exclaimed. Just them, Sir Thomas was able to get Sir Henry's coat free. "I got it, Sir Henry. You're free now!"

"Oh! Thank you, young Thomas!" cried Sir Henry, with relief.

But just as he turned around to exit, Sir Henry lost his balance and fell out of the cockpit, tangling his feet in rope in the process.

"Bow bumble!" cried Sir Thomas, trying to grab on to him but slipping in the process and falling backward onto a lever in the cockpit. Suddenly, an eerie sound began within the flying machine. WA WA WA WA! Then there was a loud backfire. Sir Henry tried to untangle his feet from the ropes as Sir Thomas was getting back up from his fall. They then realized the aircraft's engines were fully functional.

"Bow bumble, what do we do now, Sir Henry?" cried Sir Thomas, in a frenzy from hearing the engines start up.

Dr. Cumulus Primrose, in seeing the event unfold before her, screamed at the top of her lungs, "Thomas Tattletale don't you touch another thing on that aircraft, young man!"

Cumulus, in shock, dropped her plate of freshly made blueberry pancakes as the wind from the propellers blew her blue hair every which way. "Great bananas in oatmeal! I have to get the ladies and quickly!"

Running up to the second landing, she frantically screamed throughout the hallway, "Ladies wake up! Wake up! Thomas and Henry are about to take off in the new biplane!"

"What's going on?" cried Okidoki still in bed and rubbing her eyes.

"Thomas and Henry have started up the new biplane, that's what's going on!" cried Dr. Primrose.

"Oh my goodness, I'll get Countess Fanta," Okidoki replied as she jumped out of her bed.

Cumulus then ran over to Oopsi's room, "Oopsi wake up already, Thomas and Henry have started up your new biplane downstairs!"

Still half asleep, Oopsi replied, "Oh, lovely Cumulus could you shut the window? It's awfully drafty."

"Oopsi, it's not drafty in here, it's the propellers of your new aircraft that's about to take off downstairs!"

Oopsi then sat up on her bed, "Take off? Without me? How rude! Who is this upstart?" she exclaimed.

"Oopsi, it's Thomas!" Dr. Primrose said with worry.

"Well, well I didn't know that little devil could fly!"

"Oopsi, I'm going to get Bixby, wake up already and go get Amanda quickly, please!"

Meanwhile, the aircraft began to move about and was turning in circles. Sir Henry, still underneath it, was dragged by the ropes he was tangled in. "Bow bumble, if only I could locate a stop button, perhaps it would stop" Thomas cried over to Sir Henry from the cockpit. Looking around the cockpit, Sir Thomas found a purple button labeled 'OBEN' and decided to press it. "Okay Sir Henry, I've located a button labeled 'OBEN' that I think will stop it."

In pressing this button, things only got worse. The propellers on the wings retracted upward like a helicopter and began to levitate the aircraft off the ground with Sir Henry now hanging by his feet upside down in midair.

"No no, my boy! 'OBEN' means up in German!" Sir Henry cried.

Oopsi couldn't believe that Sir Thomas could be flying her aircraft, so she walked nonchalantly over to the banister. Looking down, she saw the biplane hovering in midair about to take off. "Why that little devil. I didn't know he could fly! So adorable!" Oopsi said to herself. "I simply must go upstairs and give high praise to Amanda about her little nephew!"

She rushed over to Amanda's room and knocked on her door. "Amanda, lovely, you have such a talented little nephew, I did not know he could fly an aircraft!"

Hearing Oopsi words at the door, Amanda bolted out of room, only half-dressed.

"What in the name of Mary mother of corn flakes in milk are you talking about, Oopsi! I've never taught him how to a fly an aircraft!" she exclaimed. "Oopsi, get out of the way!" She bolted past Oopsi like spit fire and ran to the banister, where she yelled out to the other ladies, "Ladies, listen to me closely. Everyone meet me up on the third floor!"

By this time, the biplane had levitated to the second floor with the sounds of Sir Henry's cry for help, who was still upside down.

"Ladies, we have no time to spare. Do you see the brass cranks on each side of this floor? Take one and start cranking!" cried Amanda, hysterically. Turning to Dr. Primrose, Amanda asked her to go get her Zeppelin started.

"You've got it, Captain. Anything else?" she asked.

"I'll let you know what to do next when we get up the roof."

"Oh lovely Amanda, does it play music?" asked Oopsi, looking at the ornate brass crank. This place is just full of surprises you know!" she added.

"SHUT UP AND GET CRANKING!" cried Amanda.

None of the ladies knew what would happen as they all took a crank on each side of the wall. Well, something very special did happen indeed. The magnificent arched cast iron cylinder glass ceiling began to open slowly.

"Faster ladies, faster, they are almost to the top!" cried Amanda.

The ladies were all in a hysterics as they tried to get a grip on the situation until Fanta thought of something. "Amanda, I have an idea. Take hold of my crank."

As the biplane approached the third level of the gymnasium, Fanta de Vol carefully balanced herself on the edge of the banister while holding onto a column, waiting for the right moment to take action. When the moment came, Countess Fanta jumped like a puma from the banister ledge, grabbing onto the very rope Sir Henry was hanging upside down on. All looked on anxiously as the three exited through the opened arched cast iron cylinder glass ceiling.

"Ladies, follow me!" cried Amanda as she ran toward the staircase that lead to the roof.

Reaching the roof, Dr. Cumulus Primrose stood at attention by her zeppelin and addressed the ladies with a salute and a handshake, then showed them a map of the area. Cumulus then predicted the weather conditions. "Today is looking quite favorable with the winds coming from the northwest, which should gear the aircraft in its heliport state towards Pattypan Pond."

"Fantastic news, Dr. Primrose. Good weather is in our favor today!" stated Amanda. Amanda then began to explain the rescue plan. "Dr. Primrose, Okidoki and Bixby will be traveling with you by air. Oopsi and I will follow by land on motorcycle."

Bixby Trumbow then interrupted with great urgency. "Need I remind everyone that we have to act fast because there are only about 30 to 45 minutes of fuel in her?"

"Countess Fanta is with them, so that should give us a better chance of catching up to them," stated Okidoki.

"Great, ladies. Let us get cracking!" replied Amanda.

Everybody began to gear up to get Sir Henry and Sir Thomas safely down on the ground.

Meanwhile, up in the air, Sir Henry Humphrey cried over to Fanta. "I say, if it isn't my gothic angel of the skies. Have you come to save me?"

"Oh, Oui Mon Cheri, I'm here to save you both! The name is Fanta and I'm no angel Mon Cheri! I shall climb up the rope and help Thomas with the gear, then I will pull you up slowly."

Thomas was overjoyed to see her climbing up the rope into the cockpit. "Bow bumble, Countess, I'm so glad to see you!" cried Sir Thomas as she entered the aircraft.

"And it is also very nice to see you in one piece, my little devil of the skies," Fanta replied.

The Countess then quickly showed Thomas which levers in the cockpit would stabilize the aircraft while she helped sir Henry on the rope. The Countess rushed over to the rope and began to slowly pull Sir Henry up. "I"d better hurry before Sir Henry passes out from the blood rushing to his head!" Fanta exclaimed. Sir Thomas was overjoyed at seeing Sir Henry being safety lifted up into the aircraft.

On entering the cockpit Sir Henry was ecstatic to be right side up again. "Oh dear Countess Fanta, I am indeed in your debt for saving me. How could I ever thank you?"

"Thank me later, Sir Henry. We do not have much time as we are running out of fuel!"

Looking out of her good eye, but not quite sure, Fanta asked Sir Henry, "Mon Cher, is that a lake or a pond ahead?"

"Oh that's Pattypan Pond, Countess Fanta!" Sir Thomas quickly replied.

"Well gentlemen, we might just have to make an emergency landing there," said Countess Fanta.

"I'm sure Lord and Lady Pattypan wouldn't mind us dropping in for tea!" said Sir Henry.

Fanta de Vol just rolled her eye in reply.

Looking out the window, Thomas could see Dr. Cumulus' zeppelin. "Countess Fanta! Countess Fanta! I can see Dr. Primrose's airship."

As it got closer, Sir Thomas could see everyone on board the airship and he shouted out to them, "Hello Cumulus! Hello Okidoki! Hello Bixby! I'm flying! I'm flying," He waved his hands out the cockpit, laughing.

Seeing Thomas waving his hands from the biplane, Dr. Primrose worried about his mental health. "Pineapples and cranberry juice, ladies, I think the boy is hysterical!"

Okidoki looked out and, waving back to him, replied "Oh no Cumulus, I think he just found Bixby's cough medicine to keep warm!"

"Well, hi dee ho, over my dead body!" cried Bixby Trumbow. Bixby ran over to the window of the zeppelin, screaming across to Thomas, "Thomas honey, if you need to keep warm, PLEASE TAKE FANTA'S COAT!"

Meanwhile on the ground, Amanda raced through the countyside tracking the plane by motorcycle, Oopsi in the sidecar. They came upon cast iron gates encrusted with leaves, gourds, and cherubs that led into Pattypan manor.

Oopsi was fascinated by the surroundings. Looking on, she asked, "What's up with all the pumpkins, lovely?"

"We are on the estate of Lord and Lady Pattypan. They raise pumpkins," replied Amanda.

"Oh Halloween must be quite a hoot around here!"

"Oh, not really. They manufacture pumpkins for motorcar fuel," replied Amanda.

Approaching the ornate gates, Oopsi sat in the sidecar while Amanda dismounted. "Hello, is anybody there? It's an emergency!"

Suddenly, a voice beckoned from a rusticated arched doorway of the gates. "Today is hide-and-seek day, no visitors!"

Amanda implored, "Please my nephew will be making his first landing and I do believe he'll make it in your pond!"

The voice called out once again from the arched doorway of the gates, but it was much softer this time, "Amanda?" the voice asked, "Amanda Cruikshank, is that you?"

"Why yes, it is!" Amanda replied with relief and asked, "Is that Crookneck?"

"Why indeed it is, young lady! Don't tell me you've lost yet another one your model flying machinea on the property, or are you just here for proper tea and a good game of hide and seek with Sunnysideup and Simon?"

Amanda, replied with haste, "Neither. I'm here to oversee a possible crash landing."

"Oh I see. Do you know the parties involved?" he asked.

Amanda explained, "Indeed I do! It's my nephew Thomas and a good friend of the family, Sir Henry Humphrey."

Hearing this, Crookneck rushed to open the massive gates. As Crookneck came out to let Amanda and Oopsi in, they noticed he was carrying two croquet maillots. "Amanda do take these and give one to your friend."

Oopsi was still admiring the grounds when she saw the aircraft approaching. "Oh Amanda! Amanda lovely, I see the my aircraft, come quickly. We must catch it!"

Amanda thanked Crookneck, mounted her motorcycle, then gave a croquet mallet to Oopsi.

Looking baffled Oopsi asked, "Why on earth lovely do we need these croquet mallets?"

"In case we bump into Sunny!" Amanda replied.

"Sunny who?" asked Oopsi.

"Oh, Lady Pattypan's daughter, Lady Sunnysideup Pattypan!" replied Amanda. "Sunny is quite strict on the hide and seeks rules, you know. Their rules are quite elementary. One hides, you see, as the other seeks. As one finds another, they bop them on the head with the croquet mallet."

"Oh, I see, not what I imagine hide and seek would be, lovely," replied Oopsi.

As they rode on, keeping a close eye on the aircraft hovering above, Oopsi was admiring the foliage of triple ball topiaries shaped like pumpkins along the way. "What a grand idea," she cried.

"What's so grand?" asked Amanda taking her eyes off the road for a minute.

Oopsi then cried out, "Watch out, in the middle of the road!"

There was a loud thud as they hit something. It was a man covering his eyes in the middle of the road dressed in a purple Little Lord Fauntleroy outfit. They continued to ride on, looking back.

Oopsi asked, "Oh lovely, I do think he's dead!"

Amanda nonchalantly replied, "Oh whoop de do he's not dead, Oopsi!"

"And why do you that say that?" Oopsi asked with confusion apparent on her face.

"Because, it's Sir Simon Pattypan, Sunnysideup's brother. Nothing hurts him if he covers his eyes!"

They were both relieved as they looked back to see him get back up, only to see him shaking his fist at them yelling, "Father shall hear of this, you game assassins!"

The Pattypan twins are the son and daughter of Lord Magnesium and Lady Juniper Pattypan. At the tender age of thirty-five years old, they still resided at Pattypan manor with their parents, and still attired in the clothing of ten-year-old children.

Reaching Pattypan pond, Amanda and Oopsi saw Dr. Primrose's zeppelin circling above the aircraft near the pond. They watched it slowly descend like a helicopter, then plummet ten feet down into the pond.

"Oh, my angel of the skies, are you okay, my love?" cried Amanda, as she ran over to the pond with her arms extended.

Popping out of the biplane with a giggle was Sir Thomas Tattletale. "Bow bumble Aunty, can we do this again?" he asked.

"Thomas Tattletale, you wicked lovely boy! You gave us quite a startle you know!" cried Oopsi. "Oh Merci, lovely Fanta for guiding and assisting these two!" she said to the Countess as she and Sir Henry disembarked the aircraft.

"Dear me, so nice to see the ground again," cried Sir Henry as Countess Fanta helped him off the aircraft.

"We were quite fortunate to have Countess Fanta aboard to help us, Aunt Amanda," stated Thomas.

Amanda was pleased everything had turned out okay. "Indeed my little angel of the skies" she said as she squeezed Thomas in her arms.

Amanda turned to Countess Fanta and said, "I can't thank you enough dear Fanta Merci Mon bon ami Fanta." Amanda gave Countess Fanta a kiss on both cheeks with a salute.

As the ladies gathered around the pond with Sir Thomas and Sir Henry, they happened to see someone coming from behind a large cone and square topiary. It was Lady Juniper Pattypan dressed in a blue and white striped evening gown in the Edwardian style, holding a croquet mallet. She was drawn toward the pond by all the commotion.

"I say, what's the meaning of this?" she exclaimed. She then cried out to her husband, "Magnesium, dearest Magnesium? Come out at once! There seems to be a flying machine in our pond."

Coming out from behind another large topiary shaped like a pyramid was Lord Magnesium, attired in a vibrant orange striped blazer and white trousers, with a croquet mallet under his arm. As he approached the pond, he took off his straw boater while gazing up at the flying apparatus in the pond. Looking on, he stated to his wife. "I say quite a change in game plan, my love."

"Oh indeed my dearest, the children will be so disappointed in our postponement of our game," Lady Pattypan replied.

As he came closer, he recognized Amanda. "I say, it's Amanda Cruikshank and Sir Henry Humphrey!"

"Is it really? Of the Humphrey Steam-powered Automobiles?" cried Lady Juniper, placing a gold lorgnette to her eye.

"Why hello, Amanda," cried Magnesium.

"Dear child, is everything okay?" asked Juniper.

"I say, is everyone in one piece? asked Magnesium, anxiously.

Then as Lady Juniper peered in closer, she saw Sir Thomas. "Oh, and look Magnesium, it's little Thomas Tattletale. We haven't seen you since you were two!" she cried.

Lord Magnesium was surveying the flying machine. "I say, it looks like someone has got their wings today," stated Lord Magnesium as he smiled at Sir Thomas.

"Indeed I did! I can't wait to do it again, but with my aunt Amanda next time!" Sir Thomas replied with a grin, as he looked up to his aunt. "Oh look aunty the others are here!"

The zeppelin landed in the courtyard and the ladies got off to join the others by the pond.

"I say Juniper, a rather odd looking blue balloon has landed in our courtyard."

"Dearest, it's called a zeppelin, and it runs on hot air."

"Oh I see, like your father in law!" replied Magnesium.

As Amanda began to explain to Lord and Lady Pattypan what had happened, Sunnysideup and Simon came storming up the pathway toward them. Sunny was dressed in a navy blue sailor dress that stopped at her knees. She ran up her mother and cried, "Mummy oh Mummy, Amanda Cruikshank is here and uninvited, need I remind you!"

"Oh Sunny, she's standing right here," replied her mother. "Amanda, do introduce me to your charming friends. Are they from your flight academy?" asked Lady Pattypan, as she peered through her lorgnette.

Amanda began to introduce her friends. "Why yes, they are my instructors at my flight academy." She turned around and started with Oopsi. "Allow me to introduce you to one of my finest stunt flyers, Ms. Oopsi Daisy!"

"Why I just adore that scarf, Ms.Daisy," stated Juniper.

"Pleased to meet you Lady Juniper, and may I say that dress is just lovely," Oopsi replied.

"Thank you, Ms. Daisy. I think your exceedingly long silk scarf is just smashing," Lady Juniper replied, clasping her hands.

"Just call me Oopsi, lovely Juniper!"

Sunnysideup was furious at the interruption of their game and said, "I say what kind of name is that, Oopsi?" She stamped her foot down.

Lady Juniper turned to her daughter and said, "Now Sunnysideup, one should take on a skill such as flying an aircraft instead of the poor skill of rudeness, I say."

"Here here, well said, dearest Juniper. Amanda do carry on with your introductions," cried Lord Magnesium.

Amanda continued and introduced Countess Fanta de Vol. "And this is my right-hand gal for adventure, explorer Countess Fanta de Vol of France. She is one of our champion long distance flyers."

Lord Magnesium kissed her hand said, "Just delighted."

"Amanda has told us of your extraordinary adventures abroad, so I insist the next time you visit, you must share them over tea and frosted lemon cookies, dear Countess," stated Lady Juniper.

The Countess replied, "I shall keep that in mind, dear Lady Juniper. Merci."

Moving on to Bixby, Amanda said, "I am privileged to introduce you to our top aeronautical engineer at the academy, Ms. Bixby Trumbow from Chicago."

Lord Magnesium shook her hand with a bow and said, "It is truly a pleasure to meet someone with such a great talent, Ms. Trumbow."

Once again the introductions were interrupted, but by Simon this time, who said, "Oh Father, Father! There is no doubt that Amanda and her uninvited friends are clearly here to sabotage our fun!"

Looking over to the ladies, Lord Magnesium whispered, "I should have named the poor boy Nincompoop!"

"She's not even playing fair mummy!" cried Sunnysideup, interrupting again. "After I found Simon and properly bopped him on the head, he told me Amanda and another uninvited friend ran over my dearest sweet brother on a motorcycle while holding croquet mallets in their hands. Mummy, really the very idea!" She had both hands on her hips, and stamped her foot.

"The very idea indeed, Sunny!" replied her mother. "Perhaps we should indulge in that rather creative idea." She then turned to Amanda and said, "Thank you, Amanda, I never thought of using motorcycles in such a manner." With a giggle, she turned to her husband and asked, "Magnesium darling what do you think?"

Lord Magnesium replied said, "I say, it sounds most delightful, dearest Juniper!"

"Well one thing for sure: she didn't get that name for her sunny disposition!" Sir Henry whispered over to Okidoki, who couldn't help but giggle.

Amanda continued with the introductions. "This is our weather forecaster, Dr. Cumulus Primrose."

Lady Juniper liked Cumulus' attire and remarked, "Dr. Primrose, I just adore your blue leather outfit."

"Thank you, it is my favorite color!" she replied.

Amanda continued to Okidoki. "Last but not least, the giggling one is our boo-boo specialist at the academy, Nurse Oki Nocadoki of Japan."

"Pleased to meet you, Nurse Oki Nocadoki," stated Juniper. "We spent our honeymoon in Tsukimi, Japan years ago, it was just so romantic with the moon and cool autumn air."

Okidoki replied "Oh yes, but the next time you go, you must visit Otsukimi. It's just across the bridge from where you were. My brother Jugoya gives tours there."

Simon and Sunny were still on a mission to continue their hide and seek game. "Father, oh Father! Are you just going to let them get away with this?" cried Sir Simon.

"Do forgive us, Nurse Oki Nocadoki, could you excuse us for one moment?" Lord Magnesium looked at Simon. "Oh Simon, why don't you go and play with your new fire engine machine you got for your birthday?"

With that said, Sunnysideup whispered something into Simon's ear, only to have Sir Simon reply back to his parents, "Yes father, good day mother."

With that said, they merrily skipped off while holding hands.

"Amanda, your friends are more than welcome to join us for lunch. We're having tuna fish salad, boiled eggs on toast," Lady Juniper invited warmly.

"Juniper, don't forget the iced tea and rainbow lemonade for drinks," Magnesium said with a giggle.

"Oh lovely Amanda, I do hope it's a Long Island Iced tea!" cried, Oopsi looking up into the air.

As they all sat down for a most scrumptious lunch filled with laughter and merriment, Countess Fanta heard something. "Say, is there a fire nearby?"

"Not that I'm aware of, why do you ask?" replied Magnesium.

"Well because I hear the sounds of a siren," said Countess Fanta.

"And I hear a bell ringing!" Added Okidoki.

"And I know I'm not crazy because I hear both!" exclaimed Bixby Trumbow.

"Oh, it's probably Simon playing with his birthday present. It's a fire engine machine. It entertains him for hours on end!" replied Juniper.

As the siren got louder and louder, everyone stopped eating and looked over to the garden from where the sounds were coming. The source of the sound was from a siren and brass bell atop Sir Simon's birthday present. There was only one problem, this was not a small toy but a full size 1918 Mack fire engine machine equipped with ladders and fire axes. Racing up to the lunch table with a screeching halt was Lady Sunnysideup. She was cranking the siren and Sir Simon was at the wheel ringing the brass bell. They were both wearing fire hats.

"Young lady, what is the meaning of this? And why you are in Simon's fire engine machine when you have your very own?" cried Lady Juniper.

Sir Simon interrupted his mother, "Oh mummy, she crashed hers into the drawing room on the way here!"

Lord Magnesium bellowed, "If I told you two once before, I've told you a thousand times! No fire engines in the house!"

Standing up in her seat with a sharpened fire axe in her hands, Sunnysideup had something to say. "Well, mummy and daddy, if you can change the rules of our beloved hide and seek, we can change the rules too! Don't you agree, Simon?"

"Indeed I do!" replied her brother.

"So, therefore, my brother and I shall count to ten with everyone finding proper hiding places," Sunny stated, a most sinister grimace on her face.

Taking turns, they both began to count. "ONE!" cried Sunny .

"TWO!" cried Simon.

Amanda was alarmed by this and said, "Dr. Primrose I don't like the way this looks."

Dr. Primrose replied, "and I don't like the way it sounds. I'll get the zeppelin started!"

"Take Thomas and the ladies with you," said Amanda. "Oopsi and I shall take the motorcycle."

Lord Magnesium, realizing the enormity of the situation offered his assistance. I say Amanda, you should head for the gates. They are prohibited from passing through it with their toys."

"Why is that, Lord Magnesium?" asked Oopsi, curiously.
"They would lose their inheritance if that rule were ever broken," he replied.

"We'll stall them for you, dearest. Just go and get your motorcycle," said Lady Juniper, Magnesium agreeing by shaking his head.

"THREE, FOUR, FIVE, SIX!" counted the brother and sister.

"Thank you, Juniper and Magnesium," Amanda said quickly, then turned to Oopsi. "Come on, Oopsi!" Amanda and Oopsi quickly jumped into motorcycle and sped off, cutting through the hedges to the main gate.

With the guests gone, Lady Juniper cried out, "Oh my darling Sunnysideup. Look, we are going to hide!"

Giggling, Lord Magnesium joined in. "That's my boy Simon. I shall close my eyes and try to find a place where you'll never find me!"

Sunny and Simon were still counting, "SEVEN, EIGHT!" They paused as they heard the laughter and giggling of their parents.

Sunnysideup turned to her brother with joy and said, "Pickles and raspberry ice cream! Mummy and Daddy approve of our new game!"

"Dearest sister, you are a genius!" said Simon as he started to cry.

"Now Simon Pattypan don't you dare start to cry!"

"Oh forgive me, dear sister, I'm just so happy!" he replied.

"Now where were we, dearest sister?" asked Simon as he wiped his eyes.

"Silly pickles, you were at number EIGHT!" she cried.

"Forgive me, dearest sister!" Simon replied as he continued to count with his sister.

"NINE! TEN! Ready or not here we come!"

As Sunnysideup cranked up the siren, Simon stepped on the gas. They ran over the dining table, smashed every blue and white porcelain dish in sight, then bolted through the manicured grounds while knocking down every ornately cut topiary in sight.

Meanwhile, everyone else started to board the zeppelin. "Come on everyone, into the zeppelin, quickly!" cried Dr. Primrose as she boarded the aircraft, carrying Thomas in her arms. "Okidoki, could you take Thomas for me while I start her up?"

"You got it, doctor!" Okidoki replied with a salute.

"Hey Doc, we might have a little problem," cried Bixby.

"Now what would that be, Bixby?" asked Cumulus.

"Well I not only hear a siren this time, but I can also see it coming toward us!" stated Bixby, pointing out of the zeppelin.

"Pineapples in gravy! Ok everyone, grab onto something and hold on tight!" cried Dr. Primrose, as she pulled a lever in the cockpit, which catapulted the zeppelin upward in one large jolt.

The fire engine headed toward them, but it missed by inches, only to crash into a marble statue of Demeter. Sunnysideup and her brother were knocked clear from the fire engine and into a nearby pond. With the sudden jolt of the airship, everyone aboard had been laid flat on the zeppelin's floor.

"Apples in banana sauce! Are we all okay back there?" asked Dr. Primrose. She clasped her hands together and grinned.

As they got up off the deck, they all replied. "Yes, we're good!"

"Bo bumble, that was fun. Can we do it again?" asked Thomas giggling.

"That was a close one!" said Fanta, holding Thomas in her arms as she got back up.

"Well heidi de ho you go, Doc!" cried Bixby, relieved.

"I didn't even know this airship could move that fast," cried Okidoki.

"Ok ladies and gentlemen, we are going to make a sharp turn back to pick up Ms. Daisy's aircraft." With that said, Dr. Primrose pressed a button in the cockpit, and three long chains with hooks on them end came down and picked up Ms. Daisy's aircraft.

On the ground, Amanda stopped her motorcycle, and she and Oopsi could see Dr. Primrose's zeppelin taking off with Ms. Daisy's aircraft getting hoisted away safely.

Running ahead of Sir Henry and Amanda, Sir Thomas bolted through the doors with excitement when they arrived back at Tattletale Manor. He could not wait to tell his mother of his adventure. "Oh Mummy, Mummy you'll never guess what happened to me today with Aunt Amanda!" Thomas said with glee as he ran up to his mother.

Lady Tatiana could see Amanda and Sir Henry in the foreground with terror on their faces. "And what would that be, my little love?"

With excitement, Thomas cried, "I went flying for the first time, and we were chased by a red fire engine machine and dined on tuna fish salad and boiled eggs!"

With a rather worried look on her face, Amanda exclaimed, "Now Tatiana, I can explain everything!"

"No need for an explanation, dear sister. When I saw the opened arched ceiling in the gymnasium with nobody present I knew my little love was in good hands," Lady Tatiana Tattletale said with a wink and smile to her sister.

CHAPTER 5
Sir Thomas Tattletale in Londinium

Sir Thomas could not help but look up to the sights and sounds as he and Sir Henry arrived in the city of Londinium. They passed the Grand West Benjamin Tower Clock as it chimed. The Grand West Benjamin Tower Clock is a Gothic Neoclassic-style clock with eight faces of time on its tower. The four faces of time at the top of the clock tower tell the Londinium time in roman numerals, while the four faces below it tell time in different dimensions of other kingdoms. The first face displayed astrological signs, the second had numeric numbers which run backwards, the third flaunted geometrical shapes, and the fourth had Egyptian numerals from one to ten.

The architecture of the city of Londinium was a combination of architectural styles that consisted of Art deco, Edwardian, and Gothic taste. In this kingdom, automobiles race for endurance and prestige. There are neither racecars nor commercial air flights - only biplanes along, air zeppelins, and ocean liners that make transatlantic crossings.

As Sir Henry drove through the congested city streets of honking automobiles, roaring three-wheeled motorcycles, and velocipedes of all sizes, he was fascinated by the movement all around him. He could see people coming and going, dressed in full attire for dinner parties and fancy dress balls. The sidewalks of Londinium had the most fashionable people that came in all different colors, shapes, and sizes, walking, running, and skipping to their destinations. As Thomas listed to the bustle of the people, one sound stood out from all the rest in the City of Londinium. It was a piercing bell sound: Ding Ding Ding. It rang out all through the city.

"I say Sir Henry, what is that sound?" asked Thomas.

"My boy, that is the sound of our newest transport system. We call it 'The Red Trolley Bus line'," replied Sir Henry.

The Red Trolley Bus line is an electric high-speed red double-decker trolley that runs on tracks that were newly installed throughout Londinium so that it doesn't derail at high speed as it made sharp turns at corners. Mechanical hands pop out of the side and hold onto a steel rail system. They were installed on every corner. Only briefly stopping at its destination, people were always running after the trolley, and jumping on and off.

The city of Londinium also has the Blue and Green Pipe Lines, the Londinium subway systems, operated completely on electricity with the exception of the elevated green line trains, which runs on steam power.

Sir Henry stopped the motorcar in traffic as another automobile pulled up. A voice yelled out from the automobile. "I say old chap, why don't you move that old steam tin can of yours?"

Then a second voice rung out from the other side of motorcar window, "Here here, now we have a dinner party to attend. Move aside. My sister frowns upon lateness, you know!"

"Steam tin can you say, indeed," exclaimed Sir Henry, as he turned around to look at both men yelling at him from their automobile.

"Well, well. If it isn't old Sir Henry Humphrey," said the first man with surprise. He was dressed in a long tan duster, with brown gauntlet gloves and white tie and tails with a white rose in his lapel.

"I say! Do my eyes deceive me? Why it is!" replied the second man, who was sitting at the wheel in astonishment. He removed his driving goggles and rubbed his eyes. He was dressed in a black tie and white spats and was wearing a half black, half white duster.

They were Sir Henry's arch nemesis, Lord Yancey Pfeiffer, and his partner in business, Count Stavros Tetradrachm. They were driving their latest collaboration, an automobile powered on peanut butter and olive oil. It was painted half white and half black in the Tetradrachm family style. They were late to a dinner party being thrown in their honor by the Count's twin sister, Countess Athena, and were partners in new developments of automotive fuels and the manufacturers of automobiles.

Lord Yancey Pfeiffer of Yorkshire England is the owner of Yancey Pfeiffer motorcars of Londinium. Lord Pfeiffer had vast real estate holdings and distilleries. Count Stavros Tetradrachm of Thoricus Greece manufactured new kinds of automotive fuels.

He partner up with his sister Athena when participating in races. Countess Athena Tetradrachm of Thoricus Greece is the twin sister of Stavros. She is the finical advisor of the family and owner of sixty percent of Tetradrachm, Inc.

"Oh I say! You must forgive me, old sport," said Lord Yancey, sarcastically. He looked down at Sir Henry's motorcar, then retracted his last comment. "On the other hand, I take it back. I think you and your automobile are both rusty steam cans." He laughed as he looked over at Count Stavros.

"I say Sir Henry, will you be entering that steam tin can in the Brighton to Londinium races this weekend?" Count Stavros asked with a smirk on his face.

Sir Henry was ready to retaliate. "I say, what skullduggery are you tacky gents up to now!"

Just then, the stoplight changed and the traffic started moving again. Lord Yancey and Count Stavros drove off in a cloud of dust, laughing.

"Bo bumble, Sir Henry! Who was that?" asked Thomas.

"Well my boy, you just met a rat with a fat cat in spats!"

Bow bumble!" he said as he bounced up and down on the seat. "I say Sir Henry, are going to enter the race?"

"Now now, Young Thomas, what would your mother say?"

"You can't let them talk to you in that manner!" Thomas cried, as he settled back down in his seat. He folded his arms with a frown on his face. Sir Thomas then stood up again pointing his finger in the air and said, "Well then I shall sit in the stands and observe while you teach a rat and a fat cat with spats a lesson in automotive tact!"

"Perhaps, young Thomas, we'll see." Sir Henry replied with a smile.

They reached their destination at Hummington's Haberdashery for the Automotive Enthusiast. As Sir Henry was parking the automobile in front of the store, Sir Thomas heard a clarinet playing and it seemed to be getting louder. A magnificent six-wheeled silver chromed motorcar pulled up across the street. It stopped in front of a music store. Sir Thomas could see three ladies dressed in little girls clothing, each in a different color, get out of it. It appeared that they were arguing about something while one of them played the clarinet. Sir Thomas could not hear what they were bickering about. He was still looking on when one of the ladies noticed Sir Henry and waved her hand toward him. She then turned to the other two ladies, notifying them of Sir Henry's presence. Both of the ladies turned to look at Sir Henry,

"Oh! Sir Henry! "Toodle-oo!" cried the first lady. She was dressed in green and was jumping up and down.

"No, No, No! Ninny poop pop," cried a second lady, dressed in pink, as she pushed the lady in green aside. "It's said Boodle Whoo, Henry! She stated, waving her hand frantically.

You are both ding-dong doorbells in the head. It's pronounced and said as such: Doddle loo," said the third lady, dressed in blue. She waved a silk scarf toward Sir Henry.

Before the three ladies crossed the street, the first one said to the other two, "Wait one moment, while I look both ways."

The first lady proceeded to cross the street alone in a hopscotch manner, but she stopped in the middle of the street and cried out to the other two to cross. She then proceeded to cross, still hopscotching.

The second lady, dressed in pink, skipped across merrily while the third lady dressed in blue just walked across the street with a frown. She passed the other two who were hopscotching and skipping happily across the street. Once she crossed, still frowning, the lady in blue just stood at Sir Henry's automobile with her arms folded. As the other two ladies reached the automobile, the ladies dressed in green and pink asked the lady dressed in blue why she looked so gloomy.

The lady in blue replied, "Because I'm cursed with two idiots!"

Sir Henry then interrupted the ladies before another argument started. "Why hello ladies. And how are Londinium's three graces doing?"

"Delightfully smashing today, Sir Henry," replied the ladies at the same time. They were looking at Sir Henry's motorcar curiously. The ladies surrounded Sir Henry on both sides and peered on with great curiosity, then asked questions one at a time.

"Oh, Sir Henry. Who is that in your motorcar? Is it a new apprentice?" asked the first lady dressed in pink.

"What are you talking about, ding-dong dumb bell. It's his long lost son!" The second lady dressed in green stated with a grin.

"You both have butter in your brains with no toast to put it on," cried the third lady dressed in blue. "It's quite obvious dear sisters. It's a woodland elf Sir Henry found on one of his countryside jaunts. Oh, and I must say he is indeed quite a find and so adorable." She clasped her hands together.

Sir Henry then interrupt them, "Ladies, ladies, please! First, I do not have a son, Tessa. Nor do I have apprentices, Odessa. And I most certainly did not find a woodland elf in the countryside on one of my holiday jaunts, Vanessa. He is the son of a dear friend in Surbiton Surrey. I'm taking him to pick up a new duster."

"Well I'll be pickled in vinegar on Sunday!" cried Odessa as she looked over at her sisters and giggled.

"Never ever seen one?" asked Tessa with surprise.

"Nor has he ever been in one!" added Vanessa, looking at Tessa with astonishment. "Indeed! Unheard of! I cannot imagine."

"Well, we will see about that," cried Odessa, looking at Vanessa and Tessa.

The three Pound sisters, Vanessa, Tessa and Odessa Pound, are triplets who started their life on the stage and as they grew up, ventured off into other investments, such as competitive automobile racing. They were worthy challengers of the racing circuit with their very own automobile called The Triple Thunder, which they developed in their garage.

The Triple Thunder was powered by garlic soup fuel. It was art deco style of polished aluminum, a six spoke-wheeled marvel, with four wheels in front and two in the back. It comfortably seated the three sisters. The three sisters had baby blue eyes and curly brunette hair that was fashionably bobbed. They always wore Mary Jane party dresses in three different colors of blue, pink, and green as if they were still nine years old. Although the sisters weighed over 285 pounds, they moved about like a ballerinas.

"Well, what's his name?" asked Tessa with a smile.

"Oh, no, no. Don't tell us. We will guess. And besides, we are known all over the Londinium for our psychic abilities you know!" said Tessa to Thomas.

"Oh indeed!" cried Odessa, agreeing with her sister. They nodded their heads in approval.

"Now let's see," said Vanessa, as she placed her hands to her temples. "Now let's see... would it be Tomato because of your rosy cheeks?" said Vanessa, smiling.

"I'm afraid not Vanessa," answered Thomas, giggling as he looked over to Sir Henry.

"So then," Tessa tried to guess his name, and said, "Now, now young man, I have it!" She added, "Your first name is Apple because you are as sweet as one."

Sir Thomas laughed. "Ha, ha, you are very funny Tessa, but that's not my name," stated Sir Thomas.

Odessa then interrupts, "Oh, Tessa you just said that because you are always eating them!" Tessa was always eating green apples.

To which Tessa replied, "Well, I can't help that! I really do love them you know. Apple pie, apple cake, apple fritters!"

Sir Thomas said with a smile, "I like apple juice."

"And I like apple juice, too," replied Tessa, smiling back at him.

"Here, here! Let me try, silly ninny. Move aside," cried Odessa, as she pushed her sister to the side. Odessa placed one of her hands to her temple and with the other she pinched her nose.

"I see an S in your name. I have it"! "Is it Sir Peter Potato? Because you are little like one," she stated with a proud grin.

Tessa cried, "Sir Peter Potato! Are you mad? That's even worse than my prediction!

"Odessa, I've never been so embarrassed," cried Vanessa.

Sir Thomas then politely tipped his top hat with a giggle and properly introduced himself. "Dear ladies, it's indeed a pleasure, but my name is not Apple, nor Tomato, you see, and it most certainly is not Sir Peter Potato if you please. My name is Thomas, like the T in tomato you see. I'm here to view my first automobile race in Brighton, you know!"

"And that you shall indeed," cried the triplets, giggling and looking at each other.

Their conversation was interrupted by a loud yell from a young girl. "Extra! Extra! Read all about the mysterious disappearance of children all over England! Glasgow Yard baffled."

"Oh what a pity. Those poor children," cried the triplets, looking at each other.

One at a time, the sisters said goodbye before driving off. "It was very nice to meet you, Thomas," said Vanessa.

"I do hope to see you and Sir Henry at the racetrack," said Tessa.

Sir Henry and Thomas arrived at number 22 Finch Berry Lane, the city home of Sir Henry Humphrey. Sir Thomas Tattletale was now the perfect Londinium dandy in his new duster equipped with the racing attire: goggles and little brown gauntlet gloves.

Yellow Baroque roses lapped over the red brick wall leading to the entrance of Sir Henry Humphrey's townhome. As they passed the rose tangle cast iron gateway to the Jacobean style townhouse, Sir Thomas noticed four round Irish yew topiaries resembling automobile wheels lining the garden. These brought them to a vivid blue door with a brass knob shaped like a turtle.

Sir Thomas heard rather spindly music coming from within the house. It sounded like a piano, but a little different. "Sir Henry, what kind of instrument is that playing? It sounds a bit like a piano."

"Why it's my harpsichord, Thomas! It is a piano, but an early form," replied Sir Henry. "I say, it must be Ms. Koukouvágia, playing it again, and at this time of day."

It was music that Sir Henry had never heard before, so he decided to investigate. As Sir Henry turned the brass door knob, he noticed the door was unlocked. Walking in, they proceeded to follow the sound down a long hallway of mahogany wood plank floors covered with little Persian carpets.

"Oh, I say! It's coming from the drawing room!" cried Sir Henry.

They each took a brass door handle shaped like a rabbit's ear and slowly opened the doors to the drawing room only to find Ms. Koukouvágia, the housekeeper, dancing with Digby Scarborough, Sir ry's assistant.

"Why Ms. Koukouvágia! And Digby! What on earth are you doing?" he cried.

They were dancing to American varsity music. They both looked over to Sir Henry without stopping. "It's an amazing new dance step called the Charleston," stated Ms. Koukouvágia.

"Do you care to join us, it's an awful lot of fun!" Digby said with a howl. "I say, who's that little man standing next to you, Sir Henry?" added Digby.

"His name is Sir Thomas Tattletale," replied Sir Henry. "Ms. Koukouvágia, what are you doing?"

"Why Sir Henry I'm dancing silly, The Charleston!" she replied.

"By Jove Ms. Koukouvágia, that's not how it's done."

Ms. Koukouvágia was just bopping up and down.
"Here! Here! Now let me show you how it's done!" cried Sir Henry as he joined them on the floor.

"Excuse me, Sir Henry, but is your home haunted by ghosts?" asked Sir Thomas as he gazed in astonishment at the harpsichord playing with no one at the seat.

"Most certainly not! They left years ago of boredom," laughed Sir Henry as he attempted to dance the Charleston, kicking his legs out and flapping his arms like a chicken.

"Why do you ask, Thomas?" Sir Henry asked.

"Well, I asked because while Digby and Ms. Koukouvágia are dancing, the harpsichord is playing on its own," explained Sir Thomas.

"It's automated dear boy. Digby altered it, the brilliant chap that he is," stated Sir Henry.

Taking off his cricket cap, Digby then took a bow, welcoming Sir Thomas to his new surroundings. Ms. Koukouvágia is employed by Sir Henry as the housekeeper. She was tragically changed into a large owl by the Duchess of Twelve Points for eating her breakfast eggs. Commonly dressed in a cricket uniform, Digby Scarborough is the faithful assistant who partners up with Sir Henry Humphrey when he races. Digby was a champion cricket player until the opposing team switched their lemonade, thereby changing him and his entire cricket team into pug dogs.

Meanwhile across town in Highcliff Regents park, Lord Yancey and Count Stavros approached the grey Abbotsford style town house of Countess Tetradrachm. Unlike the other townhouses on Highcliff Regents Park row, the Tetradrachm's home was round in shape and thus stood out from the rest.

Both Lord Yancey and Count Stavros, knowing that they were frightfully late, silently entered through a black lacquered door with an ornate silver pull decorated with snakes that intertwined on the handle.

When they reached the vestibule, the second door opened abruptly. A voice rang out. "Good evening gentlemen. Countess Athena is expecting you."

"I take it my sister is in the music room?" asked Stavros.

"No, your sister is in the dining room and you are late," replied Aráchni with a grimace. I shall escort you there."

They proceeded to follow Aráchni to the dining room. "How sumptuous," stated Lord Yancy as he adjusted his monocle and looked up at the rosettes within the coffered ceiling of portico squares.

Aráchni the Butler is a faithful servant and henchman to Countess Athena. Graced with four arms, one could say that he was great at multitasking.

Walking further along the Cosmatesque style floor of black and white inlay marble to the dining room, Lord Yancey happened to hear the sounds of violins and an accordion player in the distance. "What an enchanting music, Count Stavros! Are we also entertaining guests from Spain?"

"Not that I'm aware of," replied Count Stavros.

The music playing had a rich Spanish flair. In between each white grey veined marble column that they passed, a maid and butler stood at attention.

The maids were dressed in black and wore aprons of horizontal black and white stripes with matching headbands and curtsied as they passed. On the opposite side, white-gloved butlers had silver buttons on their tailcoats with black and white horizontal striped vests, who also bowed when they passed.

Lord Yancey and Count Stavros soon reached two large silver leaf art deco dining room doors, which two albino footmen gracefully opened. The doors depicted Dionysus on one side and Apollo on the other side. They opened up onto a magnificent oval shaped ballroom in the pantheon style taste.

"I say Aráchni, this does not look at all like the dining room. I do believe we have been misdirected to the wrong room," cried Lord Yancey.

However, as they entered the so-called dining room, they could see the guests dancing to sounds of the Tango, cheek to cheek. This room, unlike the others in the house, had a touch of color on the walls. Six modern works of art in art deco black frames with splashed of reds, greens, and yellows.

"Count Stavros, this looks more like a ballroom than a dining room, old chap," exclaimed Lord Yancey to Count Stavros.

"Oh do be quiet for one moment Yancey," exclaimed Stavros, with worry.

Anxiously, he yelled across the room to his sister, who was dancing, "I say dear sister what is the meaning of this? This does not look like a dinner party thrown in our honor!"

Countess Athena was quite a sight on the dance floor, with hair black as night and lips red as rubies. The front and back of her little black dress were embellished with pearls that were designed in a fountain style that stopped at her knees. Athena made a final dip across the dance floor of black and white inlay marble of circles and squares within a checkerboard pattern

"Oh dearest brother, there seems to have been a change of plans." Clapping her hands, she announced to the guests dancing, "Dearest friends, to your places if you please!"

The guest began to form two lines in the middle of the dance floor. Lord Yancy tapped her brother on he shoulder upon seeing this. "I say, Stavros, what is your sister up to?" Count Stavros looked back but didn't reply.

Countess Athena walked over to a brass lever on the side of the room and with one pull, the ballroom began to transform. The guests stood in two lines looking at each other with excitement. The marble inlay floor of circles and squares began to move.

Clank, clank, clank.

As the guests looked on in amazement, a slab of black marble rectangle in shape made the crisscross pattern on the floor rise up in between each guest. This formed a grand dinner table and the circles and squares from the floor elevated to form dining chairs.

The Countess extending her arms and laughed as she announced to her guests, "Ladies and Gentlemen you may now be seated!"

"Cracking," cried Lord Yancey with his monocle falling out of his eye, adding, "Well it seems we were in the dining room all along!"

Sitting down at the head of the table crossing her legs, Countess Athena nonchalantly lit a cigarette. "Oh Lord Yancey, how good it is to see you once again. Darling do have a seat." Lord Yancey proceeded to sit near Anthea. On seeing this, Athena immediately said, "No Lord Yancey not there, your seat is at the other end of the dinner table."

"I say, but I can't hear a word of what you are saying, sitting down there," exclaimed Lord Yancey.

"Darling, that's the whole point" Athena replied, laughing. She then began to explain the change of plans to her brother, who took a seat next to her. "Dearest brother, being that you are always late to most of my functions and after receiving a phone call from a last-minute guest, I've taken the liberty of celebrating someone else."

"Who could possibly master my automotive achievements," exclaimed Count Stavros.

Just then, before the grand doorway stood the last-minute guest with, Aráchni announcing him. It was the Baron François von Tickle, the guests then stood up from their seats.

"Baron von Tickle darling, welcome!" exclaimed Countess Athena as she ran up to him, holding her hand out to be kissed.

Athena turning to her brother, "You know my brother, Stavros."

"Oh of course, always a pleasure," replied the Baron.

Count Stavros extended his hand and shook the Baron's. "So nice of you to sponsor the races this year. I say, dear Baron, but aren't you near 90?"

The Baron replied with a laugh, "A gentlemen never talks about his age."

"Stavros, don't be rude," cried his sister.

The truth was that the Baron was at least 135 years old, but his appearance was that of man in his 30s.

"Why dear Baron, where is the Baroness?" asked Athena.

"She's at our winter home," he replied as they all sat down for a most enchanting dinner.

"You'll never guess who I saw on the way here, dear sister," said Stavros.

Athena gave him an exasperated look and said, "And whom would that be dear brother?" with boredom in her voice.

"Sir Henry Humphrey!" Stavros exclaimed.

"Great gads of grape juice! Has he entered the Brighton to Londinium race?" asked Athena.

Stavros replied, "Not too sure dear sister, but he was with a rather funny little boy without a duster nor goggles on. Can you imagine?"

The Baron then raised his eyebrows as he looked over at the Count and asked, "Did this funny little boy wear a top hat?"

"Why yes, he did!" The count replied.

"If you'll excuse me, dear Count, but may I have a word in private with your sister?" asked the Baron.

"Of course, Baron," replied the Countess. She then got up to take leave of her guests. "If you'll excuse us, ladies and gentlemen, I'll only be a moment."

Taking the Baron's hand, the Countess led him to a quiet part of the balcony garden of the townhouse.

"Dear Countess, the funny little boy your brother spoke of tonight is my wife's grand-nephew by the name of Sir Thomas Tattletale."

"Of Tattletale Publishing House?" asked the Countess.

"Yes the very one," replied the Baron.

"Oh do go on, dear Baron!" Athena cried with great enthusiasm. "I've discovered on a recent visit to my wife's family that he possesses a very special powerful laugh which can only be harnessed by my wife and myself."

"Oh! I see, which explains why you look so youthful, dear Baron," stated Countess Athena, caressing his cheek.

"You could say that," said the Baron with a grimace.

"And what would you like me to do about this situation, dear Baron?" asked the Countess.

"My dearest Countess, being that you are so very creative in winning almost every race you and your brother have ever entered, I thought you would be the perfect candidate for this job. As you know, accidents do happen, especially in steam operated ones. Let's just say with Sir Henry out of the way that boy would be so much easier to grab, dearest Countess," said the Baron with an alluring smile. "In return for your creative services I shall triple your prize money and a small percentage of stock in the von Tickle motorcar company."

"Oh Baron von Tickle, you make me blush. I shall see what I can think of," replied the Countess, as they both cracked with maniacal laughter.

"Are you hungry, Sir Thomas? I make the best Dodo bird salad sandwiches, you know. If not, I can just boil a Dodo bird egg if you wish?" asked Ms. Koukouvágia.

"No thank you, Ms. Koukouvágia. I'm very tired as it has been a long day," Sir Thomas replied with a yawn.

"Okay then, we'll have scrambled Dodo eggs in the morning when you awake," she said.

"Ooh yummy, my favorite!" cried Digby, tagging along.

Sir Henry Humphrey loved eating eggs prepared in all sorts of ways. He owned a Dodo bird farm on his country estate in Kent and brought some of them to roost in the backyard of his city home.

As they walked down the hallway to escort Thomas to his room, Ms. Koukouvágia and Digby twirled around, dancing and humming. Reaching the end of the hallway, Ms. Koukouvágia announced, "This will be your room, young Thomas."

As Digby opened the door slowly, Sir Thomas peered in and was amazed by the décor. The entire room, with the exception of a small mahogany Empire bed, was covered and painted in different patterns of tartan plaids. It was truly the warmest room in the house. "Nice room, Thomas, yes?" asked Digby, as he bounced up and down on his bed.

"Yes indeed. Quite cozy, Digby!" replied Thomas, giggling.

"Digby Scarborough, get off that bed this instant! Thomas has a very big day ahead of him tomorrow," cried Ms. Koukouvágia. There now, let me tuck you in, Thomas." Ms. Koukouvágia kissed Thomas on the forehead when he got under the covers and wished him a goodnight as she tucked him in.

"Goodnight Thomas, it was very nice meeting you," cried Digby Scarborough, waving his paw.

"Goodnight, Digby," replied Thomas as he fell fast asleep.

The next morning, Sir Thomas was abruptly awoken and fell out of his because the whole room was shaking. "Bow Bumble! It must be an earthquake!" cried Sir Thomas as he rubbed the bump on his head caused by the fall. Getting up off the floor, he held onto the headboard of his bed and looked around the room. It was completely different. The walls and lamps were no longer decorated in plaid but of polished redwood paneling and brass fixtures. Only the little Empire bed was the same. Walking carefully over to the window, Thomas gazed out to the countryside as the trees whizzed past his window. "Bow Bumble I am not in a house at all, but a moving locomotive," cried Thomas. Baffled, he wondered how he got on the train without his knowledge.

It was Sir Henry's private train carriage. Just then Sir Henry walked in. "Good morning, young Thomas! I am so glad to see you up and about. We shall be in Brighton within the hour old sport, so do have a proper breakfast." Sir Henry called out to Ms. Koukouvágia, "Ms. Koukouvágia! Ms. Koukouvágia! The boy looks half starved!" he cried, laughing robustly.

Within seconds, Ms. Koukouvágia appeared. "Yes, Sir Henry," she answered as she stood behind Sir Henry.

Startled by her abruptness, Sir Henry turned around with a jump, "Ms. Koukouvágia! You'll be the death of me yet!" He said.

"Sir Henry, your breakfast is already in your cabin," she replied.

"Thank you Ms. Koukouvágia," Sir Henry replied, leaving the room.

Digby then walked in and greeted Thomas. "Why good morning, Sir Thomas. Did you sleep well?"

"Oh, indeed, but how did I get on this train without waking up?" Thomas asked with curiosity.

Digby laughed said, "Silly Thomas! Ms. Koukouvágia carried you from the house."

"Yes but how did my bed get here on the train?" Asked Thomas.

"Oh excuse me. I meant Ms. Koukouvágia carried the bed while you slept on it. She didn't want to disturb your slumber," he replied.

They were interrupted by Ms. Koukouvágia. "Your breakfast is served, young Thomas! So glad you slept well. I didn't want to disturb your sleep last night so I took the liberty of moving your bed to the train carriage."

"Oh, I see! Thank you, Ms. Koukouvágia," Thomas replied.

"Ms. Koukouvágia is quite strong and also serves as Sir Henry Humphrey's personal bodyguard, when abroad," Digby explained to Sir Thomas.

The locomotive came to screeching halt when it reached Brighton. On the platform of Brighton Station, they saw a thirty piece brass band that welcomed them and the visiting competitors to the race. As the steam of the engine began t dissipate, Thomas could see the glistening seaside. Although the brass band was rather loud, Thomas could hear a fire engine siren in the distance. "I say, there must be a fire some-where!" stated Thomas.

"Wow! A fire a fire! I wonder what's burning down. Come on Thomas, let's go and watch," cried Digby as he jumped up and down.

"Hold on one moment Digby, I hear more than one kind of siren!" exclaimed Thomas.

Sir Henry had walked up to both of them as Thomas was listening. "I say, what are you two rascals up to?"

"We are going to see what's burning down," cried Bixby, with a smile.

"There's nothing burning down at the moment, dear Bixby," replied Sir Henry. "Why do you say that, Sir Henry?" asked Thomas.

"Because the first race of the day is for the service vehicles," replied Sir Henry.

Service vehicles of all sizes and colors were joining in the Brighton to London races. They consisted of fire engines, ambulances, and police paddy wagons from all over the country.

"Sir Thomas, I have a surprise for you," said Sir Henry.

"And what would that be, Sir Henry?"

"If you'll follow me please," replied Sir Henry, as he gave Bixby a signal to run ahead of them.

Bixby ran to the storage carriage of the train, and Sir Henry and Thomas followed behind. Reaching the storage carriage, Sir Thomas saw a ramp coming down. To his surprise, driving down came Bixby Scarborough, giggling in the seat of Sir Henry's newest steam powered automobile. It was a four-door yellow and black striped motorcar with a streamlined modified steam engine.

"Bow Bumble! Sir Henry, you are joining the races!" cried Sir Thomas.

"Indeed I am," Sir Henry replied, grinning from ear to ear.

"It's absolutely beautiful! Does it have a name?" Sir Thomas asked.

"Why it most certainly does, young Thomas. I call it The Bumble Bee Steamer."

Sir Thomas couldn't contain his excitement, "Bow Bumble, just smashing, I say!" he cried.

A gunfire sounded and the service vehicles were off. "Come now Sir Thomas, we mustn't be late to the starting line," said Sir Henry. Then he turned to Ms. Koukouvágia. "The luggage if you please, Ms. Koukouvágia. He addressed Thomas again he said, "Digby and I have to go to the starting line, you go with Ms. Koukouvágia. You'll be with her in the grandstands."

Two hours earlier in a striped black and white tent near the starting line, Countess Athena was informing her brother of her dastardly plans.

"Dear sister, are you mad? I want no part in this, we've sabotaged many automobiles in our time, but kidnapping?"

"It's what I thought you'd say, dear brother, Aráchni will be replacing you in this race."

"Athena, need I remind you that Lord Yancey and I had developed that automobile!"

"Very true, Stavros, but I own sixty percent of the Tetradrachm Corporation," replied his sister. Athena then turned to the butler and asked, "Aráchni could you escort my dear brother to the exit?"

"Don't you touch me. I can see myself out!" The Count exclaimed. "You will not get away with this Athena!" he said as he turned to exit the tent.

Standing outside the tent was Lord Yancey, who had overheard everything. He grabbed Stavros by the arm as he stormed out of the tent. "I say, Stavros, you're not going to let her get away with this, are you old chap?"

"Of course not. That's why I'm riding with you, old chap. We are teaming up," exclaimed Count Stavros with a grimace.

"I say, good show, but there's only one slight problem," Said Yancey.

"Now what would that be, if I may ask?"

"Well, because the new automobile has all the sabotage gadgets!"

"You are a rather resourceful fellow, Lord Yancey. Just use your imagination," said the Count.

Meanwhile back at the tent, Aráchni had important information pertaining to Sir Henry and Sir Thomas Tattletale from his spies. "Dear Countess, "Sir Henry Humphrey shall be arriving on the two o'clock train. He is being accompanied by a housekeeper and two little boys, one of whom is Sir Thomas Tattletale."

"You have to be kidding me!" The Countess cried with hysterical laughter. "The English never cease to amaze me, Aráchni. This will be easier than I thought." Aráchni lit her cigarette. "Aráchni, do see to them as they get off the train," she added.

Ms. Koukouvágia carried two steamer trunks and various bags over her shoulder as they walked toward the hotel. Sir Thomas offered her his assistance, "Ms. Koukouvágia, do you need any help with that?"

"Oh no Sir Thomas, but thank you.

Lurking in shadows, Aráchni followe their every move.

Ms. Koukouvágia and Sir Thomas arrived at the Royal Brighton Point Hotel. Its interior style was Edwardian and Gothic splendor of a white and lavender décor. Sir Thomas stopped to smell the purple hydrangea that lined the marble vestibule side steps as he entered. Entering the middle of the lobby, Sir Thomas noticed there was a three-faced Grandfather Clock, a traffic light on top.

Scratching his head, Thomas wondered, "Why would there be a traffic light on top of a clock in the middle of the lobby?"

As Sir Thomas and Ms. Koukouvágia proceeded to walk through the lobby, Thomas stopped to look down a padded hallway. Racing down the hallway was a convertible tricycle with two laughing gentlemen on it. Thomas thought nothing of this until he looked in the opposite direction. Down another padded hallway was a Penny Farthing going full speed, heading in the same direction.

"Bow Bumble, this is why there was a traffic light in the lobby!" Sir Thomas cried. He immediately noticed that Ms. Koukouvágia was in the way of the Penny Farthing, and cried out to her, "Ms. Koukouvágia, look out ahead!"

The convertible tricycle and the Penny Farthing side-swiped Ms. Koukouvágia at the same time, twirling her around, the luggage still in her arms. "Sir Thomas? Sir Thomas Tattletale, where are you, young man?" She was in a dizzy.

"I'm right front of you, Ms. Koukouvágia. The hat box is blocking your vision," Thomas cried.

She was still in a daze. "Oh dear me." She put down the luggage and, catching her breath, turned to Sir Thomas. "Thomas, could you wait for me in the lobby while I get us checked in?"

"No problem Ms. Koukouvágia, just look both ways next time," Thomas exclaimed, sitting himself down underneath the lobby clock.

Ms.Koukouvágia walked over to the concierge and rang the bell once. A silver-haired gentleman appeared in morning attire. "Welcome to the Royal Brighton Point Hotel. May I be of any assistance?"

"Oh yes indeed, I'm just checking in for Sir Henry Humphrey," she replied.

"Oh very good. Oh yes I have it here… ah yes! Suite 1921, here is your key," said the gentleman, as he gave Ms. Koukouvágia a key to the room. A bellman on a unicycle shall take your luggage up to your room in a moment."

"Come now Sir Thomas, we're going up to our room," cried the housekeeper.

"Yes Ms. Koukouvágia, I'm coming," replied Thomas, as he ran across the lobby.

Ms. Koukouvágia picked Thomas up to press the up button to the elevator. As the elevator doors opened, they were greeted by a courteous bellhop, "Good afternoon, going up?" he asked.

"The fifth floor, if you please," replied the housekeeper.

"Will you be needing any assistance with your luggage to your room, madam?" Asked the courteous bellhop.

"Oh, no thank you," replied Ms. Koukouvágia.

As the elevator began to move, Thomas was curious about something. "I say, that's rather odd Ms. Koukouvágia." He pointed his finger at the bellhop.

"Why do you say that, Thomas?" asked Ms. Koukouvágia.

"Well, the other bellhops were on unicycles, while this one is not," he stated. "Oh Thomas, don't be silly. This bellhop doesn't need a unicycle to carry luggage because he has four arms," exclaimed Ms. Koukouvágia with a smile.

"Why, what a smart little boy you are," stated the four-armed bellhop as he glared down with a grimace. "I do believe this is your floor."

"This does not look like our floor, Ms. Koukouvágia," said Sir Thomas.

"Oh bellman!" this looks like the basement. I've requested the 5th floor," said Ms. Koukouvágia, politely.

"I'm afraid you are both right!" said the four-armed bellhop.

"Allow me to introduce myself, I'm Aráchni, and the Countess is expecting Sir Thomas Tattletale for dinner." He was holding a long piece of rope in one hand as he grabbed Ms. Koukouvágia and Thomas by their arms with his other hands.

"Unhand me at once!" cried Ms. Koukouvágia, as she struck Aráchni in the head with a piece of luggage.

Sir Thomas kicked him in the knee, breaking free. Thomas tried to help Ms. Koukouvágia. "Thomas, don't worry about me. Just get back to Sir Henry! Now, run!" She began to wrestle Aráchni to the ground.

Running up the steps, Thomas headed for the main floor of the hotel. Once there, he headed out through the doors onto the main grounds to the starting line.

Reaching the starting line of the race, Sir Thomas saw Sir Henry Humphrey's automobile. Digby saw him and yelled, "I say, look Sir Henry, its Sir Thomas."

Sir Thomas got close enough to them to speak. Out of breath, Thomas attempted to explain what happened to Bixby and Sir Henry. "A tall man with four arms grabbed me and Ms. Koukouvágia at the hotel."

Sir Henry and Digby looked at him with astonishment. "Cranberries and peanut butter sauce! Thomas, how did you escape?" asked Digby.

"I escaped by kicking him in the knee!" replied Thomas, finally catching his breath.

What did he want?"

"He said he wanted me to have dinner with some Countess he works for," Sir Thomas replied. "I'm awfully worried about Ms. Koukouvágia. Should I go and assist her?" asked Thomas, looking intently at Sir Henry.

"Young Thomas don't you worry your head about Ms. Koukouvágia. She can handle anything. For now, you are going to ride with us," replied Sir Henry.

"Oh, Hurrah!" cried Digby Scarborough.

Meanwhile, all the automobiles from around the world were lining up at the starting line. "Aráchni what took you so long, and what did you do with the boy and that housekeeper?" cried the Countess. "Oh never mind, just get in the motorcar. The race is about to begin." She noticed his eye and asked "Aráchni! Where did you get that black eye and why is one of your arms in a sling? Now don't tell me a little boy and a common housekeeper did this to you!"

"I'm afraid so, dear Countess. The common housekeeper you speak of is about six feet tall and has rather sharp talons for feet! But I did manage to tie her up back at the hotel."

"And what of that little brat Thomas Tattletale?"

With dismay, the butler replied, "I'm afraid, dear Countess, that Sir Thomas Tattletale got away."

"We'll look for the boy later. Let's just concentrate on getting rid of Sir Henry Humphrey permanently along the way."

CHAPTER 6
The Brighton to Londinium Race

"Ladies and gentlemen, I'd like to welcome you all to our 75th annual Brighton to Londinium race. A very special thanks to our most generous sponsor, Baron von Tickle."

"In our starting lineup, we have, in the number one position from Hong Kong, in the green and white three-wheeled marvel, Professor Gan Quan!"

"At number two, from Greece, in the black and white automobile are the brother and sister team of the Count and Countess Tetradrachm. Wait a minute, there seems to be a change. The Countess now has a new partner, a four-armed chap."

"At number three from the Americas, from the little town of Brooklyn in the black 1910 Octoauto, sporting eight white-walled wheels, is the mother and son team of Kenneth and Johanna Skeleton."

"At number four from France in the purple 1918 electric Benault Coupe De Ville is Marcel de Monogram."

"At number five from India in the burgundy 1912 rose oil-powered Lanchester limousine is Prince Samir Nawaz."

"At number six from Egypt in the white and chrome trim 1913 Mercer electric Raceabout is Lady Farrah Cotton and her sister Afshan."

"At number seven from Londinium in polished aluminum six-wheeled automobile are the three Pound sisters."

"At number eight from Brazil in the orange 1920 electric Obrigado Por Passá lo automobile is Prince Palo."

"At number nine from Kent in the yellow and black striped steam powered automobile is Sir Henry Humphrey."

"And finally, number ten from Yorkshire in the red modified touring motorcar is Lord Yancey Pfeiffer. Well, I'll be! Lord Yancey has a new driving partner. Why, it's Count Tetradrachm! Now I've seen everything, folks!"

"Ladies and gentlemen, you may now start your automobiles!"

The race began. In the lead were Professor Gang Quan and Prince Palo. They were neck and neck so far. Down on the track, racing side by side, Prince Palo hollers over to Professor Quan who is eating French bread in his motorcar. "Say good friend, but how can you eat and drive at the same time?" asked Prince Palo, taking a whiff of his yellow Gerber in his lapel.

"Because I am a talented and gifted driver, you see, more than I can say for you, Prince Palo!" replied Professor Quan.

"Oh you must forgive me Professor, but if you were so smart you would have put butter on your French bread!" said Prince Palo with a smirk.

"I prefer raspberry jam on my French bread," replied Professor Quan.

"Oh indeed, well allow me to be of assistance," stated Palo as he pressed a button in his jacket pocket which squirted raspberry jam through his Gerber into Professor Quan'a face, blinding him.

"Ahhhh!" The Professor screamed trying to wipe the jam out of his eyes as the automobile swerved off the road and crashed into the bushes.

"Thank you, dear Professor, for letting me pass you," cried Prince Palo devilishly, waving his hand as he raced off down the road.

Pulling up to the side of Prince Palo's motorcar was Prince Samir Nawaz. "Why hello Prince Samir, fantastic party you threw last night," he cried.

"Why thank you, Palo, I try," he replied.

"Poor thing, what happened to Professor Quan, crashing so early in the race!" exclaimed Prince Samir.

"Oh indeed, so sad. As I had said before, the roads were meant for the princes," stated Prince Palo.

"Oh indeed I agree!" he replied.

"Say, but where do you get your cologne? You smell like a bouquet of roses at the end of a finish line," said Prince Palo.

"Oh thank you. I'm truly flattered but it's not my cologne, dear Palo, but the fuel in my automobile. It runs on rose oil you see," Prince Samir replied as he took out a cigar, ready to light it with one hand.

"Really? You mean the substance that's leaking from your motorcar?" stated Prince Palo slyly.

"Oh dear Palo, there's nothing leaking from my automobile. It's just being sprayed onto your tires," Prince Samir stated with a maniacal grin.

"Well thank goodness I have proper treads or I would have surely swerved and hit a tree by now with all that rose oil all over my tires," he stated with a smirk.

"So good to know, dear Palo, because rose oil is quite flammable," replied Prince Samir. The Prince then struck a match on the dashboard of his automobile, lighting his cigar. He threw the match onto Prince Palo's front tires, setting them ablaze.

"My wheels are on fire!" cried Prince Palo as he swerved off the road, tail spinning into a pond.

Looking over to the waterlogged automobile, Prince Samir yelled, "Now there shall only be one Prince on this road, dear chap!" Three automobiles raced past Prince Nawaz as he revved his engine and raced off, laughing.

Racing down the road, Prince Samir passed Lady Farrah Cotton's motorcar, parked on the side of the road. She was sitting on the running board sipping chamomile tea in long black gauntlets gloves. Dressed in the Gibson girl style, the Lady Cotton was the very picture of feminine elegance. Her blouse of navy blue and white bold stripes was complemented by a tailored white skirt, and paired with a wide black leather belt with a brass buckle.

"A damsel in distress and in need of princely assistance!" thought Prince Nawaz to himself, pointing his finger into the air. He decided to stop for here and parked only a few feet away by a tree. Exiting his automobile, he approached Lady Farah. "Could I be of any assistance my little Egyptian water lily?" Prince Samir asked, taking off his burgundy racing cap and goggles and placing them to his chest.

Upon hearing the Prince's offer, she looked up slowly in tinted goggles, and offered the Prince a cup of tea, "Do you care for some tea, dear Prince?"

"Why I would be delighted, dear Lady Cotton," he replied.

She stood up to reach over into the motorcar and pulled out a teapot and cup. "Do you take honey or sugar lumps?" she politely asked.

"I take two lumps, my little Egyptian goddess," replied the Prince, with a grin.

"Oh, dear me! It seems that I'm out of sugar lumps, dear Prince, but I do have honey," she stated.

"Never you mind, dear Lady Farah. In any case, why did you stop?" He asked.

"A nut came loose on my back tire, so I sent Afshan to go look for it," Farrah replied with a soft smile.

As Prince Samir looked around, he saw a figure approaching them from up the road. "I say, isn't that your sister Lady Afshan coming up the road now?"

Lady Afshan approached Prince Samir, dressed in a similar fashion as her sister, but sported white jodhpurs with black riding boots. Like her sister, she wore a wide black leather belt with a brass buckle.

Seeing her approach, Lady Farah turned to her and said, "Why it is, Afie! Oh Afie, do hurry or we're going to be late for the race." Reaching the automobile, Lady Afshan was out of breath. Lady Farah asked her, "Afshan, has everything been done?"

Still out of breath, her sister cried, "Yes everything is done, Farah!"

"I say, Lady Afshan, have you've located the nut?" asked the Prince.

"The only nut I've located is the one standing before me. Now get out of the way. We have a race to win!" cried Lady Afshan.

Prince Samire turned to Lady Farah. "How rude! Are you just going to sit there and let your sister talk to me in that fashion?"

"Dear Prince, my sister was being kind, now if you do not move aside, I shall indeed run you down," she stated.

"Now be gone with thyself!" Cried her younger sister as she swished her hand at the Prince.

Prince Samir was flabbergasted. "Well I never!" The Prince then stormed off toward his automobile, and was struck in head with a tea cup. "Ow! My head! What in the world," he cried, grabbing his head in pain. Then he was struck once again, but with a teapot this time. "Oh, my head!" He turned to Lady Farah and cried, "Why on earth did you do that?"

"Well, now you have the two lumps as you requested my little Vishnu God," she replied. She and her sister drove off laughing.

Prince Samir was now furious as he ran back to his automobile and set it on full throttle. Unfortunately for the Prince, as he did this, he did not realize that the back axle of his motorcar was chained to the very tree he parked next to earlier. Thus, as he stepped on the gas, the automobile was torn in half as the front of the vehicle went flying across the road and crashed into a ditch.

"Ladies and Gentlemen, oh the agony, we now only have seven magnificent automobiles left in our race," stated the commentator.

"I say Digby, are we making good time?" asked Sir Henry.

"Indeed we are so far!" Digby replied. "Sharp turn ahead Sir Henry!" The wind blew his tongue to the side of his face.

"Hold on Sir Thomas, we're coming up to a sharp turn!" cried Sir Henry.

"Weeee!" Sir Thomas was holding on to his top hat as they made the sharp turn.

An automobile pulled up next to them with familiar voices coming from inside. "Oh, Toodle-loo! Toodle-loo Sir Henry!" cried a lady in the automobile.

Sir Thomas Tomato!"

"You silly Apple head, that's not his name! It's Sir Thomas Potato," replied the other lady.

"My god! Why oh why have I been cursed with these two idiots!" said the third lady who added, "For the love of corn flakes, just call him Thomas already!" It was the three Pound sisters.

Sir Henry, Sir Thomas, and Digby took a quick glance at them.

"Hello Sir Henry, so glad to see you racing once again!" Tessa cried with a joyous giggle.

Sir Henry smiled back and said, "Delighted to be back in the driver's seat again, dear Tessa!"

"And I see you brought along little Thomas. How delightful!" cried Odessa.

"So my little Thomas, how do you like it so far?" asked Vanessa.

"Just smashing, Vanessa!" replied Thomas.

"Toodle-loo!!" cried Vanessa, blowing a kiss to Sir Thomas.

"Goodbye gentlemen," cried Odessa, waving both hands and almost falling out of the automobile in the process.

"Bye bye, and good luck, Thomas!" cried Tessa as she and her sisters raced off.

Just then, Lord Yancey and Count Stavros pulled up beside them. "I say old sport, but I have a bit of rather important information for you!"

"And what would that, be you rancid rat?" asked Sir Henry, scornfully.

"My dear sister means to have your boy kidnapped and you out of the way, old chap. Permanently, that is!"

Sir Henry did not want to anything to with them. "I'm well aware of this old chap, now be on your way!" exclaimed Sir Henry.

"Very well old chap," replied Count Stavros as he and Lord Yancey raced off and down a fork in the road.

On the racing route, not too far away, the Countess was not too far behind. She saw Sir Henry Humphrey's motorcar.
"Sir Henry, I can see the Countess's automobile!" What shall we do?" cried Thomas.

He told Thomas to stay hidden in the back seat until the coast was clear, then instructed Digby to cover Thomas with a blanket.

The Countess could also see Sir Henry's automobile in the distance and prepared to execute her plan. "I see Sir Henry's automobile ahead. Get the explosive ready!" she asked of Aráchni as she stepped on the gas. Catching up to Sir Henry's automobile, she greeted him with a smile. She was unable to see Sir Thomas covered in the back seat. Looking across, she hollered, "Why hello gentlemen, wonderful day for a race."

"Oh indeed it is, my little viper," Sir Henry replied with distaste.

"Why Sir Henry Humphrey, you make me blush, you wicked man!" she replied with cackling laughter.

While Athena was making small talk to occupy Sir Henry, Aráchni was attaching a mechanical time bomb to the back fender of their automobile.

Uncovering himself, Sir Thomas saw Aráchni attaching something to the back fender. He bolted from underneath the blanket and cried, "Sir Henry, Sir Henry, that's the man with four arms I told you about! He's put something on the automobile!"

"Hold on Thomas and Digby!" cried Sir Henry as he pulled a lever next to the stick shift, releasing extra steam to the engine, which catapulted them down the road, leaving the Countess in the dust.

"Aráchni! Sir Thomas Tattletale was in the automobile!" she cried, realizing their mistake.

"Aráchni! Nothing must happen to the boy, we must get that bomb off Sir Henry's automobile quickly or I shall be out of a great deal of prize money and benefits!" the Countess exclaimed hysterically.

Just then, Marcel de Monogram drove up behind them. Apparently, he had overheard the last bit of her conversation and slyly asked, "Bonjour Mon Cheri Athena. Did someone say bomb?" as he threw an exploding smoke bomb into their automobile and sped off with cackling laughter.

The Countess shrieked furiously, "Why you rotten swine!" as blinding smoke filled the automobile. "Aráchni, lower the roof. I can't see a thing and do hurry before we crash!"

"Right away, Countess!" replied Aráchni, as he pressed a button in the side compartment and the roof retracted, clearing the smoke. Athena and Aráchni could see Sir Henry's motorcar going up a steep hill in the distance.

The only problem for the Countess at this moment was Marcel de Monogram and The Skeleton Family, both of whom were in front of them side swiping each other as they tried to knock each other off the road. "Get out of the way you blithering idiots!" cried Athena as she tried to find a way ahead. "Why bonjour, dear Countess. So nice of you to join us," stated Marcel.

"Well you are more than welcome to pass us if you can get through us!" cried Kenneth Skeleton as his mother cocked a crossbow and aimed it toward her tires.

Marcel de Monogram just laughed as he prepared to hurl another smoke bomb into her automobile.

"Gentleman it brings a tear to my eye to know how kind and thoughtful you all are." Then, addressing her butler, she said, "Aráchni prepare the slicer." As she drove the motorcar, Aráchni pressed the button on the side panel of the dashboard. A large retractable rotating saw came out from under the automobile. As they got closer to Marcel's automobile, the saw turned vertical and began to slice his vehicle in half.

Marcel was taken by surprise by this sudden maneuver of the Countess. "My motorcar! You maniacs!" he cried, throwing his last smoke bomb at them as he jumped out of his automobile and onto the side road.

Seeing Marcel's smoke bomb headed in their direction, Aráchni took out a cricket bat and took one good whack at it, knocking it straight into the window of the Skeleton's automobile. The bomb exploded inside of their motorcar, sending it into a tailspin.

Racing alongside them laughing at the devastation was Lady Farah and her sister Afshan. They had thoroughly enjoyed the show and looked at each other, smiling. "Oh, dear sister, how dramatic they all are!" Lady Farah exclaimed.

Lady Afshan replied with smile, "Oh indeed, dear sister. Why can't they be more civil like us?"

Meanwhile in the Skeleton's automobile, Kenneth and Johanna were blinded by the smoke. "Mother! I can't see anything!" cried Kenneth, choking at the wheel from the smoke.

"I can't either, son. I'll try to locate the roll handle for the window," his mother replied. The tail was spinning out of control as she tried to locate the handle. As Johanna located the handle to open the window and pulled hard, her crossbow discharged out of the open window and landed on the front tire of Lady Farah's automobile, piercing it. Now with a flat tire, Farah and Afshan also went into a tailspin, crashing into a tree on the side of the road. Coming out of the tailspin as the air cleared off their automobile was a sigh of relief for Kenneth and Johanna Skeleton until they realized their automobile was horizontally parked in the middle of the road.

Unfortunately for the Skeletons, Countess Athena and Aráchni were headed down the road still fully armed with the rotating protruding buzz saw. The Skeletons frantically tried to restart their engine but to no avail. In a minute, the Countess' automobile was upon them and the Countess sliced right through their automobile, splitting it in half.

"Yup, he's right Sir Henry, there's something on the fender and it is ticking like a clock," stated a grinning Digby, as he pointed at the located bomb.

Sir Henry asked Digby, "Digby take the wheel and do keep it steady old chap." Turning to Sir Thomas, he instructed, "Thomas, go sit with Digby in the front." Then, as Digby took the wheel, he climbed onto the back of his automobile. Looking closely, he confirmed, "Yes gentlemen, it is indeed what I thought it was all along."

The curious Sir Thomas asked, "And what would that be, Sir Henry?"

"My boy, it seems to be a mechanical time bomb set to go off in about five minutes and the only way to deactivate this monstrosity is with a key."

As Sir Henry was trying to dislodge the time bomb from the automobile, Sir Henry saw Lord Yancey and Count Stavros approaching from the fork in the road. Stavros offered his assistance to Sir Henry nonchalantly. "I say old chap, it seems you are in a bit of a spot. Could we offer any assistance?"

Sir Henry replied, "No need gentleman, I have it!"

Digby drove while Sir Henry concentrated on the bomb as they came upon a sharp turn. Sir Henry almost fell off his automobile while trying to dislodge the time bomb, but was saved by Digby's fast thinking. Maneuvering the turn and anticipating the fall, Digby asked Sir Thomas to take hold of the wheel, while he grabbed on to Sir Henry's ankles. In this movement of the automobile, Sir Henry was able to release the time bomb from the fender. Unfortunately, he was about to lose his balance once again as the time bomb slipped out of his hands and onto the hood of Yancey and Stavros' motorcar. With only seconds left, the mechanical time bomb went off, taking off the front of Yancey and Stavros' motorcar.

Driving off, Sir Henry Humphrey apologized to them, "I say old chaps, so sorry about that, didn't mean it you know!"

Sitting in a half automobile with soot on their faces from the explosion, Lord Yancey looked over to Count Stavros nonchalantly and stated, "This is very last time I offer my assistance."

"I say Yancey, your carnation is crooked," said Stavros as he tried to fix it on his lapel only to have his hand smacked by Yancey.

Speeding like hellfire to catch up to Sir Henry, Athena noticed her brother and Yancey sitting in the partially demolished automobile. She cried out to them, "Fools!" as she passed them by. She then smelled something rather odd, and turning to Aráchni she cried, "Aráchni why don't you say excuse me! That's just disgusting," she exclaimed.

"But what did I do dear Countess?"

"It is polite to cover one's mouth when burping!" she said.

Then Aráchni replied, "But countess, I didn't burp!"

"Well, then what is that smell I ask you?" the Countess wondered aloud.

Just then, they came upon the 3 Pound Sisters singing and laughing in their automobile. "Forgive me Aráchni! I've just located the source!" exclaimed the Countess. Athena then yelled over to them, "Dear Ladies couldn't you have found a better fuel source other than garlic soup?" Her eyes began to water.

"No, not really. Why do you ask?" Vanessa replied innocently.

"I ask darlings because the exhaust coming from your automobile is just dreadful," the Countess replied with outrage.

Oh thank you, dear countess, you also have a beautiful head full of hair!" replied Vanessa giggling, waving her hand, and blushing.

"No I said dreadful not head full!" replied the Countess, rolling her eyes lined with dark mascara.

"Oh Odessa, the Countess just complimented me on my beautiful hair!" exclaimed Vanessa, puffing her hair as she drove.

"Is the countess blind? You are wearing a wig! I'm the one with the naturally curly flowing hair!" exclaimed Odessa.

"Oh my goodness! The Countess is blind I did not know that," cried Tessa in amazement as she stopped playing her clarinet.

"Aráchni it is beyond me how those three nincompoops even made it to Brighton!"

"I see them ahead, Countess. They are headed toward the Dover Mountains!" the butler stated.

"Splendid Aráchni, I have an idea! Do you have any more rope left?" she asked.

"I packed extra, dear Countess," replied Aráchni, smiling.

"This is what we're going to do Aráchni," Athena then began to explain the plan in detail. "As they make another sharp turn on the road in the mountains we shall drive alongside them. Then you shall make ready your rope lassoing the boy in Sir Henry's automobile, pulling him out to safety into our vehicle. Afterward, I shall run Sir Henry and his dog-faced assistant off the cliff."

"Superb idea, dear Countess, if I may take the liberty of saying that," replied Aráchni as he prepared the rope.

Driving up the road at a mad pace, unbeknownst to the Countess and Aráchni, was a mysterious 1900 style motor cab. One could say it was a most unlikely entry to the race.

Entering the lush Dover mountains, Sir Thomas happened to look back and saw the Countess' motorcar catching up to them. He cried, "Sir Henry! Sir Henry we need full steam ahead, the Countess is catching up to us!"

"I'm afraid we're running out of steam, Thomas," he replied.

"Well perhaps we're too heavy. Let's just throw some things over-board!" cried Digby as he looked about the automobile for items to toss over.

"I say Digby I found a picnic basket and a tool box!" exclaimed Thomas.

"Oh, Hurrah! Toss it, Sir Thomas. I'll give you a hand!" he replied with a giggle as they both began to toss the items overboard, but the automobile did not move any faster.

"Digby, what about the spare tires? We have four of them," said Thomas.

"Sir Henry, what do you think?" asked Digby.

"Toss them, my boy!"

The Countess, seeing them throwing things overboard said, "Why those ingenious little monsters! I do believe they are trying to sabotage our motorcar with all those obstacles in the way!" She swerved to avoid the tossed items.

As Digby and Sir Thomas were throwing out things, the automobile did move faster but moved backward, putting them right next to the Countess's vehicle.

"Why, Sir Henry Humphrey, so very nice to see you again. Aráchni, now!" she cried as Aráchni hurled the rope over, lassoing Thomas and pulling him out from the automobile. As he was doing so, their automobile was sideswiped by another vehicle. Aráchni lost his balance with Thomas in his arms, and fell back into Sir Humphrey's motorcar, which was now going in the right direction.

The mysterious sideswiping vehicle was the 1900 style motor cab with none other than Ms. Koukouvágia in the driver's seat and Professor Gan Quan giving directions. "I say Ms. Koukouvágia, good to see you, but what took you so long to get here?" stated Sir Henry.

"Oh, you must forgive me Sir Henry, I got tied up. Literally!" replied Ms. Koukouvágia. Then indicating to the professor, she said, "Sir Henry, allow me to introduce you to Professor Gan Quan. His motorcar was demolished during the race."

Digby, interrupted, asking, "Is he your boyfriend?" He covering his mouth, giggling.

"Digby Scarborough, he is not my boyfriend! I got lost on the road and he knew the racing route. Henceforth I asked him if he would join me."

"Nie-how, nie-how," greeted the Professor.

Sir Henry Humphrey replied. "Indeed a pleasure, Professor Quan."

"Hello Ms. Koukouvágia, I'm so glad you are okay, and very nice to meet you, Professor," Thomas exclaimed, waving his hand.

"Nie-how, nie-how, Thomas!" replied Professor Quan, laughing.

Sir Thomas was intrigued by this response and turning to Digby, he asked, "what does Nie-how mean?"

Digby explained, "It means 'hello' in Chinese, Thomas." He then bit Aráchni in the arm.

"I think you are all mad, now hand over the boy!" cried the Countess as she swerved back and forth, madly trying to shake off Ms. Koukouvágia and the Professor. "Aráchni, grab the boy and get out of that automobile this very second!" she exclaimed.

"Right away Countess, as soon as I can get the pug face boy's teeth out of my arm!" the butler replied.

With Thomas kicking and screaming under his arms, Digby took hold of his other arm with his teeth and growled. One could say Aráchni had his hands full.

"Don't you dare touch a hair on that boy's head!" cried Ms. Koukouvágia as she sideswiped them once again.

Coming up on a steep turn, all three of them collided with each other. With the Countess' automobile closest to the cliff's edge, her vehicle began to tip over the side. "Not in this lifetime, darlings. If I go, you're coming with me!" she cried with malice. Then she pressed a button in her glove compartment and a mechanical clamp came out, attaching itself to Sir Henry's running board and Sir Henry Humphrey's automobile started to get pulled over the cliff with the Countess. The automobiles turned over each other and down they went over the cliff, but with only a brief thud.

Seeing this, Ms. Koukouvágia stepped on the brake in horror and turned back. She frantically got out of the motor cab with Professor Quan and ran over to the cliff to look over. "Oh my gracious they are still alive," she cried. "Look, Professor Quan, they are alive!"

"Yes I see them, Ms. Koukouvágia. They don't have much time. We have to act fast," stated the Professor.

Fortunately for Thomas and his friends, there was a massive old dead oak tree just below the cliff which they had all landed on. But their good luck was only temporary because the tree was beginning to crack under the weight. Climbing out from under her overturned vehicle, the Countess cried out, "Just great, I've lost my best cigarette lighter! Aráchni! Aráchni!" the Countess called out to her butler.

"Yes, Countess?" replied Aráchni. "I need a light!" she demanded, holding out a fresh cigarette and sitting on a branch.

"Forgive me Countess, but I'm a bit detained at the moment," he replied.

"Aráchni, you are useless!" exclaimed the Countess.

Aráchni was indeed detained, as he was pinned hanging upside down from Sir Henry's motorcar, still holding on to the rope to which he lassoed onto Sir Thomas. He swung back and forth in mid air on the end of the rope. Digby still held on to Aráchni's other arm by his teeth. Sir Henry was hanging from the steering wheel.

"I can hang here all day if need be!" Digby muffled with a growl.

"I say Digby, don't talk with your mouth full, it is quite rude you know!" exclaimed Sir Henry.

"Oh forgive me Sir Henry" and as Digby said that, he fell off Aráchni's arm.

"Ahhhh!" cried Digby as he was falling.

"I got you my boy!" cried Sir Henry as he caught him in mid air with one hand.

"Oh, my gracious Digby. Are you ok?" Ms. Koukouvágia asked, peering down from the ledge.

"Never felt better, Ms. Koukouvágia," replied Digby with a giggle.

The Professor yelled over the cliff to Thomas, "Thomas, see if you could swing the rope toward the rocks. If so, just grab on and climb up to us with the rope around your waist."

"I'll try, Professor," Thomas replied. Thomas then looked at Aráchni and asked, "Aráchni could you swing me a bit?"

"I shall try my best, Thomas!" replied Arachni, who swung the rope twice and Thomas was able to catch on to the rocks and he climbed up the cliff, the long rope around his waist.

Upon reaching the top, he untied the rope from around his waist and handed it over to the Professor and Ms. Koukouvágia, but the weight on the branch of the oak tree began to crack and then broke and Sir Henry's automobile began to slip through the branches.

Sir Henry hollered over to the Countess, "I say how can you be so calm, you dreadful woman?"

"Because I have a parachute, darling," replied the Countess.

"You only have one, dear Countess?" asked Aráchni.

"Oh, I'm afraid so, dear Aráchni. Ta-ta!" replied the Countess as she jumped from the tree branch, parachuting toward the ground.

"Digby, are you able to climb to the top of the automobile?" asked the Professor.

"Yes Professor, I can!" replied Digby.

"Ok I'm lowering the rope to you. Just tie this to the front axle of the motorcar and make three knots," explained the Professor.

"You got it, Professor!" replied Digby, as he attached the rope to the axle and tied three knots, following the Professor's instructions perfectly.

As Digby did this, Ms. Koukouvágia tied the other end of the rope to the front of motor cab, slowly pulling up Sir Humphrey's automobile.

As they were doing this, half of the tree the Countess' automobile was tied to gave way down the mountain, leaving Sir Henry's motor car dangling in midair.

Meanwhile, Countess Athena landed safely on the ground. Taking off her parachute, she applied a fresh coat of powder to her nose. In the process, she saw her cigarette lighter on the ground and happily picked it up. "Oh what luck, my lighter!" she exclaimed. She then took out a cigarette to light it, which caused her to look up. The dead oak tree, along with her automobile, came tumbling down upon her, smashing her flat. Countess Athena Tetradrachm was no more.

Still dangling from the cliff edge, Sir Henry and Digby were remaining calm. Professor Quan gave the signal to Ms. Koukouvágia to back up the motor cab, lifting Sir Humphrey's automobile to safety.

Digby cried "Oh hurrah!" He hugged Sir Henry with joy.

Leaving the automobile with Digby in his arms, Sir Henry was ecstatic to see the ground once again.

Turning to Ms. Koukouvágia, Sir Henry thanked her, "I can't thank you and the professor enough," he said gleefully.

Bowing his head, Aráchni apologized to Ms. Koukouvágia and thanked Professor Quan for rescuing him. Then he turned to Thomas and said, "Beware of Baron Von Tickle." With that said, he disappeared into the trees

Gathering themselves together, Sir Henry and Digby surveyed the damage to the Bumblebee steamer. "I say, he's pretty banged up, Sir Henry!" exclaimed Digby.

"Nonsense I say, Digby, he has some life in him yet. Pass me a hammer in the toolbox while I straighten out the fender!" exclaimed Sir Henry optimistically.

"Oh I'm afraid we can't do that, Sir Henry!" cried Digby.

"Why on earth not?" asked Sir Henry.

"Do you remember when we had to unload some things to move faster?" said Digby sheepishly.

"Oh yes, I remember!" replied Sir Henry.

"Well, the tool box was one of them," Digby blurted out.

"Oh bow fumble, it looks like all is lost now!" cried Sir Humphrey.

"Wait a minute Sir Henry all is not lost as of yet!" cried Ms. Koukouvágia as she checked the motor cab for a hammer. "Peanut butter and sauerkraut, I found one!" she cried.

"And what did you find, Ms. Koukouvágia?" asked Sir Henry hopefully.

"I just found a blue tool box with a hammer in it!"

"I say, good show. Don't diddle dawdle now, bring it over!" he cried.

Rolling up their sleeves, Sir Henry and Digby worked feverishly to repair the automobile. As Digby worked on the motor, Sir Henry straightened out the fenders with the hammer. Racing past them were the Three Pound Sisters, but when they saw Sir Henry was in trouble, they backed up and offered their assistance.

"I say, Sir Henry Humphrey, are we okay?" asked Tessa.

"We are quite alright now, dear Tessa," replied Sir Henry.

"Oh dear me, do we need any Boo-boo Band-Aids?" asked Vanessa.

"We're quite good, thank you, Vanessa," Digby replied with a giggle.

"Well then you must be famished, here take this basket of green apples. I insist!" stated Odessa and she passed a basket over to Digby, who gave the apples to Sir Thomas.

"Bow Bumble Odessa, thank you they are just scrumptious!" said Sir Thomas, taking a bite of one. With that said and done, the three Pound sisters drove off.

"I got it running again Sir Henry," cried Digby, closing the hood to the engine.

"Splendid, Digby," Sir Henry replied.

Then, turning to Thomas, he called out to him and said, "Thomas get in my boy, we are off!" Then he shouted out to Ms. Koukouvágia, "Just follow us!"

With a loud backfire, they were off with Ms. Koukouvágia and the professor trailing behind them.

The announcer called "Ladies and gentlemen, it looks like we have only two automobiles left in the race. And they're headed for the finish line! We have Sir Henry Humphrey's Bumble Bee Steamer and The Triple Thunder driven by The Three Pound sisters. Wait a minute folks, you are not going to believe this, but catching up at a fast pace is The Skeleton family in their eight-wheeled, no wait a minute they only have four wheels now, it seems their automobile has been cut in half! Ladies and gentleman, it's half of their automobile! And our winner is the Skeleton family by a nose. In second place is The Triple Thunder followed by the Bumble Bee Steamer in third.

Back at Tattletale Manor, Lady Tatiana awaited nervously for her little Thom Thom at the foot of the vestibule steps.

Hearing the sound of Sir Henry Humphrey's automobile driving up the gravel roadway, all the servants sprang to attention and run down the steps to greet and to assist them.

"Hello, mummy!" cried Sir Thomas, as he ran up the steps to give his mother a kiss and hug before sitting in her lap. "You'll never guess what happened to us in Brighton!" he exclaimed.

"Did you have an adventurous good time, my love?" asked his mother.

"Oh indeed I did, mummy!" he replied.

Still hugging him, she said, "Well then you must tell me all about it over dinner tonight my love."

Running up the steps with panic on his face was Sir Henry Humphrey. "Dear Lady Tattletale I can explain everything!" exclaimed Sir Henry flushed.

"No need dear Henry I read all about your adventure in graphic details in our newspaper," replied Lady Tatiana calmly.

"Oh indeed!" he replied, wiping his brow.

Then with a chuckle, she added, "Besides a little adventure and mayhem is good for the bones."

CHAPTER 7
A Visit from Aunt Fanny

On this particular day, Tattletale Manor was abuzz with the excitement for the arrival of Lady Tatiana Tattletale's youngest sister, Fanny Cruikshank. A loud backfire down the gravel roadway drew the attention of all the servants, who ran to the window to see what was amidst. Lady Tattletale wheeled herself to the window with great anticipation of it being Fanny. A large blue touring automobile with five larges boxes on the hood roared up the driveway.

With an abrupt stop in front of the manor, a woman dressed in a orange wool coat trimmed with a checkerboard design on her collar and cuffs got out of the automobile and yelled "Holy raspberries in applesauce! Dear sister, you have the roughest roadways I have ever driven on. Well I'll be! That could very well be a song!" Fanny then pulled a banjo out of her luggage and began strumming as she walked up the vestibule steps, humming along the way. Mary the maid ran off giggling after taking off Fanny's coat along the way. Chris the butler and Mass the caretaker came down to help Fanny with her luggage and the mysterious boxes.

"Luggage to the guest room!" Chris exclaimed. "Mysterious boxes to the drawing room!"

Fanny threw open the doors as she entered the drawing room. She dropped her banjo and screamed "Raspberries! How's my big sis doing?" She then looked around the room. "And where in heaven's name is my little Coconut?"

Peering curiously from the side of a wooden column in the drawing room, Sir Thomas wondered who this lady could possibly be. She had dark, smartly bobbed brown hair, a long strand of pearls, and was wearing an orange dress cut above the knee with a checkerboard sash tied in a bow to the side of her dress.

Lady Tattletale threw her arms around Fanny with a big hug and kiss before wheeling over to her son and gently seating him on her lap. "This is my little sister, and your Aunt Fanny," she explained. "She hasn't seen you since you were two years old. Aunt Fanny is so excited to see you, my little Thom Thom."

Sir Thomas, looking at the boxes curiously, replied "Bow bumble! What could this possibly be?"

"Oh Sis, you're looking just smashing! How are things working out at Tattletale publishing? I'm sure you give them a run for their money, huh?" Fanny asked enthusiastically.

"Oh Fanny, as always the life of the party, and so creative. I'm so proud of my little sister's music achievements!" Lady Tattletale exclaimed.

"Ah, raspberries! You're the smarts in the family, running Tattletale publishing!" Fanny replied. "Oh, and just look at our little Coconut!" She smiled at Thomas. "You've gotten so big, Thomas! So tell me, how old are you now?"

"I'm six and a half years old," Sir Thomas replied.

Fanny beamed down at him. "Look! I've brought you something from Londinium. It's an equestrian counting book that goes up to 10."

"Thank you, Aunt Fanny, for the lovely book!"

Aunt Fanny leaned in to get a kiss from her favorite nephew, but Sir Thomas cringed, folded his arms, and looked up at his mother.

Fanny started to sing to Thomas to ease his nerves. What Sir Thomas didn't know was that his Aunt Fanny was a famous night club singer that traveled with a clockwork jack-in-the-box jazz band. Fanny walked around the drawing room and started to wind up the various mysterious boxes that the maid, butler, and caretaker brought in earlier. In tune with her delightful singing, each of the boxes opened to display a member of her jazz band. Each mechanical clockwork player wore a black tie with white spats on their shoes, and they all played a different instrument.

The first one was a clarinet player who did not move out of his box, but bopped and swayed as he played.

The second was a trombone player, who marched around the room to the rhythm.

The third box, which had been placed by an upright piano in the drawing room, included a piano player who was humming and swaying to Aunt Fanny's voice.

The fourth box held a drummer, who played with a frenetic beat as he bopped his head back and forth.

Finally, the fifth player came out of his box, but he had nothing in his hands!

"Oh, raspberries!" cried Fanny, realizing he should have been holding the banjo she was playing on the way in. She ran over to where she had dropped the banjo and gently placed it in his hands so he could begin to play. Fanny continued to sing:

I say! No kiss from my favorite nephew!
Bo whoo.
Have I got to pinch you?
If I don't get a kiss from you.
I guess this will have to do.
Be do be do be doo!
With a pinch on the cheek
Or perhaps on your little chin-chin.
Be do be do!
Guess this will have to do
Or maybe a pinch on your knee?
Be do be do be doo!
Just love you my little nephew!
Be do be do be doo!

"Bow bumble!" cried Sir Thomas, as he clapped his hands to the beat. "You're egg salad salmon on toast, you are!"

"Egg salad salmon on toast you say?" questioned Fanny. "Well, I've never been compared to a summer sandwich before, but I shall indeed take it as a compliment from my little Coconut!"

"Oh yes indeed!" replied Sir Thomas. "Have you ever tasted one? It's just smashingly jolly good, like you!" With that said, Sir Thomas gave his Aunt Fanny a soft kiss on the cheek.

"Oh thank you, my little Coconut!" replied Aunt Fanny. "Raspberries, that's it! You must come to Paris with me. No, no, Monte Carlo instead, darling! I leave in two days. You can come see me perform!"

"If mummy allows," Sir Thomas said. He looked at his mother with plea in his eyes. Aunt Fanny also looked at her sister, with a similar plea in her eyes, grinning.

"I'll leave it up to Thomas," Lady Tattletale said, looking at her sister. "I think it's a smashing idea, Thom Thom!"

"Oh mummy, I would love to go with Aunt Fanny to see her performance!"

"Well, then I shall make arrangements for you to travel with her, my love!"

"Bow bumble, mummy. Thank you!" Sir Thomas jumped back into her lap and gave her the biggest kiss he could muster.

Two days later, as Sir Thomas Tattletale prepared to leave for France, his mother wanted to show him something. Sir Thomas sat in his mother's lap as Mary the maid began to wheel them down a long, black and white marble checkerboard hallway. Chris the butler opened the mahogany doors for them as they entered the library. The Tattletale library could only be described as a mecca of exquisite grandeur, consisting of three floors of books supported by mahogany Etruscan columns under a neoclassic style vaulted ceiling. The first level of books were on fine art, sculptures, and prints. The second level was botany, medicine, and law. The third floor was dedicated to foreign language, travel, and maps.

"I have just the thing for you, Thom Thom. It's the perfect travel companion." Chris the butler silently walked behind them as Mary wheeled Lady Tatiana Tattletale toward a hand-operated brass elevator in middle of the library. "That will be all for now, Mary. Thank you, I'll take it from here." Mary nodded and headed back to the drawing room.

"Going up, sideways, or down, Lady Tattletale?" Chris asked.

"Up, Chris, to the third floor please," she replied.

Chris closed the brass gate and they went up in a magnificent brass elevator to the third floor of the library. Chris opened the brass gates and Lady Tattletale wheeled herself out of the elevator toward a dusty bookshelf. She pulled out a small book.

"I say mummy, what kind of book is this?" asked Sir Thomas Tattletale.

"This is a very special book," she replied nostalgically.

"When I was a little girl, I used the same book when I traveled abroad. It's always good to know how to say "thank you" and "you're welcome" in a different language. It's a book that teaches French, German, Italian, and ten other languages you may need."

"Thank you, Mummy. I shall put it in my duster near my heart on my journey to France!" Sir Thomas Tattletale gave his mother a kiss and a hug and left the library, headed for Aunt Fanny's blue touring motorcar.

With a tear in her eye, Lady Tattletale and the entire staff waved goodbye. With a loud backfire, the automobile was off.

Sir Thomas couldn't stop laughing as Aunt Fanny raced down the street so they could board the ship on time. He thought she was a great driver because she never once stopped for a red light. Aunt Fanny put the car in park and the ship's fork lift stored the motorcar and the five boxes in the hull. Watching from the ship's deck, Sir Thomas noticed three large black limousines approach from the distance. They stopped in front of the ship and four men got out of the limousines, escorting a lady dressed in all black wearing a tricorn hat. She had a high collar and wore long skirt. In her arms was a little girl with long curly hair, wearing a top hat with a flower in it.

One of the men gave the little girl a kiss on the cheek and gently caressed her hair and said "Glück mein Engel (Good luck my angel)".

"Danke, dass du mein freund (Thank you, my friend)," said the lady in the tricorn hat. She then turned to the luggage and sneezed, stomping her foot three times. The luggage sprouted feet and began to walk up the plank. The lady in the tricorn hat then proceeded up the ship's plank with the little girl in her arms to their cabin.

"Thomas! Oh Thomas! Come my little darling, it's raining. my love, come inside!" cried Aunt Fanny.

"Yes, Aunt Fanny," Thomas replied.

Later that evening as Sir Thomas walked along the ship's deck dressed in his favorite duster and top hat, he noticed the little girl from earlier on the floor of the deck playing with something. She was dressed in a red hunting jacket, fur muff, and a purple dress with blue polka dots. She was talking to little carved animals that she had pulled out of an elaborate box. Within the box were compartments where each of the carved animals were held. From what Sir Thomas could see, there was a zebra and a hippopotamus on the deck floor. The little girl had long, black curly hair with soft café au lait skin, and green eyes.

As Sir Thomas approached her, he greeted her with a soft smile. "I say, this is rather damp weather to be playing out here with your toys. Why don't you come inside with me?" he asked cheerfully. "I've brought my favorite toy from Surrey: a wheeled purple jockey," he added.

"Well I'm quite alright just where I am," stated the little girl. And they are not toys, but my friends and protectors from my home," she added.

"And where would that be?" asked Sir Thomas.

"Zimbawawe," she replied

"Bow bumble! You must forgive me! I have carvings back home such as this. Though, what do you mean your friends and protectors?" asked Thomas, as he curiously looked at the carved animals on the ship's deck.

"I'm a orphan, and these animals are my only friends when I travel. If I am ever in trouble or danger, they come to life to help me."

"Oh, I see! I had no idea they were enchanted!" replied Sir Thomas Tattletale.

"I was just telling them not to be frightened by the swaying of the ship."

Looking down at the carved animals, Sir Thomas Tattletale properly introduced himself by tipping his hat, and with a great big smile on his face. "Indeed a pleasure to meet you, Mr. Zebra and Mr. Hippopotamus."

Picking up the zebra in one hand and the hippopotamus in the other, the little girl beamed. "The zebra's name is Ingaway and the hippopotamus' name is Onawa." The little girl asked Ingaway if he liked Sir Thomas Tattletale, putting the zebra to her ear first. Then she asked Onawa before putting both of them back into the box. "They like you Thomas," she replied.

"Oh I'm so glad they do!" cried Sir Thomas.

"Young Lady!" exclaimed Her Governess, with a thick German accent. "Come in this very instant before you catch a death of cold!"

"But I'm not cold Ms.Gazoontiet!" protested the girl, as she walked toward the lady.

Sir Thomas cried out after her, "I say, you did not tell me your name!"

The little girl then pulled away from her governess and ran back to Sir Thomas Tattletale. "My name is Zara, Zara Zuckerman." She gave him a little kiss on the cheek before scurrying back.

"Indeed a pleasure, Zara. Good night!" he said before running back to his cabin.

Bursting in through the door, Thomas yelled, "I have a new friend!"

"Now who would that be, my little Coconut?" asked Aunt Fanny.

"Her name is Zara!"

"Zara, who?" asked his aunt.

"Zara Zuckerman, the little girl that boarded the ship earlier today, Aunt Fanny."

"Holy raspberries, Zara Zuckerman!" It was the same little girl Fanny read about in the newspapers. "I do hope you were nice to her."

"Of course, Aunt Fanny, why wouldn't I be?"

"Well, you see, Zara's an orphan."

"Yes, Aunt Fanny, she told me. Perhaps we can invite her over for tea at Tattletale manor?" Sir Thomas asked.

"Oh that would be very nice, Thomas," Aunt Fanny said.

Zara Zuckerman's father was Peter Penny Zuckerman of Zuckerman Moving Picture Theaters in Germany. Her mother was Princess Ingaway Notuwa of Zimbabwe, who owned an animal refuge on the premises. Her parents perished in a tragic air zeppelin accident in Zurich in 1920. Zara was taken in by her uncle, a man by the name of Alfred Pitter Zuckerman of Londinium. He was unfortunately mauled by some unidentified animal, and she was orphaned once again. Zara was then shipped off to her aunt, Gloria Patter Zuckerman, in Paris.

"Thom Thom, oh my little Coconut, look!" Picking up Sir Thomas in her arms and bringing him to the deck of the ship, Aunt Fanny pointed toward land. "That's the Eiffel Tower in the distance. We are approaching Paris, France!"

As Aunt Fanny and Sir Thomas Tattletale exited the ship down a long plank, everyone stared at them with amazement. Aunt Fanny was quite a sight dressed in a wool black and white checkerboard coat, with black monkey fur trim on the collar and cuffs, with a large red gerbera in her black hat. As they made their way to their motorcar, about 50 people surrounded them. One man offered her a large bouquet of red roses. Fanny put the roses in the back seat of her the motorcar. She thanked the young man. "Oh, merci, merci, darling!"

There were excited yells from the group, Thomas noticed that the people addressed Aunt Fanny, but by a different name he hadn't heard before.

"Bonjour, Fanny Flapper!"

"Welcome back, Fanny Flapper!"

"Could I have an autograph, Fanny Flapper?"

"Fanny Flapper's jack-in-the-box jazz band, welcome back!"

A lady in a red turban with six Russian wolfhounds asked, "Darling are you coming for lunch today? We haven't seen you in ages, darling. How long are you staying?

"Oh darling, just for tonight and tomorrow. Then we're off to Monte Carlo for a show. After that, back to Paris to catch up."

"Dearest Fanny Flapper, there is a party being thrown in your honor tonight at The Cat Fish Bowl Night Club. I do hope you'll be able to make it!" Hollered a tall man in a straw boater and white spats.

"Well pickle me in bathtub gin! Why if it isn't Mr. Nicolas Almondbrittle. So very nice to see you again!" She held out her hand so Mr. Almondbrittle could kiss it, then putting her hands to her hips. "How in the world did you know I was going to be in Paris today, Nicolas?"

"Not everybody has a sister that operates the largest newspaper in Europe, you know," replied Mr. Almondbrittle. Mr. Nicolas Almondbrittle, ESQ, of San Francisco is an avid art collector and "bon vivant," currently on holiday.

Fanny smiled. "I shall indeed attend!"

"I'll send my automobile to pick you up at nine!"

Sir Thomas Tattletale gazed out the window of the lights of Paris in Mr. Almondbrittle's yellow and purple motorcar en route to the club. Noticing the brilliant neon lights above an art nouveau glass awning, his first words were "Bow bumble!" He had never seen anything like this before.

They arrived at the steps of The Cat Fish Bowl Night Club. Aunt Fanny was wearing a long strand of pearls and her trademark checkerboard pattern dress. She was sporting a long white glove on one arm and on the other, a long black glove.

Crowds awaited their turn to get into the night club.
Near the entrance, horses were parked next to a fleet of limousines from around the world.

Once the mansion and city home of Baroness Lillian Gauduchon du perfume de France, The Cat Fish Bowl Night Club was built in 1880 in the age of beauty La Belle Epoch. When Lillian passed away, her sister Baroness Gertrude Gauduchon du Chocolate de France took over and transformed it into a night club, but she loved the exterior and kept it intact. However, the interior was transformed into the style and fashion of this period. Baroness Gertrude updated only parts of the rooms with art deco interiors.

Passing through the crowds of people, Aunt Fanny and Sir Thomas Tattletale managed to get into the club. They entered the pink marble lobby of la belle epoch interiors and art deco furnishings into a sea of white-tie and tail gentleman and feather couture ladies. There was also a group of French fox hunters in full dress, with one still on his horse. A man and a woman trapeze artist duo dressed in grapes flew from the ceiling. The French fox huntsman with a horse rode around them as they made flips in mid air, tried to catch the falling grapes. The other fox hunters watched and cheered him on.

As they walked down the hallway past the French fox hunters on a red carpet with gold meander pattern trim, they came upon exquisite beveled glass art nouveau doors. Sitting in front of the doors were identical twins dressed in striped black and white jackets, with black tie and spats. They were looking at each other, playing banjos, and singing.

As Aunt Fanny and Sir Thomas Tattletale approached, they turned to them and sang, "Welcome to the Cat Fish Bowl, welcome to the Cat Fish Bowl. BOO BOO DE DO!" They opened up the exquisite beveled glass doors leading into a magnificent art nouveau ballroom with an array of people wearing the latest fashions, and laughing, smoking, drinking, and dancing to the beat of rickety jazz music. There was a beautiful brass art deco bar at the end of the ballroom which had every drink in the world stocked in it. They walked over to it.

"Are you thirsty, my love?" asked Aunt Fanny.

"Oh Indeed, Aunt Fanny, I'm parched!"

Aunt Fanny ordered a vodka martini on the rocks. "Oops, pardon moi! I meant an apple juice!" Sir Thomas Tattletale ordered a tall glass of lemonade.

As they were leaving the bar, Sir Thomas tugged at Aunt Fanny's dress. "Aunt Fanny, I do believe there's something wrong with my lemonade! I think the lemons have gone bad in this."

"Oh my darling little Coconut. There, there, now let dear aunty have a sip. Holy raspberries in cranberry juice! Bartender, oh bartender, darling? Could we have another lemonade, please, but this time no embalming fluid in it, love." The bartender replaced the drink, to which Aunt Fanny replied "Merci, mon dour, merci!"

Mr. Almondbrittle, sitting with a group of friends at a table nearby, was waving to Aunt Fanny like a madman. "Fanny, oh Fanny! I'm over here! You must meet Joslyn. She is a great dancer from Louisville."

Dressed in a short red dress, Joslyn Jazz Brewster's hair bobbed with a red head band, and a long strand of pearls was holding a champagne bottle. She extended her other hand to Fanny. "Oh Fanny, I've heard so much about you, Sugar, and that marvelous mechanical jack in the box jazz band of yours," she rasped, with a southern accent.

"Thank you, Joslyn, I'm looking forward to seeing you dance!"

"Fanny, Sugar! All my friends call me Jazz Baby!" She did a delightful shimmy while laughing. "And who is this handsome escort you have with you, Sugar?"

"Everyone, now everyone, this is my little nephew, Thomas. I have him for two weeks, so I'm showing him around Paris and he's attending my performance in Monte Carlo!"

"Oh Sugar, now you have another aunty," Jazz Baby said.

"Pleased to meet you, Ms. Jazz Baby." Sir Thomas tipped his hat.

"Oh, pecan pie! You're gonna have to do better than that, Sugar! Your Aunty Jazz Baby gets a kiss and a big hug!"Mr. Almondbrittle gestured toward another woman. "This is Dr. Dorita Desmond, a brilliant doctor from Brazil. One of her clients is the Duchess of Denmark."

The doctor's style consisted of finger waves pushed back in a bun. She sported a monocle, smoking a cigarette, and dressed in a double breasted grey pinstriped suit with a yellow gerbera in her lapel. "Indeed a pleasure, Fanny!" she said, as she grabbed both of Aunt Fanny's hands and gave her a kiss on both cheeks.

"It is also a pleasure, Dr. Desmond" replied Fanny.

"Oh Fanny, come now. It's Dora to you from now on!" She looked over to Sir Thomas. "Pleased to meet you, Sir Thomas!"

"It's very nice to meet you too, Dr. Desmond."

"Oh my, you are a charmer. Fanny, you simply must keep this one!"

Mr. Almondbrittle continued his introduction. "And this is Bartholomew Banks."

Bartholomew Banks circled the table on roller skates in a frenzy, wearing a bowler hat and chesterfield coat, laughing. He stopped only to greet Fanny and Thomas Tattletale. "How do you do, Fanny!" He tipped his bowler hat and kissed her hand. "It is indeed an honor, Sir Thomas." He tipped his hat once again, and shook Sir Thomas' hand.

"I say, Mr. Banks, why do you have on roller skates?" asked Sir Thomas Tattletale.

The man smiled. "I can make friends more quickly and in less time that way, and I do love it so very much, you see! You must come to Boston, Massachusetts, sometime. Everybody roller skates there!"

Suddenly, a blonde haired woman in dark makeup yelled from across the room, "Taxi, oh taxi!" After a moment, she yelled again, "Taxi, darling, TAXI!"

Aunt Fanny then realized the commotion was directed toward her. As the blond haired lady got up from her table surrounded by men in white ties and tails, she walked toward Fanny's table with her hand on her hip. She was dressed in a purple gown with long white gloves and peacock feathers coming out of her headdress, smoking a cigarette. As the lady got closer, Aunt Fanny knew who it was, Lulu Beresford Star of Stage and Moving Pictures. She and Fanny were once in a jazz band together.

Turning to Thomas sitting beside her, Fanny said softly, "Oh my little Coconut, always remember that in a succulent bunch of grapes, there will always be a bitter one. She looked up at Lulu, but spoke to

Thomas. "Darling, why don't you take a look around at the magnificent architecture while I talk to my dear, dear friend Lulu."

"Sure, Aunt Fanny. There's plenty to look at here," Sir Thomas answered before running down the hallway to another room.

As Lulu Beresford approached Fanny, the whole room went silent. "Well, well, well," cried Lulu. "If it isn't Checkerboard Fanny Flapper!" She smiled spitefully. "Taxi, oh taxi, darling! Oops, you must forgive me. I thought you were a taxi with that dreadful checkerboard outfit you have on." Lulu laughed.

"Well, well, if it isn't my very best friend in the whole wide world, Lulu B. Oh darling, I wish I were a taxi. It would give me great pleasure to run you down in that dress that's two sizes too small on you."

Lulu then turned her back and held out her hand to show off her new art deco diamond ring. "Oh darlings, look what I just bought at Bouillon's jewelry store today." She flashed her ring to the guests at Aunt Fanny's table.

Aunt Fanny calmly pulled out a cigarette from its case and attached it to a long cigarette holder, as the men sitting at Lulu Beresford's table rushed over to light it. As Fanny took the first puff of her cigarette and twirled her long strand of pearls, she replied "Darling what's a jewelry store?" Everyone at the party roared with laughter.

"Well I never!" Furious with Fanny's witty comeback, Lulu Beresford picked up a cake and flung it toward her. Aunt Fanny ducked, and it missed her. It instead hit a wealthy patron directly in the face. The patron retaliated with a cherry pie from the same dessert trolley. That wealthy patron, also missing, hit a famous patron. A mad dessert fiasco ensued.

"Holy raspberries in applesauce!" cried Fanny.

Meanwhile, in another room of The Cat Fish Night Club called the Empire Room Gallery, the music was much softer. Sir Thomas saw a man painting a mural on the wall with his feet while drinking Scotch and smoking a cigarette. Sir Thomas Tattletale asked the man why he was using his feet, since there was nothing wrong with his hands, nor arms. The man explained that he was just taking a break.

A Japanese man dressed in a red dinner jacket holding a martini entered the room. "Just magnificent! I've never seen anything like this work of art before. I must have one!"

"Indeed, he is a wonderful artist!" replied Thomas, who turned around to face the Japanese man.

The Japanese man replied: "Oh, no! No, I'm not talking about him. I'm talking about you!" he placed his martini glass on Sir Thomas's top hat. "My god, I have never seen such a fantastic modern table top!"

"Table top?" questioned Sir Thomas.

"You're just brilliant! I must have one!"

Looking up at the martini on top of his hat, Sir Thomas replied, "Sir, I am not a table top, but a little boy."

"I think you are just a mechanical marvel of ingenuity. You're obviously the work of Von Tickle manufacturing!" cried the Japanese man in the red dinner jacket. "My wife simply must see this! Helena, Helena! Come look at this mechanical table top!"

An elegant Egyptian woman walked over, dressed in a white evening dress. "Oh my darling, he's just charming, and he talks! Simply amazing, we must have one. Where do we wind him up?"

"I don't know, but let's find out."

"But Sir, Madame, I am a little boy with my Aunt on holiday!" cried Sir Thomas Tattletale.

A crowd started to gather around him, ogling at him in with amazement.

"Wow, I want one, too!" said a man in the crowd of people.

A large woman with diamonds exclaimed "I saw him first!"

The Japanese man in the red dinner jacket in spats picked up Sir Thomas Tattletale in his arms and held firmly.

"I say, let me go, let me go! I'm a little boy!" Sir Thomas Tattletale yelled, kicking the Japanese man in the leg. Sir Thomas was able to break away from him and his wife, and ran down the hallway back toward Aunt Fanny.

The guests of the night club were in hot pursuit of him. He hid behind a bronze sculpture and watched the frenzy of
madcap people passing him by. As he approached the twins, they opened the glass doors into the ballroom once again. It was covered in cake and blueberry pie.

Sir Thomas cried out, "Bow bumble!"

"Thom Thom, where are you darling?" cried Aunt Fanny, partly covered in pie.

"I'm right here, Aunt Fanny!"

"My darling, I think it's time for us to go. The French police were called in and raided the club!"

Jazz Baby yelled above the noise, "Come with us! We know where there's a back way out!"

Aunt Fanny picked up Sir Thomas in her arms and followed Jazz Baby, Bartholomew Banks, and Dr. Dora Desmond through a secret passageway out of the night club to Mr. Almondbrittle's motorcar awaiting them in the ally.

The next morning, Aunt Fanny and Sir Thomas entered the Gare de Opéra Bastille train station en route to Monte Carlo. There was complete havoc at the terminal. Animals ran loose in the station. A giraffe was eating the leaves off a palm tree, a baby elephant was taking a bath in the fountain, a zebra ran after a conductor, two monkeys were tossing apples at a passerby from a fruit stand, and a hippopotamus was eating croissants from the bakery.

"Thom Thom, how very French! Exotic animals loose in a Paris train station. Only our second day in Paris, what a treat!"

"Aunt Fanny, these animals are indigenous to Africa, not Paris. Something is amidst!" cried Sir Thomas Tattletale. He thought for a moment. "Bow bumble! Aunt Fanny, Aunt FANNY! Zara's in trouble! We must go and help her!"

Just then, with all the panic, a rush of people crashed into them, separating Aunt Fanny from Sir Thomas Tattletale.

"Thom Thom! Oh, Thom Thom, where are you!" cried Aunt Fanny as she started to tear up. She then called over two police officers in the midst of the havoc. "Officer, oh officer, I've lost my nephew. He's wearing a silk top hat and large white collared shirt. Can you please help me?"

"Say, by any chance would your name be Fanny Flapper?" the officer asked.

"Why yes, that is my name," Fanny replied.

"And would you also be a night club singer?" The officer asked.

"Why yes, I am," Aunt Fanny replied, wiping tears from her eyes with a smile.

I hereby place you under arrest for inciting a riot at The Cat Fish Bowl night club the other night. You're also being charged with assault with a coconut cream chocolate cake!"

"Raspberries! What ever for? I've done nothing wrong!" she cried. "I know who did this. That dreadful woman Lulu Beresford did this!"

"Who in the world is Lulu Beresford," cried the officers, laughing. "A Baron F Von Chatouiller has bared witness to your actions and is the one that is pressing charges for the assault," exclaimed the officer. With that said, they handcuffed Aunt Fanny, taking her away to the police station.

She called out to Thomas, "Thom Thom where are you? I'll find you, my love, don't worry!"

"Aunt Fanny? Aunt Fanny! I can't see you anywhere!" cried Sir Thomas Tattletale.

Still searching, he came upon a little boy sitting on a large steamer trunk and crying. Dressed in a tweed knickerbocker suit in navy blue and red striped high socks, sporting a derby. There was a chain with a key on it around his neck. He had also been separated from his parents due to the frenzied crowd.

"Now, now, no need to get upset, old chap. If you were upside down, you would look like you are laughing!" Sir Thomas said, trying to lighten the boy's mood. "I say, don't cry, I'm lost too." Sir Thomas put his arm around the boy. "My name's Thomas, Sir Thomas Tattletale. Pleased to meet you!"

As the little boy wiped his still-teary eyes, he replied "My name is Chronas Clockwork. I think that's very funny." His crying began to stop as he wiped his eyes.

"What's funny?" asked Sir Thomas.

"If I were upside down!" replied Chronas Clockwork. "I was separated from my father and sister."

"Where are you from?" asked Sir Thomas.

"Chicago".

"I say, that's dreadfully far."

"My father makes clocks and repairs them, too. He was invited to repair magic clocks in France."

"What is that key for?"

"It's for my heart," Chronas replied.

"For your heart?" Sir Thomas asked curiously.

"Yes, I have a French clock for a heart. The key around my neck reminds me to wind it every 12 hours."

"I say, that's quite amazing! How did you get it in there? Bow bumble, I can even hear it ticking!" Sir Thomas looked at the boy's chest, curiously.

"Well, you see, I was supposed to deliver cherry cupcakes to my father and sister for dessert, but I ate one on the way and fell asleep. When I woke up, the clock was there!"

"Bow bumble!" cried Sir Thomas.

You're probably wondering why a French train station would have "opera" in its name. Before it was a train station, it was a grand opera house built in 1860. Ornately decorated in Venetian mosaics, friezes, and marble columns. The ceiling was adorned with cherubs, among other embellishments. Although slated for demolition, the architects and designers did not have the heart to tear it down so they combined it with the modern interiors by complimenting it with two moving picture houses and a modern train station.

"I say! That is quite an extraordinary story, Chronas," exclaimed Sir Thomas. "Come now, no need to pout. I shall help you locate your father and sister. If not in Paris, my aunt Fanny knows many people in Chicago as well. But at this moment I am in need of your help and I cannot do it by myself. A friend is in trouble. Her name is Zara. Zara Zuckerman."

Chronas Clockwork stopped pouting, got off his steamer trunk, picked up his leather doctor travel bag, and said with a soft smile while shaking Thomas' hand "You got it Thomas!"

Off they went, running through the Paris train station together holding hands so they would not get separated in the crowds of scurrying people. Thomas happened to see Onawa the hippopotamus eating croissants in a boulangerie (bakery) in the station a cross the way.

"Chronas! Grab my hand quickly.I see Onawa."

"Who is Onawa?" Chronas asked as they were running through the train station.

Thomas then explains Onawa to him. "Onawa is one of Zara's friends. Perhaps she can led us to her! We must hurry Chronas, there's no time to lose before she changes back into a wooden sculpture!"

"Changes back into a wooden sculpture?" asked Chronas.

Sir Thomas explained the story of the enchanted animals to Chronas en route to Onawa.

"Really Thomas? By Golly!" Glad you told me of this, because I found a wooden toy giraffe over by the palm trees earlier. Could this be one of her friends?" Chronas then pulled out a hand carved wooden giraffe from his pocket, showing Thomas.

"Bow Bumble, Chronas. That is one of her friends! Just put him back in your pocket, we are running out of time. Onawa! Onawa!" cried Sir Thomas Tattletale, as they grew closer amongst crowds of frantic people in the station.

Onawa recognized Thomas almost immediately. Onawa stopped eating the warm croissants and ran right over to Thomas, licking his face. Although Zara's animals do not speak, they use sign language to communicate.

"Onawa, where is Zara? I know she must be in trouble."

As Thomas talked to Onawa, Chronas looked around the vacant boulangerie for clues. He notice a turned over table and two shattered tea cups on the floor. Near the tea cups, a heavyset woman dressed in black laid in a deep sleep. Chronas called over to Thomas, "Thomas, Thomas come quickly. I found a lady on the floor!"

"I'm coming Chronas. Onawa come with me?" asked Sir Thomas. Thomas introduced Onawa the hippopotamus to Chronas. "Onawa, this is my friend Chronas from Chicago. He's here to help us."

"Pleased to meet you, Onawa," said Chronas.

Onawa replied by licking his face as Chronas gigged. As Sir Thomas approached the sleeping lady, he recognized her. "Bow Bumble, Chronas!" he cried. "This is Zara's Governess Ms.Gazoontiet. Let's see if we can wake her. Could you pass me that glass of water?"

With a cold glass of water, they tried to revive her with splashes of water on her face with his fingers tips, but to no avail. Ms. Gazoontiet was under a deep spell.

"By Golly, what do we do now, Thomas?"

Looking around the brasserie, Chronas found an ornate wooden box. "Thomas I found a funny looking box."

"I say, it's the box Zara stores her animals in!" exclaimed Thomas. Chronas, we're going to bring that box with us."

With that said, Chronas took all the wooden animals out of his pockets and placed them in the compartments of the wooden box before handing the box over to Thomas. Thomas then found a perfume atomizer with a squeeze spray near Ms.Gazoontiet attached to a note.

"I say, what this?" He read the note aloud. "Sneeze if you please furniture remover." He paused. "Sneeze if you please?" Thomas looked at Chronas, baffled. Shrugging his shoulders, he put the bottle in his pocket. Onawa began to turn around in circles, then nudged Thomas and Chronas to follow her. Thomas and Chronas ran alongside her down a Venetian-tiled corridor in the station.

"Look, Thomas! A funny Zebra is running alongside us."

"I say. That's Ingaway, the other friend of Zara! Hello Ingaway, are you here to help us?"

Ingaway nodded while running beside them down the corridor. Just then, Thomas noticed something was wrong with Onawa. She started to slow down and was changing back into a wooden sculpture!

"No, no!" cried Chronas. Just put her in the wooden box, Thomas."

Ingaway then stopped, kneeled down on one leg, as Thomas and Chronas climbed on. Off they rode down the corridor, passing by the frantic people running about. Thomas and Chronas no longer had to look in between peoples' legs to see what was going on. They had a much better view riding atop Ingaway. Through a sea of black silk top hats and grey fedoras, Sir Thomas saw something through his squinting eyes. There were a flock of exotic birds pecking at a limping man carrying a large steamer trunk on his back. Accompany him was a lady in a large pheasant plume hat that was trying to shoo them away.

"Bo Bumble, Chronas. I bet Zara's in that trunk! Faster Ingaway, faster. We're going to lose them!" Thomas cried.

They were headed for a side street where their automobile waited. "Click und Snap, can't you do something about these dreadful birds?" The Baroness exclaimed, shooing the birds with an umbrella.

"I am trying my very best, Baroness, but they will not go away." He waved his hands around the birds.

"Ahhh!" cried the Baroness! Now there's a little bird in my hat! Get away you dreadful little beast," she cried.

It was a Pygmy Kingfisher pecking and pulling the pheasant plumes from her hat. Then a Red Bishop swooped down, pulling every plume in sight out of her hat.

"AHHHHH! My beautiful hat! You horrid birds! Click und Snap, do hurry. Let's just get to the automobile and be done with these insipid birds! Perhaps if they follow us to the Château, my trolls shall dine on them. One thing about my trolls is they love sour milk and raw fish, but most of all, delectable exotic birds," The Baroness said with cracking laughter as she threw her hat to the ground. Click und Snap loaded the motorcar with a purple heron and a yellow-billed stork atop the trunk, both peering down at them.

Zara, hearing this from within the steamer trunk covered her mouth in horror. "Oh my goodness gracious," she cried. Little friends, little friends, fly away quickly and go and get help."

Hearing Zara Zuckerman's plea to her friends, The Baroness looked up to the trunk. She caressed the leather straps and replied, "Well, well. It seems we have an enchanted little girl in our midst who can talk to birds. How utterly charming. All the better, my little Coconut pie. Let's hope you can Foxtrot! Drive on to the Château du Chatouiller, Click und Snap!"

CHAPTER 8
The Red Hot Air Balloon

Sir Thomas Tattletale and Chronas Clockwork raced to save Zara Zuckerman from being kidnapped only to see the baroness's motorcar drive off into the dust. They arrived outside the station too late. Getting off of Ingaway with long faces, they sat on the sidewalk curb of the train station and put their hands to their cheeks.

Chronas asked Sir Thomas, "So what are we going to do now, Thomas?"

Sir Thomas looked down, then up to the sky. He took off his top hat and replied, "Chronas Clockwork, look up to the sky. Do you see a red hot air balloon painted with purple stars and yellow moons?"

Chronas looked at Thomas strangely and replied "What?"

"A red hot air balloon painted with purple stars and yellow moons!"

"Thomas, did you fall off Ingaway and hit your head when I was not looking?"

"Oh no, Chronas! The balloon belongs to my friend from school by the name of Phillip de Curieuse. His family is not fond of motorcars so they all travel by hot air balloons and they know every part of France."

"Thomas Tattletale, I shall believe it when I see it." He looked upward to the sky as he finished his sentence and saw a magnificent hot air balloon red in color adorned with purple stars and yellow moons. It wasn't just one balloon he could see, but three in the distance. Chronas turned to Sir Thomas in said, "By golly Thomas, there is a hot air balloon red in color in the sky with stars and moons, but there's also two more with it. A purple one with green polka dots, and a blue one with red stars!"

Sir Thomas cried, "Bo Bumble, Chronas we have to catch them. Come on, let us get back on Ingaway. We'll race to where they land."

Thomas and Chronas turned around to get back onto Ingaway, but they were too late. She had already turned back into a small wooden statue. Chronas silently picked her up gently and put her into Zara's wooden box. Once again they sat back down on the sidewalk curb. As Sir Thomas looked around, across the street from the station, he noticed an unattended orange 4-seat roadster. It was a 1913 Pope-Hartford.

"Chronas do you see what I see?" Sir Thomas exclaimed with glee as he indicated toward the roadster.

As Chronas also looked in that direction, he asked, "Why by golly, I do! But can you drive it?"

"Indeed I can. All I need you to do is to crank it up and I'll start the gas!" Thomas exclaimed.

"Say, Thomas, where did you learn how to drive a motorcar?"

"Oh I just watched my Aunt Fanny," he replied with a smile.

Thomas then got up off the sidewalk curb and got ready to run across the street until Chronas grabbed his hand. "You should always look both ways before crossing!"

Sir Thomas replied, "Bow bumble, you're right!" The boys then looked both ways before crossing the road.

Holding hands, they ran across the street giggling with excitement. Chronas ran to the front of the automobile to crank it up while Sir Thomas started the gas pull. Chaka Chaka Boom! Chaka BOOM!

"Started the automobile!" Sir Thomas cried out to Chronas, "Chronas, get in. Hurry!" He helped Chronas get into the motorcar. "Oh bow bumble!" cried Thomas in dismay.

"What is it Thomas?" asked Chronas. "My feet don't reach the foot pedal," replied Sir Thomas.

Chronas then thought for a moment. "Thomas, I have an idea," he cried. Looking into his leather doctor's bag, he found two wooden rectangle boxes that held clock parts for his father and a pair of leather shoelaces. Then, turning to Sir Thomas, he said, "Thomas, show me your feet."

Sir Thomas inched closer to Chronas, who then tied the wooden boxes using the shoe laces onto Thomas' feet. "Try the pedal now, Thomas!" cried Chronas.

"It works! It works perfectly, Chronas!" Sir Thomas replied.

With a loud backfire, they were off wobbling from side to side, racing down the Parisian streets in hot pursuit of the colorful hot air balloons. Actually, there were on the sidewalk at first, and then they were crashing through a park fence at high speed. Up and down they went on the sprawling hills of Le Bois de Vincennes.

As Thomas was concentrating on staying on track, he heard Chronas cry out, "Thomas look out ahead!"

Sir Thomas did so and saw a lady on horseback galloping toward them. "Get out of the way, silly horse," Thomas cried, swerving the motorcar and just missing the lady on the galloping horse by a hair.

Then, standing up in the seat pointing, Chronas cried, "Flock of Geese ahead, Thomas!"

"I see them, I see them Chronas!" Thomas cried.

"Honk your side horn, Thomas. It should scare them from the pathway!"

"Chronas, I can't reach the horn. My arms are too short!"

Thinking fast, Chronas jumped out of his seat and climbed to the side of racing motorcar, and pulled off the brass horn. Then he sat back in the automobile and started honking it. The geese were terrified from the noise and flew up and out of the way as the boys passed. They continued to race down the green lawns of the park through the crowds of people to catch up to the hot air balloons. Chronas was keeping a lookout for the balloons. "I can see the balloons, and we are catching up! Faster Thomas, faster!"

They rolled over the park grounds through the flowers and bushes. They were indeed catching up with the colorful hot air balloons until their excitement was interrupted by faint sounds of a French police siren. It was right behind them, getting louder. A French police officer pulled up next to them informing them in French, "Arrêtez l'automobile et tirez dessus!" (Stop the automobile and pull over!)

Chronas Clockwork could understand and speak French, and turned to Thomas to tell him to stop the motorcar and pull over. With sad faces, Thomas and Chronas slowly pulled over and stopped. They got out of the motorcar, twisting back and forth and smiling.

The French police officer slowly got off her motorcycle and approached them with a stern face.

"Bonjour, officer! What a wonderful day to go for a motorcar ride, wouldn't you say?" Chronas said in French, and with a smile.

The officer asked, "Quel âge êtes vous?" (How old are you?)

Chronas replied back in French, "Je suis âgé de 6 ans ½" (I'm 6 1/2 years old).

The officer then asked, "Oh je vois! Et votre ami conduire?" (Oh I see, and your friend driving?)

Chronas replied with a smile. "Il est 61/2 ans comme moi!" (He's 6 1/2 years old like me).

Then in English, she asked, "You are American, oui?"
Chronas continued to reply in French, "Oui, je suis de Chicago et mon ami est de l'Angleterre." (Yes, I'm from Chicago and my friend is from England).

"Your French is rather good, young man. I do speak a bit of English." From then on the officer spoke to them in English. "Could you tell me why you were in such a hurry?" she asked.

"Oh, we were going to save a friend who is in trouble and were following the colorful hot air balloons to help us!" Chronas replied.

"Oh mon Dieu!, Excusez-moi!" cried the officer, "I had no idea you were part of the entertainment!"

Looking at each other, Sir Thomas and Chronas were baffled. "I say, but what kind of entertainment are you talking about?" Thomas asked the officer, looking back at Chronas curiously.

The officer whispered loudly, "Oh, Peekaboo! I can keep a secret." She chuckled, covering her mouth.

The boys looked at each other, still baffled. Shrugging their shoulders, they looked at each other and giggled. Thomas and Chronas then both replied to the officer's comment. "I SEE YOU!"

"Oh, no, no, the hot air balloons are headed for Peekaboo Manor! It is Gloria Peekaboo's birthday. She turns 6 years old today. Everyone knows of her in Paris. She loves surprises." The officer added, "I will give you a police escort to Peekaboo Manor." Sir Thomas and Chronas just stared at the police officer. "Well don't just stand there gawking, get back into your automobile and follow me."

Thomas and Chronas then started the automobile and proceeded to follow the French police officer to Peekaboo Manor.

Gloria Peekaboo is six years old and heir to Peekaboo Cosmetics from America, currently at her boarding school in England. Her mother is Pamela Peekaboo of Porcupine Peak Pennsylvania and is founder and owner of Peekaboo Cosmetics. Pamela is a self-made woman who prides herself on the most lavish parties for her only child Gloria.

The Georgian-style estate with white marble columns where they live is located Allée Fortunée, Paris. 18th-century French baroque music was playing by Jean-Baptiste Lully in the background as everyone prepared for a grand surprise birthday party. Two ornate gazebos adorned with orange and purple balloons had been imported from America just for the occasion. The first gazebo held a massive five-tier birthday cake, which was made of chocolate with orange icing and blueberry accents. The invited children danced around it in a minuet fashion, chanting in bazaar whispers to each other, "I am Gloria's best friend in the whole wide world." The second gazebo held all of Gloria's birthday presents. On the grounds were two baby elephants painted orange, and three camels painted purple with pink polka dots. They were meant for the children to ride on after they would have dropped off birthday presents in the second gazebo.

Gloria was to be arriving at any moment from boarding school via the train station. Over 75 children awaited her arrival, dressed in their Sunday best. Ms. Peekaboo was running around frantically making sure everything was just perfect for her little angel Gloria. "My goodness, where could she be?" cried Ms. Pamela Peekaboo to one of her maids. "I sent Ferguson to pick her up at the station over two hours ago with her birthday present!" She was interrupted by the tugging of her purple polka dot dress by a little girl named Betsy Sassafras.

Betsy Sassafras was the heiress to Sassafras Soda Pop Company of Mexico. Betsy Sassafras was the very picture of perfection that a little girl could be. She was dressed in a sailor suit with a bright red bow atop her perfectly bobbed hair with pouting red lips. One could say she was sugar and spice and some things not so nice. Overhearing Ms. Peekaboo's concern over the delayed arrival of Gloria, Betsy came over and said, "Oh! Don't worry Ms. Peekaboo. Being one of Gloria's very best friends in the whole wide world, I can assure you that she's probably just reapplying the wonderful makeup you manufactured at your company to her adorable whittle face." Then, with a curtsy and grin, Betsy skipped off to play with the other children.

Meanwhile, in another part of France outside of Paris in Bois de Boulogne, the automobile approached the Château du Chatouiller, the winter home of the Baron and Baroness. The Château du Chatouiller had a slate Mansard roof with a large tower that dominated the landscape. It was built in 1880 of limestone and red brick. Hearing the automobile approach, the trolls gathered around to pull the steamer trunk from the roof of the automobile. Exiting the automobile, the Baroness approached the steps of the château. Then, turning around, she instructed the ghastly trolls, "Take our dear guest to Le Lune salle de nuit."

Le Lune salle de nuit (The moon night room) was in the tower of the château. The room was called this because of the moon night marble, which was used throughout the room on the floors and the walls. It was round in shape with eight cream Valencia marble columns. In between each column were six medieval tapestries that depicted astrological characters. Beneath each tapestry were little Victorian chairs upholstered in red damask. The ornate room had only one large Moroccan-styled window, with French doors below it. Across from this was a moon night marble carved fireplace. The French beveled glass doors opened up onto a balcony that overlooked the grand garden. Below it lay steps of solid concrete leading to the garden. The trolls brought Zara in the steamer trunk to this room.

Inside the trunk, Zara could no longer hear the sounds of her friends flying over the steamer trunk, but she could make out the sounds of the ghastly trolls carrying her up steps towards the moon night room. As the sounds of the trolls ceased and the movement of the steamer trunk stopped, she heard a soft voice call out to her, "You can come out now, my little enchanted creature."

Opening the trunk with caution, Zara peered into the exquisite room and slowly crept out. As she stepped out, she saw the Baroness standing close to her.

The Baroness looked at her intently, "Why hello, it's truly a pleasure to have you here in our winter home. I am the Baroness Giggle Von Tickle and I do hope you enjoy your stay," she said with a smile.

Zara was worried and looked around for her governess. "Where is Ms. Gazoontite?" Zara asked softly with worry in her eyes.

"Do have a seat and make yourself comfortable. We simply must have the perfect dance partner for you, my little peach," stated the Baroness with a most sinister smile.

Zara was getting worried. "What did you do with Ms. Gazoontite?" Zara asked once again in a louder tone. "I want to go home. You are not my aunt!" cried Zara with fright in her voice.

The Baroness just smiled ominously, turning her back to Zara, and walked toward the exit of the room. Her only reply to little Zara as she left the room was, "Dinner will be served promptly at nine." The massive doors shut and locked behind her as she left with a click.

As Zara sat alone in the dimly lit moon night room, she began to cry. "What am I to do? I've lost all my friends and I know no one here." Just then, Zara heard chirping coming from outside on the balcony. Wiping the tears from her eyes, Zara slowly walked over to the beveled glass balcony doors to investigate the sound. To her surprise, as she opened up the French doors, she saw little Tutsi the Pygmy Kingfisher hovering in mid-air. Unlike the other animals in Zara's enchanted box, the birds in her collection were special. So long as they did not to touch the ground, they would never change back into wood carvings. "Oh, Tutsi! How nice it is to see you! Are you here to help me?" Zara asked.

Tutsi landed on Zara's outstretched finger and Zara brought him inside. Tutsi began to talk to Zara with a series of tweets and chirps that only Zara could understand. "I shall do everything in my power to help you, Zara!" Tutsi chirped loudly with excitement. Just then, Zara heard someone at the door and she immediately hushed Tutsi. "Tutsi please, you must be quiet!" Then she quickly glanced over to the door and saw the brass door knob turning. "Tutsi come quickly." She lifted her long curly hair, telling Tutsi to hide underneath. Quickly covering Tutsi with her hair, she sat back down as if nothing had happened. With force, the doors opened and the Baroness bolted back into the room with over twenty of the troll servants. "Search the room!" she cried to the ghastly trolls. The Baroness walked in a menacing manner over to Zara as the trolls checked the room. "Well, well, well." She put one hand to her ear and continued, "Do my ears deceive me, or did I hear a bird chirping in this room?"

Zara was scared, but she put a calm front and said, "Why I don't believe so, dear Baroness Von Tickle." With an innocent smile, she said, "Your ears must be deceiving you."

Kneeling with one knee, the Baroness caressed Zara's long curly hair and said, "I dare say at my age, one is bound to make such mistakes!" Then, the Baroness stood back up and looked at the trolls. Not moving away, she looked back at Zara and asked, "Do you agree, my dearest Zara?"

"Oh indeed I do, Baroness."

Slowly, the Baroness bent toward her with evil eyes, "But on the other hand, my sense of smell has never failed me, my dearest little peach!" the Baroness exclaimed. With a sudden move, the Baroness pulled Zara's hair and Tutsi flew out into the Baroness' face. The Baroness, caught unprepared, screamed, "Ah! You foul little creature!" Then, turning to her troll army, she cried, "Ghastly trolls! The first one to catch it may bite its head off and share the rest with your brothers and sisters!" The Baroness laughed madly.

Zara yelled with fright, "Tutsi, fly out through the glass doors quickly!"

She addressed the trolls. "Close the doors at once!" With nowhere to go, Tutsi hovered over the French doors as the trolls watched him, growling and hissing. The trolls then began to climb the walls to the ceiling with their sticky feet and hands.

Zara looked on in horror as the Baroness held on to her arm, restraining Zara. "Get away from him, you horrible monsters!" Zara cried. "You are a horrible Lady and I hate you. Let me go! Let me go!" Tutsi saw the Baroness restraining Zara and flew down to peck the Baroness' face. As the Baroness tried to swat the bird away, Zara was able to break free. She cried out to Tutsi, "Watch out! Tutsi!" As Tutsi swooped down at the Baroness once again, a troll jumped off the wall and caught little Tutsi, before falling to the floor. Zara was looking on cried, "Let him go! Let him go!" As the troll laughed with pleasure and jumped up and down, he opened his mouth to bite off Tutsi's head.

Thinking fast, Zara ran over to one of the little Victorian chairs, picked it up, and smashed it over the troll's head. The troll fell to the floor from the impact, allowing Tutsi escape from its clawed hands. Zara immediately saw the opportunity and ran over to another chair. She picked it up and smashed one of the beveled glass door panes so Tutsi could escape. Without further lingering, Tutsi flew out of the broken window. "He got away! He got away!" cried Zara. With tears in her eyes, she waved a goodbye to him. Two trolls immediately approached Zara and grabbing her, dragged her back to the little Victorian chair. The Baroness walked over with sarcasm in her voice and said, "Such a pity, dear Zara. If only you had wings, you would have been able to fly away with him." Addressing her trolls, the Baroness said, "My ghastly trolls, tie our charming guest to the chair so there won't be any scurrying about this time." With a devilish smile, she turned and said, "Good night, dearest Zara Zukerman."

As Thomas and Chronas trailed behind the police officer, the police siren blared when it approaching the Peekaboo manor. The boys were ecstatic because now they could see the colorful hot air balloons about to land. The sound of a police siren caught the attention of Ms. Peekaboo, who was walking along the marble veranda. Looking toward the main gate, she could see an orange roadster in the distance as it approached, escorted by a police motorcycle. With a sigh of relief, she informed everyone to get ready. She called aloud, "Ok boys and girls! Se il vous plait. (please) Gloria is arriving! Everyone to your places. Children to your arranged seats. Se il vous plaît!" As she looked up into the sky, she saw the hot air balloons. "Oh my! Just perfect timing! The Curieuse family is arriving!" she cried as she gazed at the hot air balloons.

All the children scrambled to occupy their seats. Betsy went to her arranged seat that was next to Gloria and saw a little boy sitting in her seat. In a soft voice, Betsy asked the little boy, "Do you know sign language?"

The little boy replied, laughing, "Why of course not, silly!"

Betsy replied, "Well if you do not get up out of my seat, you are going to need classes, because I'm going to scream in your ear until I'm blue in the face!"

The little boy simply got up and ran away.

Passing the massive cast iron gates leading into Peekaboo manor, Thomas tried to slow down the automobile, but he was unable to do so. Realizing something was wrong, Thomas looked down at the brake pedal. To his horror he saw that the shoelace that held the wooden box to his foot and to the brake had fallen off.

The officer stopped in front of the house as Pamela Peekaboo walked down the steps to greet them, smiling and grasping her long strand of pearls. Thomas and Chronas raced right past them. The police officer watched as they raced past them and started to laugh, looking over to Ms. Peekaboo. The laughing officer said, "Oh! Ms. Peekaboo you have such a sense of humor! I must say, so original and a great idea!"

Pamela's eyes widened as the automobile raced past her and she exclaimed, "Officer, what are you talking about? My little angel is in that automobile!" She clenched her pearls with panic.

Now the officer could sense that it wasn't all a gimmick for Gloria's birthday. She said to Ms. Peekaboo, "Angel? There are no angels in that automobile, Ms. Peekaboo, but two little boys, the same age as your Gloria."

"What! Two little boys? Have you lost your mind, officer? I sent Ferguson over three hours ago to pick her up at the train station in an orange roadster, which is her birthday gift." Ms. Peekaboo screamed as the first catastrophe commenced.

Turning the automobile around, Sir Thomas and Chronas were headed for the backyard of the manor, where most of the festivities were. "Watch out for the orange elephants, Thomas!" yelled Chronas.

"Orange elephants you say? Oh I see, Bo Bumble!" Thomas swerved the motorcar, barely missing the elephants, only to crash into the gazebo that held Gloria's birthday cake. All the children were screaming as they ran for cover. Their happy little birthday tunes were soon turned into tears as the birthday cake flew up into the air in pieces and landed on most of them below. Sir Thomas was relieved and cried over to Chronas, "Bow Bumble, Chronas, that was a close one!" They giggled as they sped off.

Viewing the pandemonium from above, the Curieuse family hover in their balloons until it was safe to land.

Still trying to stop the automobile, Thomas and Chronas raced through the grounds, over the flowers beds, and smashing all marble and bronze sculptures in sight.

Chronas, looking ahead, screamed, "Thomas look out! There are purple camels with pink polka dots ahead!"

Squinting his eyes, Sir Thomas asked, "I say, are you sure they're not statues, Chronas? Bow bumble, you're right old chap!" he yelled, once again swerving the motorcar and just missing the colorful camels. The automobile veered off to demolish the second gazebo that held all of Gloria's presents. The presents went flying through the air and landed in the punch bowl, the fountain, and through the windows of Peekaboo Manor, smashing Ms. Peekaboo's rare collection of porcelain plates and vases from China.

Thomas and Chronas raced on, headed for a red and white striped tent which held a festive assortment of ice creams and sorbets along with hundreds of silver spoons that were ornately shaped like sea shells. The tent also contained porcelain serving bowls and cake dishes with red sea coral designs around the edges. Chronas saw the tent and, thinking quickly, got down on the floor of the motorcar. He put all his strength on the brake pedal to stop the automobile, but they collided into the tent anyway. The striped tent collapsed on them in the process. As they slowly removed the tent from their heads, they saw that they were surrounded.

Peering down on them without a sound was Ms. Peekaboo, the French police officer, and thirty servants. Ms. Peekaboo was furious. "Young men, you have no idea how much trouble you are in!" Ms. Peekaboo exclaimed. In a rage, she ran over to them and grabbed them both by their ears. "Officer, I want you to arrest both of them immediately," she cried.

Ms. Peekaboo was interrupted by a sound of an automobile driving up the driveway. It was a checkerboard taxi. It stopped at the main steps of the manor and then drove up slowly to the collapsed tent. As the taxi stopped, out popped Gloria Peekaboo and Ferguson the chauffeur.

"Crackers and milk!" Gloria exclaimed, both hands on her cheeks with joy. "Mummy! What a surprise, I just love it! Everyone looks so funny mummy! Ferguson and I could not stop laughing in the taxi on the way over!" Gloria was ecstatic and couldn't contain herself with delight. She looked over to see Thomas and Chronas with long faces standing by her mother. Gloria greeted them with a soft smile and asked, "Are you the gentleman that helped with my wonderful surprise party?"

"Um, why yes. My name is Thomas, Sir Thomas Tattletale, and this is my good friend Chronas Clockwork," Sir Thomas introduced them both as they tipped their hats.

Excited, Gloria introduced herself, "Pleased to meet you both. I'm Gloria Peekaboo. Thank you so much!" she said with a delicate curtsey and a wink. Gloria then looked up in amazement at the colorful hot air balloons about to land. "Oh, Balloons! Balloons! Balloons!" she cried, twirling around in circles and laughing. She ran over toward the balloons waving her hands, and cried out "Bonjour Philippe, bonjour Philippe!" Then, turning back to Sir Thomas and Chronas, she said, "Oh Thomas, Chronas, I just love balloons, especially the ones that hold my love Philippe!"

Seeing her daughter happy and excited, Gloria's mother was speechless and did not know what to say. Ms. Peekaboo just smiled pleasantly and wished Gloria a happy birthday with a hug and kiss. "So glad you like it, my love," she replied. Then, looking over to Thomas, Ms. Peekaboo asked, "Did you say your last name was Tattletale?"

"Why yes, I did," he replied politely.

"Of Tattletale Publishing?" further questioned Ms. Peekaboo.

"Indeed I am. My mother runs it. Why do you ask?" Thomas confirmed for Ms. Peekaboo.

"Because I do all my advertising in your mother's newspapers and fashion magazines for my cosmetics. Oh, my! How small the world can be," Ms. Peekaboo then smiled, clutching her pearls once again in relief. Clapping her hands together, she informed the servants to hose down the children before they could come into the house.

The Curieuse family gracefully landed their hot air balloon beside the striped tents as Ms. Peekaboo ventured off to greet the Curieuse family. "Bienvenue (Welcome) Augustin et Antoinette! Grabbing both of their arms as they exited their balloons, she asked, "You must tell me all about your trip to Brazil." Gloria had also followed her mother to welcome the guests. She looked over at her mother with a smile to see Philippe exiting his balloon, assisted by Bucheron the air chauffeur.

Philippe sported a tri-color cricket cap and horn-rimmed shades, and was dressed in a vibrant purple blazer with three brass buttons, a gold and navy striped tie and trousers. Looking straight at Gloria, he exclaimed, "Bonjour Gloria! Joyeux Anniversaire!" (Hello Gloria Happy Birthday). Then he saw Sir Thomas at a distance, and approaching him, Philippe exclaimed, "Bonjour Sir Thomas Tattletale, what are you doing here?"

"Bow bumble, Philippe, so glad to see you!"

Gloria was happy to see that they knew each other, and joined the conversation, "You know Thomas?" she asked Philippe.

"Why yes, we're friends from boarding school," he replied. "How adventurous you were in that roaster, Thomas. I never knew you had it in you! And who's your friend?" asked Philippe, looking at Chronas.

"This is Chronas, Chronas Clockwork from Chicago."

"Crackers and milk, an American like me!" exclaimed Gloria.

Chronas extended his hand to Philippe to shake, "Pleased to meet you, Philippe," stated Chronas in French.

Philippe was pleasantly surprised, "You speak French! Cie Bon!" he replied.

Sir Thomas then tapped and whispered into Gloria's ear, "You must forgive us but the truth is that we were actually following the hot air balloons and our brakes failed. I'm dreadfully sorry about your birthday cake."

Gloria seemed unruffled about it, and replied, "Oh crackers and milk, don't worry about it, silly Thomas. I just enjoyed seeing the cake on the faces of people I've never liked. Besides, those are mother's arranged play friends for me anyway!" Then, with a wink, she added, "Just don't tell my mother that."

Thomas smiled back with a giggle. Looking over to Philippe, Thomas then asked, "Philippe, I thought perhaps you could help us in locating a friend who has been kidnapped by rather dark characters."

Gloria was excited at the mention of something intriguing, "Crackers and milk, an adventure!" interrupted Gloria, and added, "Count me in! I shall also help you." Looking under Philippe's arm, Gloria asked, "Why Philippe, are those for me?"

Philippe was holding two elegantly wrapped pastel yellow boxes under his arm, one being a thin rectangle in shape, the other a large square shaped box with two holes on the side. Both were tied with a red silk bow. Philippe presented Gloria with the thin rectangle box first, as Ms. Peekaboo looked on smiling.

Gloria opened the first box, removing the tissue paper with a soft smile, and saw that in it was a pair of yellow suede gloves. She looked up with a bright smile and said, "Merci Philippe, I love them."

"Oh how lovely, Gloria. Just divine Philippe! This would be perfect with your Sunday dress!" exclaimed Pamela Peekaboo.

Gloria looked up at her mother and smiled.

Ms. Peekaboo was a busy host and she excused herself from the conversation. Looking at Philippe's parents, she said, "Forgive me. I have to attend to something. I'll be right back, my little angel." Gloria's mother left them briefly with Philippe's parents.

Philippe presented Gloria with the second box, "This is the real gift!" Philippe said with a grin. He added, "But first you must put on your yellow gloves!"

"Ok Philippe," Gloria replied excitedly. Gloria put on the yellow suede gloves and proceeded to open the second box. Removing the red silk ribbon, she peered in while opening the box. "Holy crackers and milk! I just love it, and it's orange!" exclaimed Gloria. Picking it up gently, Gloria asked, "Does it have a name?"

"I have named him Palo Phoneutria," he replied. Looking inside the box with much interest, Gloria asked Philippe, "Where did you find him?"

Philippe replied with a smile, "In Brazil, when I was on Safari with mother and father." It was an orange wandering Brazilian banana spider.

"He's quite beautiful! Is he venomous?" Gloria asked.
Philippe replied, "Oh indeed, that's why I gave you the yellow gloves."

Gloria looked up from the box said, "Oh Philippe, you think of everything!" She continued with her curious questions. "What does it eat?"

He replied, "Mice, frogs, fruits."

"No worms?" asked Gloria.

"Perhaps, I'm not sure."

"Let's go dig some up later after our little adventure!" said Gloria.

"Oh Gloria, you are just so wonderful. Just don't tell your mum," he replied.

Gloria cried, "Are you kidding? Of course not, silly Philippe! Merci beaucoup Philippe for the gift." Gloria then turned to Thomas and Chronas. "Okay boys, quietly go over to my automobile and wait for me while I take care of some things before we leave."

Thomas and Chronas nodded and did so.

Gloria called Ferguson over, "Ferguson, fetch me my tweed outfit, the new one with the jouphers. Oh, and don't forget to pack my trusty slingshot and bag of marbles!" she added. "I'm going on a little adventure with my new friends."

"A little adventure mademoiselle?" asked Ferguson.

"Yes. Could you also take Philippe's wonderful birthday gifts up to my room?" she politely asked, and quickly added, "And be sure not to tell mother anything of this, Ferguson."

Ferguson replied, "But of course mademoiselle."

Approaching Gloria with hands on her hips was Betsy Sassafras who clearly had something to say about this. "Gloria Peekaboo, this is simply the worst birthday party I have ever attended!" cried Betsy Sassafras with tears running down her face. "Just look at my dress mother bought me from Paris just for this party!" she screamed, pointing at her dress. Betsy's dress was covered completely with orange icing and chocolate cake.

Hearing Betsy, Ms. Peekaboo looked over and approached Gloria. "Is everything okay, my angel?"

"Nothing I can't handle mummy," Gloria replied, looking at Betsy. Turning to her mother with a grin on her face, she asked, "Mummy, could I have a word with Betsy in private? I thought perhaps Betsy could use some cheering up!"

"Oh, of course my little angel," her mother replied. Ms. Peekaboo then left to show Madame and Monsieur Curieuse her prized collection of Ming vases in the drawing room.

Gloria skipped back over to Betsy and said, "If you don't shut your big trap, I'm going to have to ask Martha and her four sisters to escort you off the grounds!"

"Martha and her four sisters?" asked Betsy. With a sour face, Betsy then looked over at Thomas and Chronas, "Don't tell me you have invited even more vagrants to your birthday party!" she exclaimed.

Gloria then held her hand out, wiggling her thumb. "Allow me to introduce you to Martha, and these are her four sisters," She wiggled the rest of her four fingers, presenting a fist before Betsy's face.

"Why I never!" Then, stamping her foot to the ground, she screamed, "Gloria Peekaboo, you wouldn't dare!"

Meanwhile, walking up the steps en route to the drawing room, Ms. Peekaboo saw Ferguson and tapped him on the shoulder. "Ferguson, could you tell me how two little boys were able to drive away with an orange roadster?"

"Well madam, it's a rather long story, but there were wild animals running loose at the train station," Ferguson started to explain.

Preoccupied with the party and Philippe's parents, Ms. Peekaboo said, "Oh I see, do tell me later Ferguson." As Ms. Peekaboo and Madame and Monsieur Curieuse were about to enter the drawing room, they heard a mind-numbing scream coming from the courtyard. It was quickly followed by another.

"What on earth could that possibly be?" Madame Curieuse exclaimed, covering her ears.

Ms. Peekaboo immediately turned around with Philippe's family, racing back toward the courtyard to see what was going on, to where they had left Gloria and Philippe and the other children.

Gloria was brushing off her pink polka dot dress and was smiling. Anxiously, Ms. Peekaboo asked her, "Is everything okay, my little angel? I thought I heard a scream."

Gloria nonchalantly replied, "No I didn't hear anything, Mummy." She quickly added, "Mummy, I just thought you'd like to know this was the best birthday surprise party ever!"

Ms. Peekaboo was overwhelmed with emotion and kissed Gloria on her cheek before leaving Gloria with her friends to enjoy the party.

Gloria then turned to her new friends and said, "Come on, let's get going. We have an important rescue!" Philippe and Gloria moved toward the automobile. "Philippe, could you crank up the motorcar?" asked Gloria, sitting at the wheel.

"Yes, Gloria. Oh, the things I do for love," Philippe said to himself as he cranked up the Pope-Hartford and all four were off on their adventure.

As they were driving through the gates of Peekaboo estate they heard the cry of a little girl. "Bow Bumble! Did you hear that?" cried Thomas.

"I did indeed!" replied Philippe. "Did you hear that, Chronas?" asked Philippe.

"By Golly Gum, I heard it too! Gloria can you hear it too?" asked Chronas.

Gloria smiled. "Nope, not at all. It must be some new kind of Koo Koo bird!" she replied, folding her arms and looking up into the air.

They were still wondering about the sound when a voice rang out from a tree limb, "Oh please help me. I'm afraid of heights. Please help me down! Oh boo whoo!" cried the voice.

Looking up, the boys noticed that there was a little girl hanging from a tree limb. It was Betsy Sassafras from the birthday party.

"Say, how in the world did you get all the way up there?" exclaimed Chronas.

"Perhaps she has wings and flew up there," stated Gloria Peekaboo with a grin.

Betsy could hear Gloria and screamed, "Why Gloria Peekaboo, you are a liar! I can hear you, you know. Just wait until I tell my Mama and Poppa on you!"

"Betsy Sassafras, if you don't shut your face I'm gonna give you a fat lip, see!" exclaimed Gloria, shaking her fist.

"Ok let's just get her down before she falls and breaks her neck," stated Chronas, looking concerned. "Thomas, could you give me a boost up the tree?" he asked.

"You got it, Chronas!" Thomas replied. "Wait a minute Chronas, I see a ladder on the side of the road."

"Well, the very ladder I was forced up by none other than Gloria Peekaboo," cried Betsy.

"Betsy, I'm warning you! You are gonna get it!" exclaimed Gloria.

Thomas looked towards Philippe for help and asked, "I say Philippe, could you stand in front of the tree to catch Betsy in case Chronas slips and drops her?"

"Oui Oui. Thomas, I'm ready," Philippe replied.

"I'm going to die! I'm too cute to die, and in this dress! Oh boo whoo!" cried Betsy.

"Oh for grace of crackers and milk, I do hope Chronas slips and Philippe sneezes!" cried Gloria Peekaboo, folding her arms and pouting as she looked on at the rescue effort.

Slowly and steadily, the boys were able to get Betsy safely down from the tree. She politely thanked Chronas while sticking her tongue out at Gloria.

"Great, you are out of the tree. So be on your way! We were on an important rescue mission," cried Gloria.

"An important rescue mission sounds quite exciting. Can I come?" asked Betsy.

"No! It's only for professionals," replied Gloria.

"Oh, really? Like you are? Applesauce, I say!" Betsy said sarcastically. "And by the way, where is your driver, Ferguson?" she asked.

"I gave him the day off, Sassafras!" replied Gloria, exasperated.

"Well I'm just going to have to march right back up to Peekaboo manor with tears in my eyes and explain how you drove off without Ferguson in an automobile with strangers," stated Betsy with a grimace and a mischievous look in her eyes.

"Betsy Sassafras! You are a rotten little apple with worms!" cried Gloria Peekaboo. "Okay. Just come along, Betsy. Perhaps you could be helpful," stated Sir Thomas.

"Oh goodie, my first adventure rescue mission!" Betsy cried with glee.

As everyone headed back to the automobile. Betsy had something to say. "Just a minute." Betsy ran over to the tree where she was stuck and kicked it. A little purse fell from it and landed into her hands. Then, running back and joining the rest in the motorcar, Betsy said, "A girl is never fully dressed without a proper purse!"

"Unbelievable!" cried Gloria with irritation, and laid her head on the steering wheel.

"Amazing!" stated Chronas.

"Bow Bumble!" exclaimed Sir Thomas.

"Well I'll be!" stated Philippe, as he cranked up the motorcar.

With a backfire they were off on their adventure.

CHAPTER 9
Le Jardin et Chateau du Chatouiller

Driving along the road on their journey to rescue Zara Zuckerman, Philippe turned to Thomas and asked, "Do you have any idea as to who could have taken her?"

"She was abducted by my grand aunt, The Baroness Giggle von Tickle." Thomas could only remember her last name in English.

"Tickle, you say?" Philippe thought to himself while scratching his head. "I'm afraid I don't know anybody in this region by that last name, Thomas."

Chronas then shared his thoughts on the matter and said, "Funny name, Thomas. In French it would be Chatouiller if that would be any help."

"Ah wait, I know now! It is the Château du Chatouiller. It's in Bois de Boulogne!" exclaimed Philippe.

"Say, it's not too far from here!" stated Gloria at the wheel as she glanced quickly at the others.

"The owner is one of the most famous inventors in all of France Le Baron Francois Von Chatouiller!" exclaimed Philippe.

"That's it! That's it! Chatouiller!" cried Thomas. "Thank you Chronas, Philippe!" exclaimed Sir Thomas.

Betsy had something to say and interrupted Thomas with a poke on the arm. "You mean to say your grand aunty is married to this person?" she asked curiously.

"Unfortunately yes, Betsy," Thomas replied with a frown.

"Oh! I can't imagine," she stated.

Meanwhile back in Paris down at the police station, Aunt Fanny had but one phone call to make and her only hope was Mr. Nicolas Almondbrittle, the brilliant attorney from San Francisco whom she and Thomas had dined with earlier. "Officer, oh officer darling, could I make a phone call?" asked Fanny politely.

"Okay, two minutes and that's all," replied the officer with a straight face. Unlocking her cell, the officer escorted her by the arm to a desk with a phone on it.

"Oh thanks, love!" she replied with relief. Sitting down, Aunt Fanny began to crank the phone up. Upon reaching the operator Fanny began to talk, "Oh operator, could you connect me to the Hotel Coochie Coo on boulevard Saint Hiccups?"

"One moment please," stated the operator. After a few moments, the connection was made.

"Bonsoire (Good evening) Hotel Coochie Coo. This is the concierge speaking."

If you please, could I have Mr. Nicolas Almondbrittle's room?" asked Fanny.

"Why, is this Fanny Flapper?" cried the concierge, recognizing her voice.

"Why yes it is!" she replied.

"What a pleasure it is, dear Fanny, I shall connect you immediately," he said.

Upon reaching Mr. Almondbrittle, Fanny told him what had happened.

"I shall be there within the hour, my dearest Fanny!" cried Mr. Almondbrittle.

174

Hanging up the phone with worry in her eyes, Fanny thanked the officer and was escorted back to her cell.

As the children were en route to the Château du Chatouiller in Bois de Boulogne, Betsy turned to Chronas and asked, "So what's in that funny looking box you're holding?" She tried to reach over to touch it.

"Don't touch! It's to be given to Zara only, by golly!" cried Chronas, who made a sour face.

"Ok ! No need for the sour face, I just wanted to see what was inside," replied Betsy.

Chronas replied, "I wasn't making a sour face at you. I just have to go to the POTTY by GOLLY! Okay, if I show you what's inside the box, will you promise to guard it for me while I go to the potty?"

"Cross my heart," she happily replied.

Opening up the box, Chronas showed Betsy what was inside. Betsy in turn kept her promise with Chronas as she giggled like a mad goose. After relieving himself of number one, Chronas headed back to the automobile, when he saw something quite amazing. He instantly called over to Thomas. "Look Thomas, it's that little bird we saw at the station." It was little Tutsi, the Pygmy Fisher.

Thomas got out of the automobile to get a closer look, "Bow Bumble! You're right, Chronas!"

Then, looking back up, he shouted, "Hello little bird! Are you here to help us find Zara?"

The little Pygmy Fisher just tweeted and fluttered around their heads, then gracefully landed on Sir Thomas's silk top hat.

"Well Chronas, it looks like we have another friend to help us on our journey," he stated gleefully. "Come on, let's get back to the motorcar."

Back at the motorcar, the young ladies were arguing about something. "Get out of my extra stash of marbles, Betsy!" cried Gloria.

"I don't like marbles anyway. Here take them. I have a magic box instead!" Betsy exclaimed, picking up Zara's special box and placing it in her lap.

"Say, what's all the fuss about?" cried Chronas, looking at the arguing girls.

Gloria turned to answer, "BETSY SASAFRASS is touching things that don't belong to her!" she cried.

As he realized that Betsy had just picked up Zara's box, Chronas shouted, "Betsy, I had told you to hold on to that box!"

Betsy looked at him calmly. "Oh I just put it down for a second," she replied with a grin.

"Hey! Where did that little bird come from?" asked Philippe, pointing to Thomas's hat.

"Well Philippe, let's just say we have a special friend to assist us on our mission," stated Thomas.

As Philippe cranked up the Pope Hartford everyone loaded back in the automobile and resumed their journey to rescue Zara, Tutsi leading the way only a few feet from the automobile. The children began to sing funny little songs to each other. As they approached the Château du Chatouiller, they could all see the looming tower from the distance. Stopping by the gilded cast iron gates of the Château, they saw a large yellow-billed stork perched high atop the gate. It was the very same yellow-billed stork that Thomas and Chronas had seen at the train station. Tutsi, seeing the stork, immediately flew off of Thomas' hat and up to the stork perched on the gate. Tutsi started chirping madly and flew about the stork's head in circles. The stork in return replied by squawking and flapping its wings.

Thomas looked closely at both said, "Bow Bumble everyone! I think they are going to guide us toward Zara!"

The stork flew off its perch and swooped down to land on the hood of the motorcar. Flapping its wings, it flew off and started to circle above their heads, indicating that they should follow it. Tutsi then flew alongside the yellow-billed stork as they all followed behind.

"Come on guys, hurry, let's follow!" exclaimed Thomas.

Before they ventured farther, Gloria had an idea. "Wait a minute. Let's hide the motorcar outside the gates in the bushes and head up to the Château on foot, cutting through the back way of the garden," stated Gloria.

"Good idea, Gloria!" stated Chronas.

"So then does everyone agree on this plan?" asked Gloria, looking around at everyone.

"I agree!" replied Philippe.

"Me too!" cried Chronas.

"Count me in," stated Sir Thomas.

Betsy on the other hand was just looking at her nails.

"Well Betsy, we're all waiting. What do you think?" cried Gloria, with a grave look on her face.

"Well, I don't know about this," cried Betsy. "Not only do my feet hurt, but do you see the shoes I'm wearing? And besides, there could be mud or worse, bugs, out there! And I only have three hours of fresh bubble gum reserved!"

"You have got to be kidding me!" cried Gloria Peekaboo as she balled up her fist.

Chronas then intervened, holding Gloria back as he recommended an idea. "Betsy, you can stay here and guard the motorcar until we come back."

"Smashing idea!" exclaimed Thomas.

"Yes, I agree, and out off our hair!" stated Gloria.

"Oh that's such a relief," cried Betsy, puffing her hair as she put a fresh piece of bubble gum in her mouth.

Ignoring Betsy, Gloria packed her trusty slingshot and a sack of marbles tied around her waist with string. "Does everyone have what they need for our rescue mission?" asked Gloria.

Thomas looked over to Chronas and asked, "Do you have Zara's special box?"

"I do, Thomas! It feels a bit heavier than before, but I have it!" replied Chronas, giving Thomas a thumbs up. In turn, he asked Thomas, "Do you have the sneezing atomizer we found?"

"Got it right here in my pocket," replied Thomas with a smile.

"I do hope this plan works, Thomas," stated Philippe de Curieuse.

"Don't worry, Philippe. "What could possibly go wrong?" stated Thomas.

"Fantastic, we are off!" cried Gloria.

Setting off through the back way of the garden, the children tiptoed through rosemary bushes that were edged with lavender and guarded by cypress trees. They could all smell the aroma of the flowers and plants around them. As they got closer to the cypress trees, they could see a large geometric green hedge flowerbed in the distance. This led to the back door of the chateau. Venturing on through the bushes as the sun set, Thomas heard a rustling in the shrubbery behind them. Alarmed, they stopped dead in their tracks.

Thomas turned around asked Chronas, "Did you hear that, Chronas?"

"Why yes I did Thomas," replied Chronas.

"Me too!" whispered Philippe.

"Ok guys, I heard it too. Just take cover and don't say a word," Gloria added softly. The boys immediately hid behind the topiaries that were shaped like obelisk while Gloria hid in the shrubbery and cocked her slingshot for action as she surveyed the area. "I don't hear it anymore. I think it's safe to come out," she cried. Getting up slowly, Gloria peered out and was face to face with Betsy Sassafras. "Ah! What are you doing here Betsy? You were supposed to be guarding the motorcar!" exclaimed Gloria.

"Yeah what happened?" asked Chronas.

"Oh boo whoo, a bug flew into the automobile and it was getting dark." cried Betsy Sassafras.

"Couldn't you have just put the top up and locked the doors?" exclaimed Gloria.

"I couldn't because there wasn't a chauffeur present to give assistance," cried Betsy.

"Betsy Sassafras you never cease to amaze me. You have raspberry bubble gum for brains!" cried Gloria.

"Come on then Betsy, just be very quiet," stated Thomas, taking her hand.

"Okay, but may I say one thing?" she added.

"Great potato salad in the morning! What is it now?" Gloria cried.

"I'm not sure, but I think we have company!" She pointed to the bushes.

They all turned around to see giggling little green eyes glowing in the bushes. It was the ghastly trolls.

"Everyone, head for the back door while I hold them off!" cried Gloria, taking out her trusty slingshot and taking aim. "Got one! Only 26 more to go," she cried. Reaching for her sack, Gloria realized she was running out of marbles. "Oh, apple fudge! I left my extra marbles in the motorcar!" she exclaimed. Slipping the slingshot in her back pocket, Gloria began to run.

Tutsi and the yellow-billed stork saw Gloria from the air and joined in by swooping down to peck at the ghastly trolls. Outnumbered, Tutsi and the stork then flew off, abandoning the children to fend for themselves.

"My goodness they are ugly!" cried Betsy to Gloria as she ran beside her.

"Well for someone's feet to be hurting, you sure are a fast runner!" cried Gloria.

"Let's just say I have been spiritually motivated!" Betsy replied.

Betsy reached the door first. She was so frightened that upon entering, she slammed the door shut behind her, forgetting about the others outside. As the rest reached the door, they all began to bang on it, screaming, "Betsy Sassafras, open the door! The trolls are right behind us!"

"Bow Bumble chaps, it seems were doomed," cried Sir Thomas as the trolls got closer.

Just then, the skies turned dark with an eerie sound as hundreds of birds filled the sky. The children saw Tutsi and the yellow-billed stork leading the massive flock. Tutsi and the yellow-billed stork had not abandoned the children after all, but had gone to get help from the local birds of France. As the children looked on in amazement, there were over 353 species of French birds swooping down pecking at all the trolls until they all retreated.

Meanwhile, inside the Chateau with her back to the door in fright, Betsy heard a hypnotic music coming from down the hallway. Mesmerized by the music, Betsy failed to hear the cries for help of her friends from outside the door. Betsy walked as if under a spell away from the door toward where the music was leading. The music stopped suddenly, breaking the trance Betsy was under.

Snapping out of it, Betsy instantly remembered the others outside. "Goodness gumdrops, Gloria and the boys!" she said aloud before running back to the door and rushed to open it. Betsy only found their shoes scattered about the ground. As Betsy closed the door in sadness, two birds flew in silently. It was a purple heron and a red bishop. The very same birds that were at the French train station earlier. Ignoring the birds that flew in, Betsy only thought of her friends and the empty shoes outside the door and began to cry. She wondered aloud, "Oh my goodness gumdrops! The trolls have eaten my friends! They're probably saving me for desert because I'm the sweetest. Oh what will I do! Oh boo whoo," Betsy cried as she collapsed to the floor and covered her face.

The red bishop and purple heron appeared once again with only the sound of the flapping of their wings. The red bishop softly landed on Betsy's head.

She then screamed, "Get away, silly bird. Can't you see I'm grieving?" she cried, swishing the bird away.

Then a voice cried out, "I've said it before and I'll say it again, BETSY SASSAFRAS, you have raspberry bubble for brains!" It was Gloria Peekaboo.

As Betsy looked up to meet the voice, she saw Gloria and the boys standing before her. "Oh, goodness me! I thought the trolls ate you all up," Betsy said with surprise. "How did you get in here?"

"We came in through the kitchen window on the other side," replied Chronas.

"The yellow-billed stork showed us the way," explained Philippe."

"But how do you explain your shoes outside the door?" Betsy asked curiously.

"We didn't want to make any noise coming in through the kitchen window," replied Thomas.

"Okay, now are we all filled in, Betsy?" stated Gloria.

"Well I guess so!" Betsy replied, wiping her eyes.

"Great! Now shut your mouth before more of those trolls hear you blabbering on!" Gloria added.

Chronas took Betsy's hand and said "Come on Betsy, just tiptoe."

As they were putting their shoes back on, Philippe noticed the two birds fluttering about in the hallway. Unlike the other birds, these did not make a sound.

"Look Thomas and Chronas, two more birds. Should we follow them?" asked Philippe, pointing. "

"Yes indeed, Philippe. Come on Gloria and Chronas!" cried Thomas.

Behind a dark blue lapis marble column, someone was watching the children. A voice beckoned from within, "Well it seems we have guests." The shadowy figure disappeared from the column, giggling.

The children followed the red bishop and the purple heron down a grand hallway of black and white marble herringbone floor. They were amused by the interiors and giggled, glancing up at the arched ceiling which depicted cherubs chasing dragonflies in a field of irises. As they reached the end of the hallway, there was a magnificent floor to ceiling arched window that overlooked the main garden. Turning the corner of the hallway, the children came upon yet another long hallway. In this section of the château, the floor pattern was in the checkerboard style made of empress green and grey-veined white marble. The arched ceiling, art nouveau in style, was gold-leaf decorated with large emerald green dragonflies that lined the hallway, forming the arch. Underneath each opulent dragonfly against the wall were wheelchairs of different periods. Although there were many doors along the hallway, the birds only perched themselves atop a marble broken base pediment above coffered double doors of mahogany at the end of the hallway. Beneath the marble pediment was a hand carved mahogany medallion of Medusa with seated mermaids on each side. The doorknobs were large polished brass beetles.

As the children reached the ornate doors, Sir Thomas ran up and tried to open them, grabbing on to one of the brass knobs. He was unable to open it.

"Perhaps one needs to turn both at the same time," suggested Philippe.

"Sounds like a good idea," replied Gloria. "Come on, I'll help you, Thomas." Once again, Thomas took hold of the brass beetle door knob, Gloria on the other. "Okay, on my count. Thomas, turn slowly," stated Gloria.

They both began counting together slowly. "Five, four three, two, one," and as the knobs began to move, the doors began to open, opening to reveal a sumptuous drawing room of purple damask walls and empire style furnishing upholstered in hunter green velvet. There were also Greek and Roman-looking marble statues in the room with one holding a sword and another with a bow and arrow. The statues looked as though they were yawning.

The two birds flew in ahead of the children and silently perched themselves atop another pediment at the end of the drawing room. When the children entered the room, they noticed the statues of people in different positions. Thomas looked up at the statues and wondered aloud, "I think they are Roman."

"I've seen statues like this in a museum, but they were nude," added Chronas.

Philippe giggled at Chronas's comment.

"My mother has stuff like this, but they were wearing togas and not modern clothes like these," stated Gloria.

"Oh, banana oil! Who cares," cried Betsy as she spit out her bubble gum and pointed to console tables with bowls of candy on them. Near the statues were gilt wood console tables with large crystal bowls of candy of every kind.

"Well, we could use some energy after a long trip," stated Gloria.

"Oh! I'm dreadfully hungry," cried Thomas.

"Me too!" cried Chronas.

"I guess they wouldn't miss any candy if we took only one piece!" stated Philippe.

The children rushed over to the different consoles in the room and started to stuff their pockets with candy. Seeing the children filling their pockets, the red bishop and the purple heron swooped down off their perch above in a frenzy. They started to squawk and chirp madly above the children's heads.

As he was stuffing candy in his pockets, Sir Thomas heard the birds' erratic squawking and looked over to Philippe. "That's rather strange. The birds have not made a sound since we've been here until now. Could it be the candy?"

"I don't know. Perhaps we should share it with them?" stated Philippe, grinning."

"Are you boys nuts? I'm not sharing anything with those birds!" cried Betsy from the other side of the room. She stuck out her tongue as she was about to put a piece of candy in her mouth. The red bishop swooped down and pecked her hand, knocking the candy away. "Ow, you crazy bird! You made me drop my candy!" she cried.

As Betsy attempted to pick up the candy from the floor, Gloria cried out, "Betsy! Thomas! Philippe! Don't eat the CANDY!

"Why on earth not?" cried Betsy.

"Look at the statues closely! I thought something was funny about these statues after Chronas's remark. I also found pictures of children on the floor. They are about the same age as us!" Gloria added.

In a closer examination of the marble statues, they realized the statues were not yawning but were eating the candy which in turn had turned them all into marble statues. As they emptied their pockets of candy and onto the floor, they discovered more pictures of children scattered about the floor in the room.

"Bow Bumble! These must be the children abducted in the past and the marble statues were their parents!" stated Chronas.

"Yes, searching parents who had located their missing children. Look at the birds! They've stopped squawking," stated Gloria.

The birds once again flew back up to the base pediment above the doorway at the end of the drawing room. The children looked up to where the birds had perched themselves.

"Come on, this door must lead to where Zara is being held," exclaimed Thomas.

As they all ran over to the door, Chronas paused and asked, "One minute guys, I almost forgot something." Running back into the drawing room, Chronas took a pad and pencil from a desk and wrote some-thing down. Then he placed the note on one of the nearby consoles, turned back to join the others, and said, "Okay Thomas, I'm finished. Let's go."

As they opened the doors at the end of the drawing room, they saw double helix stairs made of limestone which led to the tower of the château. There was a sign in the stairwell with fingers pointing in both directions: 'To Le Lune Salle de Nuit (The Moon Night Room)'. The children were baffled.

"Bow Bumble, which stairwell to take?" cried Sir Thomas.

Just as they were still wondering which stairwell to climb, the birds flew in from the drawing room into the stairwell. The purple heron flew up the right stairwell and the red bishop took the left.

"Hey, each bird went up one stairwell!" cried Chronas.

"I know, why don't we just spilt up?" Philippe suggested. "Thomas and Chronas can take the left stairwell and I'll take the right with Gloria and Betsy," he added.

"Wait a minute!" cried Gloria. "I do not want that bubble gum nin-compoop with me!"

"Okay, okay. Thomas could you pleases take Betsy?" asked Phi-lippe.

"Fine with me," he replied. "Okay with you, Chronas?"

"I don't care," he replied. Fine by me, let's just go. Thomas, the birds are leaving us behind."

Splitting up, the children set off on the two sides of the double helix stairs, following the birds. Reaching the second landing of the double helix stairwell, Philippe and Gloria came upon a purple door with the sound of hissing coming from within.

"Oh Gloria, let's just keep walking. It sounds like there is a large snake inside!" cried Philippe.

"But look at the bird, Philippe!" cried Gloria, pointing at the red bishop, which had perched itself above the protruding door frame. "I don't think a bird would rest by a door if it would hear a large snake on the other side. I think it wants us to open up the doors and go in!"

Philippe and Gloria walked over to the purple doors and cautiously tried to open them. The only problem was that it did not have any door knobs. Gloria and Philippe then pushed and pushed on the doors, with no luck.

"Wait a minute, Philippe!" cried Gloria, "I see a doorbell." There was an oval-shaped brass doorbell to the right of the doors that they had not seen before. "Perhaps we are supposed to ring it and someone will come to open it for us?" said Gloria. Standing at a distance, Gloria pressed the doorbell. "That's funny!"

"What's funny?" asked Philippe, puzzled.

"It made no sound," replied Gloria. Gloria pressed the button once again, but again it made no sound. The only sound they could hear was the hissing coming from within, which was now getting louder. "Okay, let's just walk up the stairs, Philippe." She turned to Philippe and pulled his arm.

Turning their backs to the door to walk up the stairs, the purple doors opened to reveal a magnificent steam-powered elevator that was made of solid brass in the art nouveau style. It was not a large snake after all, but the sound of steam. With their mouths open like codfish, Gloria and Philippe entered the elevator with astonishment. Flying in behind them was the red bishop, which perched itself on the brass control lever of the elevator.

Looking at the lever, Philippe leaned in to read the destination directions aloud. "Main floor, up, across, sideways, Moon Night Room. But which one?" Philippe looked over to Gloria, who then turned to the red bishop and repeated the destination points. The red bishop replied with a squawk when Gloria said Moon Night Room.

"Well, then I guess it's up to the Moon Night Room!" Gloria then closed the doors and they went up.

As Thomas' group reached the second landing, there were two carved gilt wood red tapestry salon chairs beside a green door.

"What adorable chairs! Could we sit for a moment? My toes are hurting," cried Betsy.

"No time to rest, Betsy! We have to follow that bird!" stated Thomas.

As they came upon the third floor, Thomas, Chronas, and Betsy heard uproarious laughter coming from behind a red door. The sign above the door read: Théâtre de la Monotoniea (Theatre of monotony). Like the floor below it, there were also another pair of carved gilt wood tapestry salon chairs by the door on both sides, but in green damask. Distracted by the laughter, the children stopped to investigate, letting the purple heron fly up to the next floor. Hearing the joyful laughter coming from within the red door, Chronas was most curious and put his ear to the door and became even more fascinated.

"Whatever it is, it must be very funny!" stated Chronas. Can we go in for a quick second, Thomas?"

"I think it would be okay, Chronas, but just a few seconds," replied Thomas.

"But what about the bird, Thomas? We're supposed to follow it," cried Betsy, pointing toward the purple heron flying up the next floor.

"Oh come on Betsy, let's go in! You'll be able to rest your toes," said Chronas, smiling.

As they approached the red door, Chronas opened it and led them onto a third-floor balcony of an exquisite opera house. The people seated in the theatre were dressed in late 19th century evening attire, which consisted of white tie and tails and ball gowns of various festive colors. As Thomas, Chronas and Betsy proceeded to walk down the red-carpeted aisle looking for seats, a white-gloved, red cap usher approached them. He was elegantly dressed in a red double-breasted jacket with gold buttons.

"Your tickets, if you please," asked the usher, politely.

"Tickets? I'm afraid I don't have tickets," replied Thomas.

Then the usher looked over to Chronas. "Your friends, tickets if you please?" asked the usher once again.

"I'm afraid I don't either!" Chronas replied.

As the usher turned to Betsy, she replied, "No need to ask here, I don't either!"

"Oh, pardon me. You must be a guest of Lady Regina Repetitive."

"Why do you say that, sir?" asked Chronas.

"Because you each said don't in your sentence. Walk this way if you please while I show you to your seats," the usher stated.

Admiring the different textures of red in the theatre, Chronas asked Thomas, "Why did they stop laughing?"

"It must be an intermission," replied Thomas, as they followed the usher.

"How do you know it's the intermission?" asked Betsy, as she looked up at the frolicking gold-leafed cherubs on the ceiling.

"Because we heard them laughing earlier and now they are all seated talking to each other with the curtains closed," Thomas stated.

Sitting in the front row of the balcony was an elegant lady dressed in a lavender gown, wearing elbow length gloves with three vacant seats next to her. "Why good evening, you must be Countless Routine's children. You are quite late, you know! You've missed over 24 intermissions already! No worries my darlings, you are here now," said the lady in lavender.

"Bow Bumble, I've never heard of 24 intermissions before," Thomas cried.

"Never heard of such a thing? Oh you poor dear," exclaimed the lady in lavender. "Allow me to introduce myself. I'm Lady Regina Repetitive."

"Who is that?" whispered Betsy.

"I have no idea," replied Sir Thomas, shrugging his shoulders.

"Let's just play along. We'll get a free show out of this!" stated Chronas, giggling.

"I say, couldn't help overhearing the conversation, but did he just say that he never heard of 24 intermissions?" stated a stout gentleman who was seated behind them.

"Oh, I'm afraid so, Lord Trevor!" replied Lady Regina Repetitive.

"Oh, what a pity, Lady Regina," exclaimed the wife of Lord Trevor who was sitting beside him.

"Oh, I agree dear Lady Terry," replied Lady Regina.

"Well they are in for a most delightful treat because there are 98 more intermissions to go!" cried Lord Trevor smiling at the children. The children looked on with shock on their little faces.

Tapping Lady Regina and addressing her in a soft voice, Thomas asked, "I say, but who was that stout fellow and lady?"

"Why, that's Lord and Lady Tedious of Londinium, the inventors and manufacturers of all the string that gets tangled in things."

"Bow Bumble, I had no idea!" Thomas exclaimed.

As the lights of the theater dimmed, the curtain went up. A musical introduction was presented by a little girl playing a two-headed kazoo. As the young lady left the stage, a man dressed in white tie and tails came out. He bowed to the audience and began his performance by taking two pieces of fruit from his pocket then placing a banana on his head.

"I bought an apple and a banana with one little raisin today. Which one shall I eat first?" exclaimed the man in white tie and tails, comedic rage on his face. Uproarious laughter rang out throughout the theater as the children's mouths hung open in shock.

"Are you okay, Betsy?" asked Chronas.

"Yes I think so, I just wish Gloria was here," she replied.

"Why do you say that?" asked Chronas.

"Because I wouldn't be the only raspberry bubble gum for brains here!" she replied.

"Bow Bumble, I agree with you on that one, Betsy!" Thomas cried.

As the curtains closed for intermission once again, Betsy and Thomas were anxious to leave. "This is our chance, let's go!" cried Betsy.

"Wait, perhaps there's more to come!" stated Chronas.

"I don't know, Chrona. It seems to be frightfully uninteresting," stated Thomas.

"Sir Thomas Tattletale, uninteresting is not the word to describe this," cried Betsy."This is the most boring and tiresome thing I've witnessed!"

Just then, two voices hollered up from the second balcony. "I say, do you want something little girl?" cried a gentleman.

Then another voice cried out asking, "Do I know you, young lady?" Immediately, Lady Regina stood up to reply back to them.

"Oh, you forgive us, Mr. Boring. Just a misunderstanding." She looked over to Countess Theresa Tiresome of Tibet. "So sorry about that mix-up, darling. Tea next Thursday, Countess?" stated Lady Regina as she sat back down, smiling nonchalantly. The commotion settled.

"Come now Betsy, Thomas, it's all not that bad. Perhaps the next act will be different," Chronas stated enthusiastically, smiling. As the lights dimmed and the curtains rose once again, the same little girl came out, but this time she played a tin drum with one drumstick. Leaving the stage, the gentleman in white tie and tails returned again only to repeat the very same lines as before.

Grinding her teeth and turning as red as a tomato, little Miss Betsy Sassafras couldn't take it anymore and yelled out, "Say, Mister, why don't you just add a scoop of chocolate ice cream with that banana and throw away that god awful raisin for heaven's sake!"

The audience gasped in horror at her comment. "I say what a rude little girl!" cried one lady.

"Just the most vulgar thing!" cried another.

"Come on, let's get out of here, Chronas! Thomas, come on," cried Betsy.

"I thought it was going to be different!" exclaimed Chronas.

With that said, the children jumped from their seats and high-tailed it toward the red door from where they had entered. Upon reaching the red door, the children were met with an unpleasant surprise. They did not realize there were two other identical doors right beside it, and they couldn't remember from which one they had come.

"Bow bumble. Gloria, Chronas, which one did we come in from?" cried Sir Thomas.

"I don't know!" said Chronas, baffled as the others.

"Thomas, let's just pick one!" cried Betsy. Opening the first door, they saw a kitchen with a ghastly troll eating raw fish. Closing the door quickly, Betsy recommended the other door. "Let's try the next one!" she stated.

As everyone looked at her, Chronas reached out to open the other door, "Ok I'll open this one." As Chronas opened the second door, the purple heron flew out of it and perched itself on the third door, a sign above the door said: To The Moon Night Room.

"Well, that must be our door!" Chronas exclaimed.

Opening the third door, they saw a magnificent wooden spiral staircase with what looked like wedges cut into the steps.

"Oh for heavens grape juice, more steps!" cried Gloria.

Painted in yellow a sign in the hallway read: Hold onto banister firmly. Reading the sign, the children were baffled, "Perhaps the steps are in need of repair," stated Thomas.

As Chronas and Betsy started to climb the steps to test to see if they were stable, Chronas cried, "Say, they are not wobbly nor broken at all Thomas!"

"Wait a minute, Chronas. I see a blue button just below the banister. Should I press it?" asked Thomas.

"Why not, we have nothing to lose!" cried Betsy.

As Sir Thomas pressed the button, the steps began to move upward. "I say, these are mechanical steps!" cried Sir Thomas. It was a wooden escalator.

"Hurry, Thomas. Get on!" cried Chronas and Betsy.

Thomas ran and jumped onto the wooden escalator.

Thomas and his friends were finally en route to the Moon Night Room. They were enjoying the mechanized stairs when the escalator stopped abruptly at the floor of The Moon Night Room. The children immediately jumped off, exiting through a magnificent La belle époque-style revolving door onto a Persian-carpeted hallway. In the middle of the hallway was a statue of the Baroness in marble with her arms extended. Directly across from it were two large French gothic doors which led into the Moon Night Room. Flying out through revolving doors was the purple heron, which silently perched on the head of the statue. At the end of the hallway were art nouveau sliding doors decorated with Egyptian water lilies and golden beetles.

The children stood in the middle of the hallway and heard a strange sound coming from the doors. "Say! What is that sound?" asked Chronas.

"It's coming from those doors!" replied Betsy, pointing her finger at the doors.

"It sounds like a radiator," replied Thomas.

"Yeah! It also smells like one," cried Betsy, holding her nose.

Just then, the doors slid open, the red bishop flying out down the hallway and landing on one of the arms of the statue. Gloria and Philippe popped out through the doors.

"Why, hello there!" cried Betsy.

"Hey, you made it up here at the same time we did!" Chronas beamed upon seeing his friends.

"How was your trip up?" asked Sir Thomas.

"Don't ask! I'm never taking this elevator again," cried Gloria.

"Why do you say that?" asked Chronas, curiously.

"Because it took us forever to reach the top of this floor, that's why!"

They all turned to face the doors of the Moon Night Room. Seeing that the large doors were too heavy for one person to open, they decided to work together by pushing on it together. Opening the doors, the children entered the Moon Night Room. "Oh, what a darling room!" Betsy said, twirling in circles.

"You should have thrown your birthday party here, Gloria," cried Betsy as she stuffed two pieces of blueberry bubble gum into her mouth.

Gloria turned to her and gave her a dirty look. The first thing Thomas noticed in the room was Zara tied to a chair. Running over to her, Thomas tried to untie her as fast as he could. "Are you okay, Zara? Your friends led us here!"

"Oh, Thomas! I'm so glad to see you, but be careful. The Baroness is as cruel as she is beautiful," said Zara. The two birds flew in quietly and perched themselves on two separate brass rods that held the medieval tapestries in place. Seeing the birds fly in, Zara was overjoyed and greeted each by their names. She looked at the red bishop. "Oh thank you, Coco." With a smile, she then thanked Miranda, the purple heron.

There was a loud bang as the French gothic doors closed. They turned around to see the Baroness standing in front of them, smiling. To the side of the room, rubbing his hands together and seated in his wheelchair was the Baron, accompanied by 20 ghastly trolls.

The Children gasped in horror. "Why, grand aunty, you have quite a charming place," Sir Thomas said with a stutter.

"Well, well welll! If it isn't my favorite grandnephew and his adorable little friends," cried the Baroness Giggle von Tickle, wickedly.

"You've been most hospitable, but we really should be going now," said Sir Thomas, holding Zara's hand firmly.

"Going? Why, you've just gotten here, my lovely little coconuts!" she exclaimed. "I see you did not like Medusa's candy in our drawing room," stated the Baroness.

"That was most unfortunate, my dearest Arborvitae," stated Baron Von Tickle, looking over to his wife."

"And I see you are not into grand entertainment either," stated the Baroness.

"It just wasn't our cup of tea," stated Betsy with a grin.

"Why, not only are you enchanting, but witty too. How delightful. I do think that the Baron and I could entertain you much better here in our charming Moon Night Room."

When the Baroness and the Baron looked at the ghastly trolls, they ran to try and grab the children, who ran in different directions. They tied the children up in chairs.

Chronas yelled over to Zara, "Zara, I have your box!" He quickly slid it over to her on the floor, but a troll grabbed it midway and handed it over to the Baroness.

"Well, well! What do we have here?" asked the Baroness. "Could this be a box of enchanted magic to kill my dear sweet husband and I?"

She gripped the box, trying to open it. Unable to do so, the Baroness turned to the children. "Well, my dear little friends of Zara Zuckerman, I think not!"

The Baroness threw the box into the fireplace, laughing impishly as Zara and Thomas began to cry.

"My ghastly trolls, do make sure our guest are tied well," she said. Thomas and Zara looked on with anguish as the ornate box snapped and crackled in the fire. Zara's animals were no more. The trolls had huddled them together.

"Excuse me, Chronas, but why are they crying?" asked Betsy."

Because the animals come to life for Zara when she is in need of help. But now it is too late, as they have been burned to a crisp," stated Chronas, as he also began to cry.

"No, they not, silly gander goose!" replied Betsy.

"What do you mean, they are not?" cried Philippe.

"It's just what I said. They are not dead, silly! They are back in the motorcar," stated Betsy.

"Back in the motorcar?" asked Chronas, with amazement.

"Yes, remember when you had to go potty?" she asked, looking at Chronas.

"Yes…" replied Chronas.
"Well, I switched the animals into Gloria's extra marbles bag. I thought they would be more comfortable in there than in that old stuffy box."

"But what did you do with all those marbles?" asked Chronas."

"Oh, I put them in your box," replied Betsy.

"By golly gum, that's why the box felt heavier!" He looked over to Thomas in amazement.

"Bow bumble! Gloria, do you still have your slingshot?" asked Thomas.

"Yes I do, but it's in my back pocket and my hands are tied. I can't reach it!" Gloria answered in desperation.

"The marbles should fall through the box at any moment!" said Betsy with excitement. "Oh, what wonderful news. Thank you, Betsy, for your fast thinking!" said Zara.

"Fast thinking? No, I just wanted them for myself to play with later!" she replied, giggling.

With her hands folded behind her back, the Baroness looked over at the children to see which one would dance first and said, "Well, well. Now, which one shall I choose to dance for the Baron and me, first?"

CHAPTER 10
Dance of the Innocent

"Why, what a lovely place you have here, dear Baroness. It's just most unfortunate that we have to be tied up like this," stated Betsy, with a pout.

"Oh dear, where are my manners? My ghastly trolls, do come and untie our most charming guest," said the Baroness with a most unsettling grin.

After being untied, Betsy whispered over to Chronas, "I think she's off her nut."

"Well, well! What a charming little girl and adorable little boy. Perhaps you'll like to be the first to dance for the Baron and me," said the Baroness, maliciously.

"Is she talking about us?" whispered Chronas to Betsy.

"Why, indeed I am, my little angels," replied the Baroness. Turning toward Betsy, she continued, "Oh, and I do like cashews."

"Betsy!" cried Chronas. "She heard you what you whispered to me!"

"Click und Snap, crank up the gramophone!" cried the Baroness, as she grabbed them both by the arms and led them toward the gramophone player. As the music began to play, it sounded like 'Stumbling' by Zez Confrey. The Baroness clapped her hands and instructed them to begin. "Around and around you go, my dearest hearts," she sang as she giggled with maniacal joy.

"This isn't so bad after all," stated Betsy, still chewing bubble gum as she and Chronas began to dance around the gramophone player.

"Come on, let's go faster," cried Chronas, giggling.

As they did, Betsy started to giggle, and then they both started laughing. As they made a third turn around the ornate two horned gramophone player, something started to go wrong. The Baron was neither feeling nor looking younger, but was short of breath and shook back and forth in his wheelchair.

"My dearest, are you okay?" asked the Baroness.

The Baron clenched his chest in pain and replied, "If my ears do not deceive me, my little arborvitae, I hear the faint sounds of chewing gum and ticking of that of a clock."

Putting her hand to her ear the baroness could also hear it. "This must be the source of the problem," she cried. "Click und Snap! Stop them at once!" the Baroness added with anxiety. "Hold them fast, Click und Snap, while I conduct a closer examination of these two."

Zara, Thomas, and the others still sat tied to the little Victorian chairs, and looked on with amazement.

Approaching Betsy first, the Baroness asked, "Dear child, are you chewing gum?"

"Oh indeed I am, do you care for a piece?" she replied, smiling.

"No! I most certainly do not, young lady," cried the Baroness angrily. "You are to spit it out immediately, you dreadful little girl!"

Spitting onto the floor, Betsy just smiled and curtseyed.

Then, turning to Chronas, the Baroness asked, "Are you carrying a pocket watch, young man?"

Chronas replied politely. "Oh no, but my father has a very nice one. It's made out of gold!"

The Baroness was getting impatient with every passing minute. "Never mind about your father. What is that ticking sound?" she exclaimed.

"It's my heart," he replied, smiling.

"Your heart, you say?" asked the Baroness, puzzled. Putting her ear to Chronas' chest, the Baroness could hear the ticking. She looked closely and noticed a silver chain around his neck with a brass key on it. "Now what is this key for?" she asked curiously.

"Oh! It's for my heart. I have a French carriage clock for a heart and the key is to wind it every 12 hours or I shall go to sleep."

Turning to her husband with a most ghastly grimace on her face she stated, "Well, well! Francoise it seems we have a magic clock in our possession!" With a cold gaze, the Baroness snatched the key from around Chronas' neck.

"Give it back, give it back!" cried Chronas.

"You are a horrible lady, give it back," cried Gloria.

Holding Chronas by the arm, the Baroness twirled the chain with the key on it, then placed it in her vest pocket. Turning to her husband, she said, "Oh my dearest Francois, I'm afraid these children are of no good to us."

"You know what to do, my little arborvitae. Untie the other two quickly, my love. There is not much time left," the Baron cried to the Baroness.

The Baroness then called in more of her ghastly trolls. "My ghastly trolls of the night, bring in the purple steamer trunk."

The trolls immediately complied and brought in a large purple steamer trunk that they placed on the side of the room. The Baroness then told Click und Snap to throw the children into it. Click und Snap then grabbed them both by the arm and dragged them to the purple steamer trunk. Hearing this, Betsy struggled and broke free of Click und Snap, then ran back over to the Baroness.

Betsy grabbed the Baroness around the waist and pleaded with tears in her eyes. "Oh please, dear Baroness, have mercy on me! I am afraid of the dark and small spaces."

The Baroness looked at her chauffeur with disgust in her voice and said, "Click und Snap, do get this dreadful child off of me."

Grabbing her once again by the arm, Click und Snap dragged her off to the purple steamer and threw her and Chronas both into it.

Back at the Paris police station, arriving within the hour, Mr. Almondbrittle was furious upon entering the police station. "I demand to see the captain!" Nicolas Almondbrittle exclaimed. "On what grounds do you have the right to hold my client?" he asked.

An officer replied, "Monsieur Almondbrittle, not only do we have a witness to the event, but the witness himself was assaulted by Fanny."

"With only one witness out of hundreds of people in attendance at the night club and with no medical records to indicate such an assault on your witness, I do indeed smell a rat!" exclaimed Nicholas Almondbrittle, with a frown.

"Monsieur Almondbrittle, the laws in this kingdom are quite different from the Kingdom of San Francisco," the officer replied.

"Indeed they are!" interrupted an elderly lady elegantly wrapped in an ermine coat. As those very words were uttered, the entire police station went silent. Walking in gracefully, the lady took off her fur and laid it over her arm. As she did, one could see a large emerald and diamond brooch shaped like a dragonfly pinned to the shoulder of her the gown. It seemed to move about her dress. "So, dear captain, who could have made such an accusation?" The elegant lady put her hand on her hip.

"A Baron Françoise von Chatouiller, your Serene Highness. He's one of our most respected pillars of the community!" replied the captain.

"Oh really? I did not know that the Baron had any authority in this territory to merit such a complaint," she replied. She then added, "Respected? Pillar of the community? Indeed! You are to release the young lady at once."

"Right away, your Serene Highness!" exclaimed the police captain, bowing his head.

Nicolas and Fanny were curious as to who could this grand lady possibly be. The elderly lady immediately approached Fanny and said, "Come quickly, my child. There are people waiting for you outside." Taking Fanny's hand, the elderly lady escorted her and Nicolas out of the police station.

Parked in front of the station was a magnificent purple 1919 Bellanger limousine. The chauffeur standing at attention wore a long striped winter scarf wrapped around his face. Seated in the automobile was a Caribbean-looking gentleman dressed in a high collar and bowler hat. A young girl in pigtails sat beside him, and on the opposite side sat a young boy dressed in a black velvet Fauntleroy style suite with a large lace collar. The boy had long curled black hair and was holding a croquet mallet. His appearance looked like that of a marionette. In the seat next to the chauffeur in front sat a stout lady crying and blowing her nose. Tied to the roof of the limousine was a large toy sailing boat with little red wheels and in it sat a pudgy little boy dressed in a sailor suit wearing boxing gloves. He had a hysterical look on his face as he waved his hands over to Fanny and Nicolas.

The chauffeur greeted them joyously as they approached. "Bonsoire Madame et Monsieur! So happy we are safe!" He clapped his hands and hopped up and down. Then, he unraveled his long wool scarf to reveal a face of a silver tabby cat. He then properly introduced himself. "My name is Mercredi," he stated, bowing his head.

A little taken aback, Nicolas and Fanny turned to the grand elderly lady with questioning looks. The elegant elderly lady took Aunt Fanny's hand and explained to her, "Whatever you see before you is not to startle you, dear child. We are but friends." She then proceeded to explain the situation her nephew was in. "I fear your little nephew is in grave danger, dear Fanny. I sadly cannot travel into the territory of Chatouiller because my powers are limited there, but I do have some friends that could help you."

Almondbrittle had been looking on in surprise and understood that they were with helpful friends. "With all due respect, madam, to whom do we have the pleasure of addressing?"

"Forgive me, I'm Princess Penelope Papillion de Champagne," the elderly lady replied gracefully.

Looking over with curiosity at the two boys in the automobile, Fanny clenched her hands together in anticipation and asked The Princess, "Are you the Princess of Toy Land?"

"Oh no, my child. I am most certainly not," she replied politely.

Interrupting the princess, the little pudgy boy in the boat lashed to the automobile's roof yelled out. "Are you daft, lady? That's the Witch of Champagne!" he said with cackling laughter.

"Shut up! Punch, I'll knock your head off with my croquet mallet!" cried the other boy in the automobile in the large lace collar.

"Not if I take off my head and throw it at your porcelain face, Smash!" replied the little pudgy boy.

Fanny and Nicolas were a bit startled by the children. The elderly lady interrupted the two bickering and said, "Smash, put that mallet down, and Punch, put your head back on! We have guests and you are both being quite rude!" cried Princess Penelope.

"Yes, Princess," replied the two boys, with somber faces.

"Do forgive us, Fanny and Nicolas. The Gauduchon brothers can be a bit trying sometimes, but they mean well."

"Princess, who are the other people in the motorcar, may I ask?" stated Nicolas Almondbrittle.

"Mercredi, if you please," asked Princess Penelope. The chauffeur then opened the door for the Clockwork family. "Fanny, Nicolas, allow me to introduce you to Mr. Charles Clockwork and his daughter Seven from Chicago. Your nephew Thomas is with his son Chronas."

A little girl popped out of the motorcar first with skin the color of chocolate milk and hair pulled back into pigtails. With a curtsy, the little girl introduced herself, "Hello! My name is Seven. Are you here to help us find my little brother?" she asked.

"Oh, I do hope so, Seven," replied Aunt Fanny.

Seven held Fanny's hand as she introduced her father. "This is my father."

"Indeed a pleasure, Fanny. I'm Charles. We lost our Chronas at the train station at the same time you lost your nephew. We've been frantic ever since," he said with anxiety.

"Well, it's good to know that we have something in common," Fanny stated with a smile. Then she turned around to introduced Nicholas to Chronas's father. "Mr. Clockwork, this is Nicolas Almondbrittle, one of my dearest friends."

Charles leaned forward to shake hands with Nicolas. "Pleased to meet you, Mr.Clockwork. Just call me Charles."

Both exchanged cordial smiles.

"Well, I've met everyone except one," Fanny said, looking over to the automobile at the stout lady dressed in black, wearing a tricorn hat. She was still crying.

"Oh! That's Ms. Gazoontite, Zara's Governess. I'll run and get her!" exclaimed Seven.

"The poor dear was just heartbroken when she found out Zara was kidnapped right from under her," stated Princess Penelope.

Walking over to console Ms. Gazoontite, Seven gently put her arm around her. Ms. Gazoontite was overwhelmed with guilt and said in a thick German accent, whimpering, "I am a failure and I've lost my little angel."

"Ms. Gazoontite, there's no need to cry now. There are people here to help us find Zara and my little brother," said Seven. After she had wiped her eyes and blew her nose, Seven gently took Ms. Gazoontite by the hand and escorted her over to Fanny and Nicolas. "This is Ms. Gazoontite," Seven said politely.

Ms. Gazoontite said, "Why hello, you must forgive me, Zara was like my own child, you see. I was informed that your child went to rescue her," she stated.

"Oh now don't you worry! We are here now to help you find her and my nephew," exclaimed Fanny.

"My darlings, enough chitter-chatter. Time is of the essence. The children were headed toward Le Château du Chatouiller in Bois de Boulogne, the home of Baron and Baroness Von Tickle (Le Baron et Baroness du Chatouiller). Do you have transportation, Monsieur Almondbrittle?" asked the Princess as she brought Aunt Fanny up to date with the events.

Nicolas was listening to her intently and replied, "I do Princess!"

"Magnificent. The clockwork family and Ms. Gazoontite will travel with you then!" she exclaimed.

Hearing a bizarre humming sound coming from the police station, both Fanny and Nicolas turned around to look and saw that it was covered with hundreds of large dragonflies. Then, as they turned back to the limousine, to their surprise they saw that it was no longer there. In its place was the Clockwork family and Ms. Gazoontite.

"Charles! Seven! Ms. Gazoontite! Where did Princess Penelope's limousine go?" asked Fanny in amazement.

"It doesn't make any sound!" shared Seven, with a giggle and shrugging her shoulders.

"No sound? How is that possible!" exclaimed Nicolas.

"Because it runs on Champagne, that's why," replied Ms. Gazoontite.

"Oh, I see well. I guess that answers my question," stated Nicolas with confusion on his face as he looked over to Fanny.

"Well, then folks, to the Bois de Boulogne!" cried Fanny, as they all jumped in the automobile and raced off.

"Well, well, it seems that we now only have four real adorable little peaches left," cried the Baroness. Turning to her trolls, she instructed, "Untie the next two, my ghastly trolls."She addressed Gloria and Philippe. "Would you do us the honor of joining us on the dance floor?"

Philippe, frightened of the Baroness, screamed out, "Never, you horrible old lady!" He held Gloria in his arms.

"Need I remind you young man, that I am not that old, but I can be quite horrible," the Baroness stated, with crackling laughter. "My ghastly trolls of the night, take this purple steamer trunk and throw it into the pond in the garden and make sure it sinks to the bottom!" she said to the trolls.

Gloria and Philippe looked at each other with despair. "Okay!" they pleaded. "We shall dance for you, but please spare our friends!"

Inside the dark steamer trunk, Chronas spoke to Betsy. "Say, why are you so calm? I thought you were afraid of the dark and small spaces."

"I lied!" she replied, giggling.

"By golly gum, are you still chewing gum? I thought that was the last piece you had," he asked Betsy.

"Yep, it was," Betsy replied.

But Chronas could hear in her voice that Betsy had something in her mouth. "Well, what do you have in your mouth? I can hear something in your mouth," he cried.

"Okay Chronas, just hold your hand out," she said mischievously.

"What!" replied Chronas

"Just hold out your hand, silly soda pop!" Betsy said.

Chronas held his hand out as Betsy spit out the silver chain with the brass key on it.

"By golly gum, how did you get it back, Betsy?" Chronas asked, ecstatic.

"Let's just say that I'm a very good actress and a great pickpocket," Betsy replied giggling as she gave Chronas a kiss on the cheek.

Chronas rubbed his cheek and asked Betsy, "Why did you do that?"

"Because you are a good dancer," she replied with a warm giggle. "Thank you, Betsy!" replied Chronas.

Back on the dance floor with sorrow in their eyes, Gloria and Philippe said their last words to each other. "Are you afraid, dear Philippe?" asked Gloria.

"Not at all, as long as I'm with you," he replied lovingly.
With that said, they slowly began to dance around the gramophone player.

"Come now children, a little faster!" cried the Baroness as she turned to help Francois from his wheelchair.

As the children were dancing, the Baron and the Baroness joined, dancing counter clockwise around them. In doing this, the Baron felt much better and he even started to giggle a bit. "A perfect match, my dearest Arborvitae!" he cried happily.

"Indeed they are, if I may say so myself," the Baroness replied with joy as they danced around the children, laughing.

As the children made the third turn around the gramophone player ,Gloria's boot got stuck on something which caused the children to trip and fall to the floor. The children were having fun and still laughing hysterically. Philippe asked Gloria, "What did you get stuck on?"

"I don't know," Gloria replied, looking around as she crawled back to her boot, pulling it off the floor to look underneath her boot. "Why, it's Betsy's bubble gum!" she cried.

As the children stumbled and fell, so did the Baron and Baroness von Tickle. The Baroness was furious and she screamed, "Ah you fools, get up this very instant!" The Baroness was frantic with the Baron lying on top of her on the floor. "Oh, my dearest Pineapple! Are you okay, my love? Shall I put you back in your wheelchair?" she asked the Baron.

"I'm just a little winded, my arborvitae. We don't have much time left, just get rid of those two," the Baron cried feverishly.

"Click und Snap, collect these two imbeciles and throw them in the Silent Green Steamer Trunk," the Baroness cried. The Baroness then turned to her trolls. "My ghastly trolls, do untie our featured guests quickly, as we have no time to waste!"

Gloria then screamed at the Baroness. "Who are you calling an imbecile, lady!" She kicked around while Click und Snap dragged her and Philippe to the green steamer trunk.

Philippe then said, "Wait, Gloria. I have an idea!" Immediately, he turned toward Thomas and Zara and yelled just in time before he and Gloria were thrown into the silent green steamer trunk, "Thomas, Zara, laugh backwards!"

"Laugh backwards?" Thomas and Zara both wondered as they looked at each other.

"Ah yes! It almost sounds like a donkey!" Just try it with me when I do it!" stated Zara. As Thomas and Zara walked up to the two-horned gramophone player, they began to dance.

The Baroness heard an annoying sound from the ceiling as they started to join the children during the dance. "What is that annoying sound?" she cried, looking up at the tapestries that circled the room. It was the red bishop and the purple heron. They were pecking on the bass rods holding up the tapestries. "Oh, it's those insipid birds again. No time for this nonsense!" Still dancing, she asked the trolls, "Dear trolls, after Thomas and Zara have finished dancing, do climb up there and get rid of those horrid creatures!"

As they were dancing, Thomas whispered over to Zara. "Zara, I found this by your governess, Ms. Gazoontite."

Zara looked at it and said, "It is a perfume atomizer. I think this may give us some time."

As Thomas and Zara circled the gramophone player dancing hand in hand, Zara held the bottle while Thomas held the squeeze ball. Around and around they went, spraying the mysterious substance in the air. Thomas asked Zara, "Bow Bumble, nothing is happening. Am I doing something wrong, Zara?"

Zara was calm and she said, "I don't know, Thomas. Just keep spraying it!"

The Baron and Baroness were dancing counter-clockwise around the children when the Baron smelled something peculiar and said, "Why do I smell potato chips, my love!"

The Baroness' first thought was that one of the trolls had farted, but then she smelled barbeque sauce. "I smell it too, my dearest pineapple, but it smells more like barbecue dipped potato chips," she exclaimed.

Just then, a troll sneezed with the slowly spreading smell in the room. "I say, cover your mouth, ghastly troll!" cried the Baroness, angrily.

The smell was overpowering by now, and it had reached the far corners of the room. The ghastly troll sneezed once again, but turned his head and sneezed onto one of the little Victorian chairs. Then another troll sneezed across the room and then another! The Baron looked around in surprise at the trolls sneezing one after another. "That's strange, my love. I thought trolls couldn't catch colds."

The Baroness was equally amazed, but she was wickedly clever and said, "No, they cannot, my Pineapple, unless magic is used!" Realizing that it was Zara and Thomas, she turned toward them and fiercely said, "You little monsters! Just you wait until I get my hands on you!"

But the Baron thought that it was better if they continued and said, "Don't stop dancing, my little arborvitae. They will be turned into ghastly trolls soon enough!"

Sir Thomas and Zara were dancing close to the Baron and the Baroness and upon hearing the Baron's comment, they began to worry. Sir Thomas asked Zara, "Bow Bumble! What will we do, Zara? We are going to be changed into ghastly trolls."

Just then, the little Victorian chairs began to move. They started to move like bolting horses running about the room. The trolls tripped up as they tried to catch them. Sir

Thomas felt a funny sensation and said to Zara, "Zara, I feel funny, as if there are bubbles in my stomach." They made a second turn around the gramophone player and the feeling increased as Thomas began to giggle.

"Thomas, don't giggle! Look at me and take a deep breath, then repeat after me!" exclaimed Zara.

"EEEH AAAW. EEHAAW!" Zara started to laugh like a donkey to show Sir Thomas what to do.

Thomas then took a deep breath and he also began to laugh like a donkey.

Still dancing around them, the Baroness cried out, "What is the meaning of this? Stop this nonsense right now, you little monsters!"

It seemed Philippe's idea was working. In the arms of the Baroness, the Baron started to lose his hair. The three-legged wooden pedestal that held the ornate gramophone player also began to move, and then smashed to the floor. The Baron and Baroness ran over to the gramophone with dented horns on the floor. They tried to put it back together but to no avail. Not only was the wooden base cracked, but the record was shattered to pieces.

At this point, the Baron was feeling sick and was growing worse. He collapsed into the Baroness' arms. "My dearest arborvitae, it's not working! I can hardly stand up."

"No, my dearest Francoise!" she cried vehemently as they both fell to the floor, the Baron in her arms. Francois took his last breath, grabbing his chest in pain, before turning to ashes. The Baron Francois von Tickle was no more.

The Baroness screamed in pain. "You've killed my poor sweet husband, you little monsters!" she cried in anguish.

Sir Thomas was surprised that the Baroness still looked the same and said, "I say! How come you did not turn into ashes?"

The Baroness replied, "Because, dear boy, my curse is quite different!"

Sir Thomas was taken aback with surprise, "Bow Bumble!"

Then, the Baroness turned toward the trolls. "My ghastly trolls of the night, open up the balcony windows." As the ghastly trolls opened up the French doors to the balcony, a flock of birds flew in and landed on all of the brass rods that held the tapestries in the room. As they landed, they began to copy the pecking motion of the red bishop and purple heron. The Baroness was now vengeful and turned toward her butler. With a menacing tone, she said, "Dear Click und Snap, grab our charming guests and throw them off the balcony to the concrete below!" Hearing the Baroness' horrific orders, the birds started to bang louder and faster on the brass rods. "Oh, the noise of these creatures is driving me mad!" cried the Baroness, covering her ears. She then summoned her trolls for a new order. "My ghastly trolls of the night, you may dispose of those dreadful creatures immediately!"

The ghastly trolls began to climb the medieval astrological tapestries. The children screamed as Click und Snap picked them up and headed for the balcony. As he did, he heard a creaking sound from inside the room. Click und Snap paused in his tracks, holding the children underneath his arms and looked up to the tapestries. It was the brass rods that were giving way under the weight of the trolls crawling up on them. The birds were not just making noise to annoy or distract the Baroness but were loosening the screws that held the brass beams in place. The medieval tapestries came crashing down to the floor one by one to reveal magnificent 18th century gilded pier mirrors. The ghastly trolls were all trapped underneath the fallen tapestries.

The Baroness then happened to gaze upon her beauty in the mirrors and started to adjust her hair. As she did, she began to change and in fright, she screamed, "No, no, you horrid birds!" She covered her face. With this, the Baroness' voice began to change and her beautiful hair began to fall out. Her stomach started to bloat, popping all the pearl buttons on her vest.

The children looked on in horror as the Baroness removed her hands from her face to reveal a ghastly complexion of bluish-green. The children were aghast at this revelation. "Bow Bumble! That's why the Baroness did not turn to ashes as her husband did. She was a troll herself!" cried Sir Thomas.

"Well, well. I must say, what a brilliant observation!" cried the Baroness, with a scratchy voice. As the ghastly trolls made their way out of the fallen tapestries, they looked over to the Baroness and started to call her Mama, holding out their arms.

"Oh shut up! I'm not your mother!" screamed the Baroness with disdain toward the ghastly trolls. "As you can see, my dear Thomas Tattletale, my curse was very different," she cried with crackling laughter.

Before Lady Galina Cruikshank was a Baroness, and after inheriting the Cruikshank family fortune in 1914, she threw lavish parties in Paris and Londinium. One night after a dinner party, she was visited by a Troll Princess by the name of Eliana. The Troll Princess asked if she may have but one dance at one of her parties as she could only be human for one night a year. In exchange, the Troll Princess promised a six strand pearl choker with a large emerald centerpiece surrounded by diamonds to Galina. She requested for one stipulation, according to which Galina should cover all the pier mirrors in the ballroom. Galina Cruikshank agreed to the request.

The next night, Galina was set to throw a large party for a handsome publisher, whom she fancied. The publisher was from England by the name of Lord Titus Tattletale.

As the night approached and the guests arrived in Edwardian splendor, Galina searched for the arrival of The Troll Princess but she was nowhere to be seen. Disappointed, she went to look for her guest of honor Lord Titus Tattletale and was also unable to find him. As Galina walked along the hallway in search, she heard laughter and modern music, ragtime in style, coming from the ballroom. Walking down the hallway, she opened up the French doors into the ballroom. As she entered, she saw her guests were dancing in a large circle, hand in hand around a gramophone player. She noticed that with Lord Titus with a beautiful woman dressed in a purple evening gown, dancing. She seemed to be laughing and enjoying herself. Seeing this, Galina began to laugh, and taking a dance partner, she joined in on the merriment.

As she came closer circling around Lord Titus, she noticed the necklace of the lady who was dancing with Lord Tattletale. It was very necklace that the Troll Princess had spoken about, a six strand pearl choker with a large emerald centerpiece surrounded by diamonds. It was, in fact, the Troll Princess. Upon witnessing the necklace, Galina's joyful demeanor changed into jealousy and hatred. "How could this be? Trolls are ugly!" Galina thought what she could possibly do. Looking around the ballroom, Galina thought for a moment. She began to run around the ballroom, laughing ripping down all the covers from the pier mirrors. Upon removing all the covers, she stood in the middle of the ballroom, as she had an announcement to make. "Ladies and gentlemen, may I have your attention. Look upon my mirrors at the most beautiful woman in the room." The guests all stood silently in horror as they gazed upon the reflection of the lady in the purple gown in the pier mirrors. She was, in fact, a monstrous troll, but her true form was visible only in the reflection of the mirror. Horrified, all guests quickly but silently left the party without even thanking their host. In the middle of the dance floor, the Troll Princess sat alone on the floor, covering her face as she cried distressfully with heartache. "There is no need to cry about this, my lovely," stated Galina as she approached her. Then she deviously added, "You never specified when I should uncover the mirrors, dearest. I'm just so very sorry about that. Now then I believe you owe me something." Galina then held her hand out toward the Troll Princess for the necklace.

Still crying, the Troll Princess gracefully took off her necklace and as she did, two tears fell upon the emerald in the necklace. She handed it over to Galina, then spoke her last words, casting a spell, "Remember this! You shall never more feel the ravage of time upon your soul, so long as you never gaze upon your beauty ever more in a pier mirror." Then, the Troll Princess disappeared through the French doors of the ballroom.

The Baroness spoke to the children. "Now my dearest Thomas and lovely Zara, I must bid you both farewells. Click und Snap, you may now throw them off the balcony."

"Please let us go, Click und Snap, please!" Zara cried as he walked over onto the balcony with her and Thomas under his arms.

Nicolas Almondbrittle's motorcar was racing up to the château with Fanny and Charles Clockwork, ready to get out in a frenzy. As they approached, they looked up to the balcony and saw Thomas and Zara from the balcony. Fanny began to scream hysterically as the motorcar screeched to a halt.

When Thomas saw his aunt below, he cried out, "Aunt Fanny! Aunt Fanny, help us!"

"Oh, my little coconut! We'll be right there, my love," cried Aunt Fanny as they all ran into the Château.

"Oh, my angel!" cried Ms. Gazoontite.

Just then, Thomas remembered something that Sir Henry Humphrey had mentioned at the dinner table to the Baron back at Tattletale Manor. He immediately shouted and pleaded to the butler, "Prince Henrik! Please put us down."

With that said, Click und Snap paused and put them down, grabbing his head in confusion.

"You fool, what are you doing? Don't listen to them. Throw them off the balcony this very instant!" cried the Baroness.

"Prince Henrik, you say, boy?" asked Click und Snap, still dazed.

"Why yes, that is your name, Prince Henrik von Schnapps! You used to own The Von Schnapps Motorcar Company, but were in a terrible accident along with my father and mother." Thomas looked at Baroness and pointed toward her before continuing. "Somehow, the Baron and Baroness acquired your company."

Click und Snap then came out of the trance. Apprehending what he was doing, he remembered the entire episode of the accident. "Please forgive me, Thomas and Zara. Danke mien freund."

Looking over to the grotesque physique of the now monstrous Baroness limping toward them, Prince Henrik asked her, "Is this true, Baroness?"

"Indeed it is, my dear poor broken Prince, I am the one who sabotaged your motorcar that day. It worked out perfectly for the Baron and me, you know.

The Baron would acquire your company through your misfortune and I would move a bit closer to inheriting the Tattletale publishing fortune," she added, nonchalantly.

"You killed my father!" cried Sir Thomas, with anguish.

"I'm afraid so, my scrumptious little apple," the Baroness replied with a smile.

"Just you wait until I tell mummy of this," cried Sir Thomas.

"I'm afraid, Sir Thomas, this will be one tattle you will not be telling dear boy!" cried the Baroness with ghastly laughter. As they all stood at the edge of the balcony with nowhere to go, the Baroness lunged at them to push them all off. Prince Henrik quickly pushed the children to the side as the Baroness and Prince Henrik Von Schnapps went over the balcony's edge to the concrete below.

Meanwhile in the Purple Steamer trunk, Chronas' special key had opened the locked trunk from inside. "Say, how did you do that?" asked Betsy as they exited the trunk.

"I'll tell you later. Let's just get Gloria and Philippe out of their trunk!" stated Chronas Clockwork.

Running over to the silent green steamer trunk, Chronas knocked on the trunk and shouted, "Hello Gloria, Philippe, are you okay in there?" There was no answer. Betsy decided to kick the steamer trunk, but still there was no answer. Betsy said, "I think they've suffocated and collapsed already!"

"By golly! You are so silly, Betsy!" It is called a Silent Steamer trunk because it is sound proof from the inside. In other words, they cannot hear us!" answered Chronas.

"How do you know that?" asked Betsy, to be sure.

"Because they make them back home in Chicago!" explained Chronas.

Placing his special key into the peephole of the lock, Chronas tapped it three times as the lid popped open.

"Chronas, thank you!" cried Gloria as she popped out of the trunk with Philippe.

"Oui Oui Merci mon ami," cried Philippe as they both hugged him. Chronas then said, "You should thank Betsy because she got the key from the Baroness!"

Betsy stood with hands behind her back, twisting back and forth grinning.

"Holy apple juice in the morning!" cried Gloria, amazed at Betsy's quick wit.

"Really!" cried Philippe.

"Yes, really!" stated Betsy. "Just thank me later, let's just get to Thomas and his new friend!"

"You mean Zara," stated Chronas.

"Oh yeah, Zara," replied Betsy, rolling her eyes and looking up into the air.

Running over to the balcony, the gang were all pleased to see Thomas and Zara.

"Zara, Thomas, are you okay?" asked Chronas.

"Yes, we are okay now," they replied.

"Where's Click und Snap and the Baroness?" asked Philippe impatiently.

"They both fell over the balcony!" exclaimed Thomas.

"She pushed him," further explained Zara.

The children were very anxious to learn what had happened while they were locked inside the trunks.

"Why, are those dreadful trolls were leaning over the balcony crying for mommy?" asked Betsy, puzzled.

"Because the Baroness changed into a mommy troll!" replied Zara.

"You're kidding me!" exclaimed Betsy.

As the children were busy talking, there was a loud noise at the doors. Hearing the brass door handle rustle, the ghastly trolls scampered through a secret passageway in on the side of the fireplace with terror. Just then, the large French gothic doors swung open and Aunt Fanny, Charles Clockwork, Seven, and Ms. Gazoontite along with Mr. Almondbrittle bolted in.

"Oh! My little Coconut, are you okay?" cried Aunt Fanny, running up to Sir Thomas to give him a big hug and kiss.

"Poppa, poppa!" cried Chronas. He ran up to his father and jumped into his arms.

"Chronas my boy, I was so worried about you!" said Charles, as he began to cry and picked his son up in his arms before twirling him around. Resting Chronas on his knee, his father presented him with something. "Chronas, this is something that will remind you to wind your heart in the event that you were to forget." It was his gold pocket watch.

Chronas happily replied, "By golly gum, poppa, thank you. I shall cherish it always."

"And after all we went through in the kingdom of Gauduchon, we lost you in a Paris train station!" stated Seven Clockwork, as she joined her family in a group hug.

"I see my big sister has not lost her sense of humor," Chronas replied, giving her a kiss on the cheek.

"Zara, is that my Zara!" cried Ms. Gazoontite.

Zara rushed toward her Governess. "Ms. Gazoontite, so glad to see you. So much has happened!" She hugged her.

"I was worried sick about you. I'm so glad you are safe now, thanks to your little rescuers."

Thomas wanted to tell his Aunt Fanny the big secret. "Aunt Fanny, Grand Aunt Galina was a monstrous troll!"

She replied lovingly, "Oh darling, I'm not surprised at all!" and added. "That's why I left home at an early age."

Thomas softly said, "Aunt Fanny?"

"Yes Thomas."

"Do we still have time to see your performance in Monte Carlo?"

"Well after we check in with your mother back home, why yes, if you're still up to it!" she replied warmly.

"Aunt Fanny?"

"Yes, Thomas?"

Thomas sheepishly asked, "Could my friends come?"

"Why of course, darling," Fanny replied enthusiastically.

"Say, Chronas, who are your new friends?" asked Seven.

"Allow me to introduce you to Zara Zuckerman. She has enchanted animals that come to life, but we left them back in the motorcar."

"You mean the orange motorcar partly hidden in the bushes as we drove up?" stated Mr. Almondbrittle.

"Yes, the very automobile," stated Chronas Clockwork.

Nicolas was amazed, "You mean to tell me that you drove that all the way here?" asked Mr. Almondbrittle.

"Oh no, silly! Gloria did the driving, it's her automobile," Chronas explained.

"Pleased to meet you, Seven," stated Zara, with a smile.

"This is Gloria Peekaboo and Philippe de Curieuse. She's very good with a slingshot and he flies by hot air balloon and sometimes eats bugs!" Chronas introduced Seven to the rest of the group.

"Did you say eat bugs, son?" his father asked, to make sure he had heard right.

"Yup! Thomas told me that," stated Chronas.

"Pleased to meet you both," stated Seven as she shook their hands.

Then, turning toward Betsy, Chronas said, "And this is Betsy Sassafras. She's rather crafty!"

Seven said, "Nice to meet you, Betsy."

"Oh it's also nice to meet you, Seven. I am the cutest one here!" stated Betsy with a smile and curtsey.

Then, turning toward Thomas, Chronas said, "And last but not least, my best friend Sir Thomas Tattletale!"

Seven looked at Thomas warmly and extended her hand, which Thomas took. "Indeed a pleasure to meet you, Seven. Your brother has told me a lot about you and your adventures in Chicago and France!"

"It is also a pleasure to meet you, Thomas. You must come and visit us in Chicago sometime!" replied Seven.

"Oh, indeed! I shall be honored if you and your family would like to be my guest of honor at my Aunt Fanny's performance in Monte Carlo."

Nicolas had been surveying the scene and noticing that the Baron was missing. He asked, "Say, where is the Baron?"

"Oh he's on the floor," replied Gloria.

"On the floor? There's nothing here but clothing and dust!" stated Nicolas.

"That's because he turned into ashes," explained Thomas.

"My god, he must have been over a 100 years old!" cried Fanny."

And where is The Baroness?" asked Mr. Almondbrittle.

"Yeah, where is that monster? I'd like to give her a piece of my mind and my fist!" said Aunt Fanny ,angrily looking around the room.

"Oh! She went over the balcony with Prince Henrik," stated Betsy nonchalantly as she pointed her finger toward the balcony.

"What! She fell over the balcony?" cried Fanny, looking at Mr. Clockwork in horror. Aunt Fanny, Charles Clockwork, and Nicolas ran to the balcony and looked over the edge. They could only see the body of Prince Henrik von Schnapps, who lay motionless with his mechanical prostatic limbs shattered and scattered about the ground.

As the children ran up to take a look they all gasped in horror for the Baroness' body was not there.

"Say, wait a minute. We saw them both go over the balcony, Aunt Fanny!" cried Sir Thomas, amazed at the Baroness' disappearance. Looking closer at Prince Henrik from the balcony, Philippe and Thomas noticed something. He was still moving, which meant Prince Henrik was still alive. "Aunt Fanny, Prince Henrik moved!" cried Sir Thomas.

"Come on, let's get down there quickly to help him. We'll worry about the Baroness' whereabouts later!" cried Aunt Fanny.

They all bolted out of the doors and rushed down the steps to the garden. The first ones out of the doors were Thomas and Zara. They sprinted toward Prince Henrik and upon reaching him asked, "Is there anything we can do?"

Taking Thomas' hand, Prince Henrik whispered into his ear, "You must shatter the mirror as she gazes upon it again." With that said, Prince Henrik von Schnapps took his last breath and was no more.

As the rest joined Thomas and Zara in the garden, Aunt Fanny asked Thomas what had happened. "I thought he was still alive?"

"He just passed away, Aunt Fanny," replied Thomas. Thomas never told Aunt Fanny of Prince Henrik's last words.

The authorities were called in the next day and after their investigations of the demise of the Baron and the disappearance of the Baroness, it was decided to grant all property and holdings to the Tattletale Family.

CHAPTER 11
The Malachite Mansion of Margret Ming

Arriving in the Kingdom of Monaco over the majestic hills, the group found themselves amidst the opulent splendor of gold leaf Baroque and Beaux arts architecture. In a blue touring automobile, Thomas, Zara, and Ms. Gazoontite traveled with Aunt Fanny and her mechanical jazz band. Nicolas Almondbrittle and the Clockwork family followed behind them in their automobile with Gloria Peekaboo in her orange birthday roadster, which was driven by her chauffeur Ferguson trailing not too far behind. Up and down they went through the winding hills of Monte Carlo.

Driving up a steep hill en route to Margret Ming's mansion, Charles saw something rather peculiar out of his window. "Say! There's a blue zeppelin with a bulls-eye design on it and it is landing on a rooftop ahead!" They all stopped and got out of their automobiles to look up.

"Why, it's absolutely beautiful!" Gloria Peekaboo exclaimed. They all gazed at it in amazement.

"I wonder who it belongs to," said Zara, looking up with admiration.

"I say! That's Dr. Cumulus Primrose's airship, Zara!" exclaimed Sir Thomas, pointing his finger.

"Raspberries in applesauce! He's landing on Margret's roof top! Well, it looks like the party is starting without us, folks. Come on, let's get cracking!" exclaimed Aunt Fanny.

"Excuse me, Aunt Fanny?" Thomas asked, tugging at her coat.

Aunt Fanny turned around and looked at Thomas, "Yes Thomas?"

"It's not a he but a she, Aunt Fanny, and she's a meteorologist," Sir Thomas stated smiling.

"What is a meteorologist, Thomas?" asked Zara Zukerman.

"Aunt Amanda told me that it is a person that studies the atmosphere around us, the weather, you could say," replied Thomas, with a smile.

Just then, Seven Clockwork saw something else in the sky and cried, "Hey wait a minute. Poppa, I can see a hot air balloon with yellow moons and purple hearts and it's landing in the same place." She pointed at the hot air balloon.

"Crackers and milk! My true love Philippe is here!" Gloria Peekaboo said with a sigh. "Who's Philippe, Gloria?" asked Seven.

"The love I speak of is Philippe de Curieuse!" stated Gloria as she placed her hand on her forehead.

"Your boyfriend flies in a hot air balloon?" asked Seven, curiously.

"Yeah, his folks aren't too fond of automobiles, you see, so they all travel that way," Gloria replied.

"Oh, how romantic!" exclaimed Seven, clasping her hands to her chest and looking up.

As everybody raced back to their automobiles, a loud backfire of a biplane approached. It whizzed toward them, doing loop de loops.

"Everyone just stay calm!" cried Nicolas Almondbrittle, frantically. "Never mind, just hit the dirt!" Nicolas exclaimed as he grabbed his straw boater and dropped to the ground.

A voice rang out from the biplane as it raced past, "Well, whoop de doo, 'lil sis!" a voice cried out and then the biplane abruptly flew back up into the air.

"Who in the world was that?" exclaimed Nicolas Almondbrittle as he got back up, still holding onto the brim of his straw boater with both hands for dear life.

"Well, I'll be! It's my big sister Amanda!" cried Fanny, waving her hand up to her.

"By golly, that looks like a lot of fun!" cried Chronas, laughing with his sister.

Swooping down once again, Amanda cried out to Thomas, "Hello, my angel of the skies! Whoop whoop de Doo!"

"And a whoop de doo to you too, Aunty!" Sir Thomas cried back, waving his hand and laughing as she flew off towards Margret's mansion.

As they approached and parked their automobiles in front of the Ming Manor, they saw three butlers standing at attention outside on the steps. The butlers were dressed in purple 18th-century footmen coats and wore festive bird masks. Unlike other mansions in Monaco that were made of limestone and marble, Ming's home was made entirely of green and blue malachite. It was a palatial manor in a Beaux-arts style.

"Bonjour madams and monsieurs, and welcome to Madame Ming Manor," the first butler cried.

"Merry Masquerade Eve!" the second butler cried, throwing confetti into the air.

"I am Roulette, at your service. Walk this way if you please," the first butler stated.

"Someone will tend to your luggage and automobiles shortly," the third butler stated joyously.

Roulette then introduced the second butler to the group. "This is Baccarat, and he'll show you to your rooms."

"Indeed a pleasure, welcome! You'll find your costumes in your rooms," he stated gleefully.

"Oh! Dear me, I had no idea that there would be so many guests at once!" Baccarat cried, as he looked at the group.

Turning to the third butler he asked, "Dear Blackjack, could you give me a hand?"

"It would be my pleasure, Baccarat," he replied.

Baccarat politely signaled toward Aunt Fanny's group, while Blackjack handled Nicolas Almondbrittle's group along with Gloria Peekaboo.

Gloria asked Sir Thomas, "What is Masquerade Eve?" as they walked down the hallway to their rooms.

"I don't know, Gloria, but I'm afraid we are going to find out soon enough!" replied Sir Thomas.

Aunt Fanny looked about the hallway for Madame Ming, and when she couldn't spot her, she turned to the butler and asked, "Baccarat is Margret here?"

"Oh, I'm afraid not at the moment. Madame Ming is having sunflower cake and tea with the King and Queen at Le Casino de Ballet," he replied.

Blackjack overheard this conversation. He instantly intervened, "I'm afraid you are wrong, dear Baccarat. It's lemon tea and chocolate sunflower cake!"

"Oh dear me, do forgive me, Blackjack. You are right!" cried Baccarat.

Roulette was walking behind the entire group and with a stern look clearing his throat he announced, "Madame shall be here within the hour." He jetted off to welcome the other guests that were arriving.

Fanny and Nicolas' groups followed the individual butlers to their rooms down a hallway of green and blue Malachite checkerboard floor. On the way, they paused for a moment to admire the gold leaf-coffered ceiling as angelic chamber music played in the background.

"What lovely music, I wonder where it's coming from?" asked Gloria as she looked around curiously.

"Yes, it is quite lovely, indeed," stated Nicolas Almondbrittle.

"To answer your question, Mademoiselle Peekaboo, it's coming from the ballroom. They are warming up for tonight's masquerade," replied Blackjack.

"The sound reminds me of the fall season," stated Seven Clock-work as she twirled around to the music.

"Why Mademoiselle Clockwork, you have quite an ear, because this piece is by Antonio Vivaldi called 'Autumn'," replied Baccarat with a smile.

Her brother Chronas made a sour face and said, "But she said fall not autumn!"

His father then got down on one knee to explain. "Fall and autumn are the same seasons depending on where you live, Chronas."

"Oh, you are so right, Monsieur Clockwork," Baccarat said with crackling laughter as he pulled large dry oak leaves from his pockets and threw them into the air like confetti above their heads.

"I do agree, Baccarat. It is indeed simply the perfect season for masquerade you know, not too hot nor too cold, you see, but just right!" he replied with cackling laughter.

Blackjack took Seven's hand and began to dance with her, twirling in circles. Stopping at the end of the hallway, they came upon two spiral staircases each leading separately to guest rooms to the north and south sides of the mansion. They saw that at the foot of the north spiral staircase stood someone in a red rooster mask.

"Cock-a-doddle-doo!" the person cried, flapping their arms.

Everyone was startled by this and stopped at a distance. Gloria Peekaboo was not stunned, but rather fascinated and ran over toward the red rooster with a grin. Coming face to face with the masked red rooster, Gloria put both hands over her eyes and said, "Oh I just love surprises. Could you take off your mask?" she asked, giggling with joy. As the rooster took off his mask, Gloria was thrilled to see that it was none other than Philippe de Curieuse. "Oh, Philippe you always know how to surprise me," she cried, giving him a hug.

Then a boisterous voice rang out from the south side of the spiral staircase. "Well, whoop de do! Gloria Peekaboo, you are truly something to behold! Philippe has told me all about you." It was Amanda Cruikshank in a hawk mask and Dr. Cumulus Primrose in a condor mask, both laughing.

"Oh crackers and milk, you make me blush, silly," Gloria replied.

Amanda and Cumulus took off their masks and introduced themselves. "Nice to meet you, Gloria! I love a girl with a little sauce in her step," Amanda exclaimed.

"Pleased to meet you both! I just love your flying machines," Gloria said cheerfully with a curtsy.

By this time, the entire group had gathered around Amanda and Dr. Cumulus. "Me too, my name is Seven." Chronas' sister came forward and introduced herself.

"Indeed a pleasure, young ladies," replied Dr. Cumulus, shaking both of their hands in a crisscross fashion.

Looking over to her sister, Amanda couldn't restrain her excitement. "Oh and a whoop de doo! If it isn't my talented little sis, Fanny!" Amanda yelled as she ran down the steps to greet her.

"Oh, raspberries! I'm not so little anymore. And how is Europe's finest stunt flyer and academy dean doing." cried Fanny, giving her a hug.

"Just grand, on vacation you know, en route to Vienna! Just thought I'd stop by," she replied.

The truth was that Lady Tattletale had wanted Amanda to keep an eye on her sister and Thomas, just in case they needed any help along the way

"Who's your friend with the blue hair?" Fanny asked.

"Oh, forgive me! Allow me to introduce you to Dr. Cumulus Primrose."

"The meteorologist I've hear so much about. Nice to meet you, Doctor," Fanny gestured toward her guests, introducing them one by one. "This is Charles Clockwork, and my good friend Nicolas Almondbrittle."

With the introductions done, the groups proceeded to their rooms. Reaching and entering their guest rooms, they noticed that on their beds, masks were already placed. Sir Thomas Tattletale and his friends were in for quite a treat because this particular night was the masquerade eve. Masquerade Eve was a law proclaimed by the King and Queen of Monaco to protect the citizens of Monte Carlo from the deadly plague of boredom. The law dictated that one must throw a masquerade ball every Friday of the month, and the ball should end on Sunday evening. For whosoever did not partake in the festivities, their penalty would be imprisonment and exile. The plague of boredom was taken quite seriously in this kingdom. Long before the law was decreed, hundreds of people in the Kingdom had perished from this dreadful plague. This particular law, on the other hand, worked out perfectly for Madame Margret Ming because she was cursed to throw costumed parties or she would be transform into a peacock. Her curse had begun in the city of Xinjiang at the tender age of six. The only child of a wealthy malachite and quarts merchant, her parents lavished her with gifts every week. As her parents ran out of gift ideas, they decided to ask Margret what she would like.

"I want a colorful bird each week, from all the kingdoms of the world," replied Margret.

To fulfill her wish, her parents set out on a journey throughout the kingdoms of the world looking for the most exotic birds. Each week, Margaret would receive a colorful exotic bird. On her father's last trip to India, he discovered a magnificent peacock. Capturing the mesmerizing peacock, he brought it back to Xinjiang and presented it to Margret in a large ornate gilded cage.

She was overjoyed to receive it and said, "Oh thank you, Father, I love it I shall cherish it forever!" She was ecstatic with the gift of a peacock. Later on that evening as she prepared for bed, Margret placed the gilded cage on a pedestal near her bed. She had fallen fast asleep when she was abruptly awoken by the peacock's plea.

"Please let me out," cried the peacock.

As she woke up in surprise, "Say, you can talk!" exclaimed Margret, rubbing her eyes in amazement.

"Yes, I can indeed," replied the peacock. "If you could let me out for one night a week to spread my wings, I shall return to you the next day.

"What if I were to forget?" asked little Margret Ming.

"Then I would lose my plumage and die, and for whomever owned the gilded cage on which I reside would take on the form of a peacock," replied the peacock.

"Well then I shall never forget, dear peacock," stated Margret. Letting the peacock out of the cage, Margret watched it fly off the balcony. Then she returned to the bed and, blowing out the candle, fell fast asleep.

As the Indian peacock flew off the balcony under the moonlight over a garden of pink Chrysanthemums, it soared up through the cherry blossoms with ecstasy, then perched itself on a Chinese maple tree. In all the excitement of being set free, the Indian peacock forgot to tell Margret what to do in the event that she was to forget.

Flying back frantically, the peacock flew in through Margret's room window and landed at the foot of her bed. He then proceeded to wake her by flapping he wings madly, but to no avail. Instead, the peacock whispered into her ear as she slept, "To show homage to me, you must throw a costume party once a night on the 7th day of the week. Only in doing this you would never be transformed into a peacock."

On her 10th birthday, she did forget, henceforth the curse began.

The guest arrived dressed in various costumes of lizards, snakes, woodpeckers to toucans. They waltzed to music reminiscent of Shostakovich's Ballet Suite, 'The Lyric Waltz'. Sir Thomas giggled at the costumes as the guests arrived. The last person to arrive with her face hidden behind a blue velvet mask embroidered with baroque pearls was Madame Margret Ming. As she entered the ballroom, everyone stood silently admiring her exquisite masquerade gown. Her gown was designed in the early 17th-century style taste, in colors of blue and green with the collar of the gown adorned with peacock feathers. Her long black hair was braided and turned up on her head with long protruding pearl stick pins that held it in place.

An hour had passed of waltzing merriment when cutting through the ballroom of waltzing masquerades, Sir Thomas happened to notice a rather funny looking costumed duck among the guests. It seemed that the duck had six little children dressed as chicks that followed behind her. They waddled past the waltzing guests into the hallway and down the steps toward the exit. As they moved, they made a rather funny sound unlike a duck's quack, which Sir Thomas thought was rather odd. As he caught up to the strange sounding costumed duck and her chicks, Sir Thomas asked, "I say, I've never heard a duck make a sound like that before."

"Boronk!" sounded the duck. "That's because I'm a Norwegian duck, dear boy," replied the costumed duck.

"Well, mummy and I have been to Norway and have never heard a duck's quack like that," replied Sir Thomas.

"Why how observant of you," the costumed duck replied. "Young man, since you are so observant, could you tell me what I'm dangling in my hand?" Asked the costumed duck.

"Why it looks like Chronas' key to wind up his heart! Bow bumble! You are not one of the invited guests, you're the Baroness!" cried Sir Thomas.

It was indeed the Baroness Giggle Von Tickle herself who had come uninvited to seek revenge and had brought along her ghastly trolls. As the Baroness and her ghastly trolls took off their masks, she addressed Thomas in a soft voice, extending her skinny clawed hand to caress his face. "Why my little scrumptious, I am just so touched that you would know your sweet old grand aunt!"

"Let me go! Let me go!" Thomas cried as he struggled to break free. He then asked, "What did you do with Chronas, you horrid monster!"

The Baroness smiled wickedly and asked, "Now, now, is that any way to talk to your favorite grand aunty?" Then she added, "I'm afraid your tic-tock friend doesn't have much time left, seeing that he does not have this key to wind up his little heart. But if you come with me quietly, I shall see that he gets it back in time, perhaps."

In hearing this, Sir Thomas went quietly along with the Baroness and the ghastly trolls.

Sitting at a table nearby, Madame Ming, Nicolas, and Seven clapped their hands to the joyous music of the waltz. After dancing, Fanny and Charles also joined them at the table. The evening was progressing splendidly and Aunt Fanny and her mechanical jazz band were about to go on.

"Well folks, I go on in an hour. Wish me luck. Have you seen Thomas? I do not want him to miss my performance!" exclaimed Fanny.

"He's probably with Amanda on the dance floor," replied Margaret.

Just then, Amanda and Dr. Primrose walked over. "Good luck on your performance!" stated Dr. Primrose, as she shook Fanny's hand.

"Yes, good luck, sis! Amanda added. "Have you seen my little angel of the skies? I was saving the next dance for him," Amanda asked Fanny.

"Why no, I haven't seen him. I was rather hoping he was with you, Amanda," replied Fanny.

"Well, whoop de doo me! He's probably with Chronas," replied Amanda.

The sisters were now starting to get worried. "Charles, have you seen Thomas around?" asked Fanny.

"Why no, I was about to ask you the same thing about Chronas," replied Charles. Then he added, "Perhaps they are with Zara?"

Overhearing this conversation, Philippe and Gloria raced over. "Say, we were looking for them too!" stated Philippe.

Gloria then interrupted. "I thought the masquerade theme was of birds and reptiles?"

"What made you bring that up?" asked Charles.

"Because there's a four-legged zebra trotting across the dance floor!" she replied, pointing to the zebra in the room.

"Well, whoop de doo me! It's a real zebra!" cried Amanda.

"Raspberries! Zara must be in trouble again!" cried Fanny, getting worried.

"I don't think so because she's standing right next to Ms. Gazoontite talking to that zebra," stated Seven, pointing across the dance floor.

They were now getting worried on the whereabouts of Thomas and Chronas. Fanny cried, "Come on folks, let's get to the bottom of this!"

They rushed over to Zara and Ms. Gazoontite. Surrounding them, Fanny asked, "Zara are you okay? Thomas had told me that whenever you are in trouble, your animals come to life to help you."

"Very true, Aunt Fanny. I was baffled by this as well," Zara replied, and then looked into her box. She noticed that all the birds were gone.

"This has never happened before," stated Ms. Gazoontite, as she looked into the box as well.

Ingaway was frantically turning in circles. "Everyone! Ingaway is trying to tell me something." Zara got closer to the zebra and put her arm around Ingaway. She began to talk to her. Everyone looked on as Zara spoke with her Zebra. With an alarmed look, Zara turned around and said, "Ingaway says that Thomas has been taken by a large duck with little chicks."

"A large duck and little chicks? Are you thinking what I'm thinking Philippe?" Gloria exclaimed.

"Yes! The very same, Gloria! It's none other than the Baroness in disguise," he replied.

Just then, the zebra kneeled down on one leg as Zara mounted her. They both bolted up the steps and through the doors.

"Raspberries! Everyone to your vehicles. Follow that zebra!" cried Fanny Flapper.

They all raced from the ballroom to their automobiles and flying machines. A mad frenzy ensued as the host and guest followed, joining in on the madness.

Twenty minutes earlier, the Baroness and the trolls discarded their costumes en route to their escape with Thomas in their possession. Thomas asked the Baroness with sadness, "Why would you want Chronas? He's done nothing to you."

The Baroness replied, "Well, you see my dearest Thom Thom Tattletale, your tic-tock friend is in possession of a very powerful magic clock. It belonged to the Gauduchon sisters of France. It now lies in his chest as a heart. I intend to extract the clock from within him and harness the powerful magic to bring my dear husband back from the ashes and to restore my great beauty. As for you, dear Thom Tattletale, you shall witness the reincarnation of my husband and me, on which you shall dance for us once again."

As the Baroness reached her motorcar and in shock, she stopped dead in her tracks. Looking at her automobile she screamed with fury at the trolls. "Why you imbeciles! I told you to sabotage the other automobiles, not mine!" She looked around, infuriated at the engine of her automobile, which was torn apart and scattered about the ground. The trolls sheepishly moved away out of fear of the Baroness' wrath. "Never mind, you blithering idiots! We have no time, we'll just take that blue automobile!"

Sir Thomas was still in the clutches of the trolls and exclaimed, "But that's Aunt Fanny's Motorcar!"

"Step lively, dear Thom Thom Tattletale, because we're going on a little journey! I do hope you have your sea legs on." The Baroness laughed maniacally as the trolls entered the motorcar with Sir Thomas, and they raced off.

The Baroness said this because they were headed for the grand pier, where a magnificent six-mass sailing schooner awaited.

At Madame Ming's manor, everybody ran frantically to their vehicles. Some were in for a rather cruel surprise. "Ah! My baby is gone!" cried Aunt Fanny. She and the others reached the garage, realizing that most of the automobiles had been tampered with.

"Baby? Say, I didn't see you with a baby," said Gloria.

"She means her automobile, Gloria," replied Seven.

"Crackers and milk, you mean her automobile has been pinched!" exclaimed Gloria.

"I'm afraid so," replied Seven.

Gloria then had an idea and tugging on Aunt Fanny's dress. "Say, why don't you just take my orange roadster? I can fly with Philippe."

"Why, that's just grand of you, Gloria! Thank you!" replied Aunt Fanny, thankfully.

Gloria turned to Ferguson and asked him to give Fanny the keys. "Yes, Mademoiselle," Ferguson replied promptly as he handed over the keys to Aunt Fanny.

They quickly got into the orange roadster and without wasting a minute, she and Nicolas sped off in her automobile.

Meanwhile, on the rooftop, Dr. Cumulus Primrose frantically began to start up her zeppelin and was about to take off when she was interrupted by a yell. "Amanda Cruikshank, requesting permission to board!" Amanda saluted her.

"Blueberry in cream corn! What on earth happened to your biplane, Amanda?" asked Cumulus, puzzled.

"Well, doc! On approaching my aircraft, I noticed that parts of it had been thrown all over the place. Hence I cannot fly the blasted thing!"

"Not another word, Amanda. You are coming with me, just get in. We are losing time!" exclaimed Dr. Primrose.

"Oh, whoop de do! We are off to save my nephew! Thanks, doc!" cheered Amanda, smacking her knee.

On the north side of the roof, Philippe's air chauffeur Bucheron helped him prepare to take off in his hot air balloon. He was interrupted by Gloria, who cried out "Bonsoire Mon Philippe! Oh Philippe, could I travel with you? Fanny's motorcar has been pinched so I gave her my automobile!"

"No problem, my dearest, get in! Bucheron, could you give her a hand up?" Philippe asked.

"Right away, sir!" replied the air chauffeur.

As the hot air balloon took off, Gloria gave Philippe directions and said, "Just follow my orange roadster, Philippe!" They went up and floated among the clouds.

As the Baroness and the trolls raced down to the pier, one of the ghastly trolls saw something out the back window of the automobile and grunted over to the Baroness, pointing his finger madly in that direction. Turning around with great dismay, the Baroness saw that Zara Zuckerman was chasing her from atop her majestic zebra. "Well, well. It looks like we might have a little company!" the Baroness exclaimed, stepping on the gas as she sped off through a wooded area.

"Hurry Ingaway, they are headed for that wooded area. We are going to lose them!" said Zara with worry. Just then, Zara looked up to see her birds above her head. She called out to them. "Tutsi! Coco! Miranda! Where were you?" The birds then informed Zara in their language that the Baroness was escaping by a sailing schooner on the pier. Zara thought quickly and instructed her birds. "Fly ahead of me and keep a close eye on the Baroness and the boys." The birds acknowledged her and flew away. As Zara turned back, she saw a barrage of automobiles behind her. She could make out Aunt Fanny, Nicolas, and

Madame Ming's guests in their automobiles who were driving furiously.

Zara slowed Ingaway down so that the others could catch up to her and she yelled over to her new friends to inform them. "Everyone head for the pier! The Baroness and her trolls plan to make their escape by sea." She bolted off through the wooded area to follow the Baroness.

Earlier partway through the wooded area, the Baroness had stopped her automobile to get out and survey the area. Looking around closely, she summoned one of the trolls and said, "My ghastly troll, pass me The Wounded Flute." The troll immediately passed on the musical instrument to her, which she began to play instantly. In doing this, the trees began to bend and wilt and lose their leaves as if they were sick. They then began to crack and break and fell onto the roadway, blocking the pathway. The Wounded Flute is one of the many enchanted musical instruments that were acquired by the Baron and Baroness through sale or theft abroad. It possessed the power to heal trees, but in the wrong hands, it did the reverse.

As the automobiles followed Zara into the woods to give assistance, they came upon the large downed trees, which posed no problem for Zara because Ingaway just jumped over them. Unfortunately for Aunt Fanny and her friends, they were unable to make it through. As for the others, they crashed into the fallen trees and the motors stalled, stuck in the mud.

Coming out of the woods and down a hill, the Baroness and her trolls finally reached the sailing schooner. "Escort my dear grand nephew to the hull," the Baroness exclaimed to her trolls. Following the orders, they locked Thomas in a room with a brown steamer trunk. As they set sail under the moonlight and left the dock, the Baroness waved a laced handkerchief and mimicked crying over to Zara, as she was too late in catching them. "Goodbye, sweet Zara Zuckerman, until we meet again. Boo whoo!" cried the Baroness, as she looked up with a ghastly grimace.

Calmly, Zara just pointed up into the air in the direction of the Baroness and then waved goodbye. The Baroness curiously looked up to where Zara was pointing and wondered, "What is that mad girl pointing at? I don't see anything." She decided to ignore her gesture and said aloud to her trolls, "Never mind, she's too late anyway." She began to move below the deck.

Meanwhile, in the hull, Sir Thomas saw a steamer trunk in the middle of the room and called out to it, "Hello is anybody in there?"

"Yes!" replied the voice within the steamer.

"Chronas, is that you in there?" Thomas asked.

"Yes, by golly! So glad to hear your voice, Thomas. I don't have much time," he exclaimed.

"Don't worry, Chronas, I'll get you out," Thomas promised his friend.

In another part of the ship, as the Baroness lay resting in her cabin, one of the trolls tapped her to draw her attention to something. He was grunting frantically and pointing up and out of the porthole window of the schooner. "Oh, what now!" she bellowed, walking over to the window and gasped as she looked out. "This can't be! I thought you would have handled this, you fool," she yelled at the troll standing before her.

It was Dr. Primrose's zeppelin in hot pursuit. Walking up to the deck, the Baroness looked up at the zeppelin with 20 trolls ready for her command. She ordered them to man their crossbows and aim at Dr. Primrose's aircraft. The Baroness halted their action midway and said, "Hold on for a moment." The Baroness was seemingly fascinated by something and said, "Let's just watch them for a moment."

Meanwhile on the zeppelin, Amanda and Dr. Primrose raced to catch up to the Baroness' ship. Amanda asked with anxiety, "Are we going full speed, Cumulus?"

Dr. Primrose looked over and checked the speedometers and replied, "That's strange. We are not moving at the maximum speed." There was a creaking sound in the foreground, then Dr. Primrose listened in closely and said, "Wait a minute, do you hear that Amanda?"

Amanda had also heard the noise, "Why yes I do, what is it?"

"I think it's the helium. Oh blueberries, it could be a leak. Let me go and check just to make sure it's not." She asked Amanda, "Could you take the wheel until I get back?"

"Aye, aye, captain!" replied Amanda.

As Dr. Primrose went to investigate, Amanda stood at the wheel of the zeppelin, keeping a close eye on the Baroness' sailing schooner. As Cumulus examined the interior walls of the zeppelin on an elevated plank, she discovered cuts in the wall of the airship, the source of the problem. When she saw the damage, she began to make repairs immediately. Dr. Primrose heard laughing from above her head. Looking up, Cumulus noticed that two ghastly trolls of the Baroness were hanging on to ropes that connected the inner skin of the zeppelin's wall. "Just you wait until I get my hands on you saboteurs!" said Cumulus as she picked up a nearby broomstick and went after them.

The trolls just laughed and split up, going in two different directions on the airship. As they went, they cut even larger holes with their claws into the zeppelin wall. The trolls escaped through a massive hole they had made earlier, diving off the airship and into the sea below.

"Blueberries and cream corn! We are going down! Amanda! Amanda, cut the engines. We are going down!" cried Dr. Primrose.

Amanda was quick to her feet. "I know! I've prepared the life preservers!" exclaimed Amanda.

"Oh blueberries, Amanda, we won't be needing those," said Dr. Primrose.

"And why do you say that!?" asked Amanda, puzzled.

Dr. Primrose replied calmly, "Because by my calculations we should be making a graceful landing." Dr. Cumulus Primrose said this because the base of her zeppelin was structured like that of a sailing boat.

The Baroness was overjoyed with dark laughter as she monitored the slow descent of Dr. Primrose's zeppelin into the ocean.

Swimming toward the starboard side of the ship were the two trolls that jumped from airship earlier. The Baroness then looked over to them. "Well! It seems that my ingenious plans have finally worked out. It's just most unfortunate that I'm surrounded by idiots that work at a snail's pace around me!" Then, turning to the rest of the trolls who were aboard the ship, she screamed, "Now retrieve your brothers from the ocean, and don't disturb me again until we've reached our destination!" Saying this, she stormed off down the steps to her cabin to rest.

The trolls noticed another flying apparatus in the foreground. It was floating in mid-air and was red in color with purple hearts and yellow moons on it. The ghastly trolls had never seen anything like this before and were terrified of this floating object. They debated with one another whether or not to wake the Baroness from her slumber to inform her. The trolls took a vote and agreed that they were more horrified of the Baroness' wrath than a red floating monster. The trolls decided to gathered their crossbows and await the red floating monster.

Meanwhile, on the red floating monster were none other than Philippe and Gloria. "Crackers and milk, Philippe. Dr. Primrose's airship has gone down in the ocean!" Gloria cried with panic, pointing her finger at the airship.

"No need to fret, my dearest. Look, they are floating," replied Philippe, with a giggle.

"Crackers! It's floating like a boat!" said Gloria. As they got closer to the schooner, Gloria could see the trolls discharging crossbows from the air toward them as they got closer. She had an idea. "Philippe, the sun will be up soon. They can't see us too well now, so we must work quickly. I need you pull on that cord as we need more hot air."

Philippe understood her idea and decided to apply it. In doing so, the hot air balloon moved about the ship like a sleek hawk. With this, Gloria took out her trusty slingshot and began to knock each troll off the schooner's edge. With only three trolls left on deck, the sun began to rise. As the hot air balloon approached the Baroness' ship, the trolls were able to see the hot air balloon much better and with two shots of their crossbow arrows, they finally punctured Philippe de Curieuse's magnificent hot air balloon. Philippe and Gloria plunged down into the ocean.

As the wicker basket floated on the water, a cry rang out, "Philippe! Philippe! Where are you, my love?"

A soft voice rang out in reply, "I'm in the water, my dearest. Are you okay?"

"Yes," replied Gloria.

Looking around, Philippe saw Dr. Primrose's airship and cried out to Gloria. "See here Gloria, Dr. Primrose's airship is not too far from us." Then he asked her, "Can you swim?"

"Oh, of course, silly crackers." Diving into the water, Gloria joined Philippe as they swam over to Dr. Primrose's floating zeppelin.

All looked on in sadness as the Baroness escaped into the sunrise with Sir Thomas Tattletale and Chronas Clockwork.

THE END

Oh, you must forgive me, boys and girls, I forgot to tell you. Remember as Zara stood at the pier pointing up and then waving goodbye to something the Baroness could not see? Well that something was her enchanted birds that she asked earlier to follow the Baroness and the boys. The birds had silently perched themselves on the mizzen mass of the Schooner. But I'm afraid that is another story entitled "The Peril of Sir Thomas Tattletale in Turkey."